To a friend
from back Pacific
way with fond
memories.

C. S. Callahan

HELLBENT

C. S. Callahan

1663 Liberty Drive, Suite 200
Bloomington, Indiana 47403
(800) 839-8640
www.AuthorHouse.com

First published by AuthorHouse 05/18/05

ISBN: 1-4208-3641-2 (sc)

Library of Congress Control Number: 2005901852

Printed in the United States of America
Bloomington, Indiana

This book is printed on acid-free paper.

Foreword

It's been said that it takes a village to raise a child. A book is rather like the child of one's imagination and it takes more than the author to bring a book to fruition. I'd like to thank those who put up with me on a daily basis, particularly during my absent-minded place while writing—Mary, Malia, Michelle, and Anne Margaret. They not only endured through it all but also readily helped with proofing and critical feedback.

I also want to thank Pat and Phyllis for their reading and helpful comments. It is a joy to write and now it is my joy to share the fruits of my labor. Behold, *Hellbent!* I hand it over to its readers, hoping that they find entertainment, a bit of suspense, and the pleasure of reading.

Prologue

The little man with wisps of hair nearly standing upright on his head knelt reverently on the tiled floor as if he were in a church. He looked at the beautiful woman lying before him. He bent forward carefully. Her eyes were closed in sleep. He was almost afraid to breathe lest he waken her; yet he wanted to come closer. He carefully slid nearer to her side. Her blonde hair lay spread out around her head, forming a kind of halo.

He felt compelled to reach out, ever so tentatively, to touch it. His stubby fingers transformed themselves into instruments of delicacy as he caressed the long strands of hair near his hand. He felt a thrill go through his body as he realized he had not awakened her.

He glanced down, his eyes tracing her form, stopping at the hand that rested against her left thigh. Dare he touch her hand? What if she awoke? She would surely rebuke him! He hesitated, but somehow a physical urge overpowered his caution. He briefly and lightly touched her hand. An onlooker would have thought he had touched a fire, but his touch had instead ignited a fire within him, for once again, he felt a surge of thrill that was almost painful. She had not awakened.

He remembered another woman like this. Blonde hair splayed out on the sands of some beach. He could almost hear the roaring and the splashing of the waves as they gave themselves to the beach, but the roar he experienced was deeper and inside his ears as his heartbeat increased, sending his blood pounding to his extremities. His passion was totally aroused now. He touched the neck and rested his fingers on her blouse and slowly unbuttoned the first little latch. Slowly and painstakingly, his clumsy fingers revealed the rounded treasure beneath the frail, white covering that had shielded it from him.

His breath caught as he saw at last what he had longed to see. This beautiful woman who kept her eyes closed tightly would be his, and as he touched the forbidden treasure of her breast, he realized that she was far better than the one he kept hidden downstairs!

****

Terry Hogan stood near the left side of the woman. She seemed from that angle to be sleeping. Her blonde hair radiated out from a face that was quiet and pale. Coming on her suddenly, lying there like that, he would have thought he'd come on someone who had fainted or had lain down to catch a few winks and had fallen into an unintended deep sleep.

Detective Terry Hogan knew better though. He only had to step over the body to see the side of her head where a heavy object had struck her temple. Whoever had struck her had been bold enough to do so from the front. The force of the blow had sent her falling backward. Her right arm lay at a near ninety-degree angle, indicating that she had tried to ward the attack off, but she had been too late to deflect that killing blow.

And then there was the blood. It had trickled from the wound down the side of her head and congealed there on the tiled floor with her hair, making the pool of blood seem like a large nail which held her hair as well as her body to the floor.

This did not disturb Terry Hogan. He'd seen it so many times in his career as a homicide detective. What did disturb him was that there were signs that she had been raped here in this quiet room where she had probably felt safe. He wondered if forensics would find that the disheveled clothing had occurred before or after the blow to her temple had been delivered. In other words, had she been conscious during the rape? More so, had she been alive at all? Terry Hogan knew that this would create a different profile for the man he would be looking for.

A light from the police photographer's camera blinded him. He stepped back, closing his notebook. Well, in this day of equal rights, he wondered if she had indeed been raped or if a woman had done everything to make it look like an attempted rape. Nothing was too far-fetched these days. He had to cover every angle, including those that seemed the least likely.

He pocketed his notebook, and in turning to leave the room, he stopped and glanced once more at the serene side of the body that lay on the floor. Then Terry Hogan found himself doing something strange. He made a sign of the cross when he turned to leave as if he were leaving a church.

Chapter 1

"There you are, Mechtilde." Becky placed the painted aluminum tea tray on the little table with its scarred maple veneer. The table was placed close at hand to the woman who sat in a wheelchair with a worn mustard-yellow pillow propped behind her. Becky always thought of yard sales when she caught a glimpse of that ugly pillow.

The older nun smiled appreciatively, her soft blue eyes glowing in the kind of merry way she had. Becky smiled back and wondered why it was that as a person aged, her hair and skin seemed to lose pigment, while the eyes remained so full of color and expression. That was certainly true of Tilly whose eyes shone so beautifully and gratefully for the least kindness shown her. She sat in a wheelchair most of the time although she did come to the dining room using only a walker, which stood perennially waiting for her at the little elevator door downstairs.

St. Genevieve's Convent was an old three-story red brick building. The brick was old enough to have been hand cast. That meant the bricks were heavy and substantial and that quality was bestowed to the building itself, suggesting that a sum was equal to its parts. In the old days, it had been chock full of busy, teaching nuns, but this was 1975, and the glory days were over. Now the convent at the corner of Elias and Stanton held only four nuns who confined themselves to the first and second floor but still felt as if they were in a rambling mansion.

"Now, don't wait for me to finish this, Becky dear. I'll take my time, you know, and you have studies that are calling you, don't you?"

"If you need anything, just ring, Mechtilde." As Becky slipped out the door, the name of Mechtilde played in her mind, translated into the old words of a Harry Belafonte song her father used to sing on Saturdays as he puttered in his basement hideaway: "Matilda, Matilda!" She took some dance steps into her room. She did have midterms to study for. The pressure of getting her Master's was beginning to prove a drag in this her last semester.

In some ways, she found herself as restless now as she had been when she was a novice. She had thought taking vows would end that, but it hadn't. Maybe she was just a restless person, period, she sighed, as she flipped open the book at the top of the stack on her desk and ran her fingers through her short, black, curly hair.

She could hear the voice that came through the wall. The phone room was right next to her bedroom and had she been the prying type, she thought to herself, she could have listened in on everyone's conversation. The muffled tone told her it was Maria talking in the next room. Just for the heck of it, Becky walked to the wall, pressed her ear against it, and listened to see if she really could make out the words.

Becky smiled as she deciphered the sounds, discovering that Maria was talking to Mr. Clayborn about the price of sheet music. She needed him to lower the price. Her music department was already over-budget, and Becky knew that Gretchen was on her case about it. The discussions between Gretchen and Maria sometimes erupted into the dinner conversation.

"Are you sure you can't discount this any further? It's for education." The pause, Becky knew, was Mr. Clayborn trying to explain that he'd already given her a reduction for that. "Yes, I do appreciate that, Mr. Clayborn, but don't you have a reduction for churches too? I mean, we're a religious school too?" Another pause. Had she managed to work Mr. Clayborn down so that he had given her an additional discount? Becky found herself rooting for Maria.

"Well, I appreciate your situation. I really do, Mr. Clayborn. You are always generous with St. Genevieve's. I'll see what I can do on my end. Now, have a good evening and tell Mrs. Clayborn hello too." The door to the room closed softly and judging by the slow steps that padded down the hall, Maria had not only been unsuccessful but also had lost her usual happy disposition.

Becky stepped out into the hall. "Maria," she called to the retreating figure. "How'd it go?"

Maria turned, tilted her head, so that her hair touched her right shoulder, and came back down the hall. "Not so good. I have to get the choir ready for the final concert; people expect this year to be different than last year's, but I can't afford the price. Back in the good old days, people used to give us things, but no more. The dog-eat-dog world has arrived at the convent door."

"I'm sorry, Maria. Maybe we can think of some way to get money. How about a fundraiser?" Becky preferred to solve Maria's problems rather than concentrate on her own--namely, a Shakespeare exam tomorrow.

"I can't. We used up our quota. Gretchen refuses to allow us to do any more car washes or bake sales. We've done four already, and she says that's enough 'nickel-and-diming of the same old people.'" Maria sighed heavily and then looked at Becky, "We took a vow of poverty to get out from under all this materialism, and here I am in the middle of it, scraping for money as if it were the end all and be all of my life!" Maria moved her head from side to side just as the doorbell rang. "I'll get it."

At the same moment, Becky heard the little silver bell next to Mechtilde. "Coming." As she turned into the room, she saw Mechtilde trying to rearrange the pillow behind her back. She needed one to help her sit forward; being so small, she seemed to sink down uncomfortably in the chair. Becky reached forward to help her, and Mechtilde smiled benignly at her.

"Mechtilde, is it difficult to have to sit in one place all day?" Becky had the question on her mind since she'd come to live at St. Gen's.

"Where one sits is not of such importance, I think, Becky, as much as how one sits. This pillow refuses to cooperate with me today."

"Well, I hope I'll have your sense of humor when my day comes," Becky said as she adjusted the pillow.

"You'll have plenty of time to develop one, if indeed you need one, before that day comes. Becky, would you ask Maria to come by, preferably before dinner? I do hope she can eat a decent meal tonight."

Becky looked thoughtfully at Mechtilde, wondering if she'd heard the conversation too. After all, Maria and she had been talking in the hall. "Sure. She went to answer the doorbell. If she isn't tied up with someone, I'll ask her to come now."

"Thank you, dear. Oh, Becky, I'll be praying my rosary for you tomorrow." The reminder tweaked Becky's conscience. She believed that God would reward her only if she did her part. No use asking for miracles, Gretchen would say.

Chapter 2

Maria was in a reasonably good mood at dinner that night, and Becky wondered if Mechtilde's talk with her had done the trick. Gretchen was tense, but that was normal for her. "Rebecca, would you pass the butter, please?" Gretchen always called her by her full name. She quietly handed the butter over. Occasionally, Maria would pretend to be elsewhere in her thoughts, and then, as if by coincidence, she would imitate Gretchen's penchant for full names. Becky wondered if she would do that again, seeing as she was in a pretty good mood.

Becky watched as Maria used her left hand to brush her long, blonde hair behind her ear as she deftly forked a fried potato with the other hand. Her choice to wear her hair long vexed Gretchen who thought nuns looked more professional with shorter hair. Then Maria glanced up innocently, "How are classes going, Rebecca Ann?" She did it! Becky and Maria smiled at one another conspiratorially. They shot sidelong glances at Gretchen, but she hadn't seemed to notice.

"I have a mid-term tomorrow. I'll need you to pray."

"I hope you aren't expecting any miracles. God helps those who help themselves." Becky, looking down at her steamed carrots and placing the edge of her fork carefully across one, caught herself mouthing the syllables as Gretchen said them. Becky looked over at Mechtilde then, who was serenely cutting her bread into four pieces to better manage it. Even bread felt heavy to her trembling hand.

"Mechtilde must believe in miracles. She says she'll pray for me and never asks if I've studied."

Mechtilde looked up quickly on hearing her name. "Becky, I know that you do your part. Anyhow, I couldn't do much about it even if you didn't, could I? My life is only full of time for prayer now."

"Mechtilde, what would we do without you? You are such a gem!" Maria was being effusive. Her mood must have gone up another notch, thought Becky.

Gretchen noticed the change too, glancing up at Maria, but she directed her words to Mechtilde. "We all love you, Mechtilde. But, I know that you also agree that we have to do our part. God doesn't just barge into our lives and dramatically change everything around; God works through evolution, not revolution!" Becky had noticed that Gretchen loved to play with words; in fact, Becky felt that Gretchen liked to package her sentences neatly, an over-all characteristic of Gretchen's: to package things and people and problems neatly.

"I'm not sure that's altogether the whole truth of it. God can do as God pleases. I doubt there is a divine precept that hems God in quite the way you say." Becky nearly rose to kiss Mechtilde for that remark! Not even Gretchen would contradict Mechtilde!

Instead Gretchen turned to Maria; the pecking order was about to take over: "Maria, the choir left the chairs in a shambles after practice. Can't you remind them to leave the room as they found it?" Gretchen's self-esteem was now in order.

"Oh! I'm sorry. I was in a hurry to call Mr. Clayborn."

"Are you placing a new order?" Gretchen's face warned of an approaching storm.

"No, I didn't. I don't need to. Mechtilde sent me into the attic this evening to find some old sheet music. The copyright has run out, and they are lovely old melodies. I'll make some copies, and we'll visit days of old for our final concert this year."

Score another one for Tilly, thought Becky. Her own spirits were lifting. She just might be able to tackle her Shakespeare notes tonight.

"Before I forget," Gretchen was indomitable, "Suzanne is coming tomorrow. She said she'll arrive later than usual. She'll stay the weekend. She has a meeting with the council tomorrow and plans to spend the rest of the day at the motherhouse.

Becky and Maria exchanged smiles at the news. Suzanne had been living as a hermit out in the country. She'd felt called to spend her life out in nature and to concentrate on God alone, which reminded Becky of Walden Pond and Thoreau. The whole idea seemed a little romantic to Becky, so much so that she had given such a life some consideration for herself. Although she found herself thinking of the possibility more at the end of a semester as exams approached than at other times. But at the news of the impending visit, Becky felt her spirits lift because Becky liked Suzie whom she found to be both pleasant and lots of fun, quite a contrast to Gretch.

The weekend! That was great because Becky's last mid-term was tomorrow and would be followed by spring break. This weekend would be totally free, and she could spend time with Suzie without feeling Gretchen's censorship about Becky's frivolous use of her time.

Chapter 3

John Hotchkiss sat nursing his scotch and soda. The television flicked varying degrees of bright light across his face, which wore a scowl. Hotchkiss had just finished grading a stack of essays from his English class at St. Gen's and had piled them on the lamp stand at his right. They had not helped his TV dinner settle any better in his stomach. He rummaged under the papers and pulled out the ashtray and lit another cigarette. Several essays fell to the floor, but he didn't care.

He hated his life. His wife, no, his ex-wife now, (he still had to remind himself that he was a divorced Catholic) had told him he was depressed. He hated that word nearly as much as he hated his life. He had taught for eight years at St. Gen's now, and it was that fact that daily reminded him his teaching career was going nowhere. He had been teaching at the prep seminary for ten years before they closed it. All the priests and religious on the faculty had been transferred to the other diocesan high schools, but laymen like himself had to shift for themselves.

All he could get was a position at St. Genevieve's, the only inner-city Catholic high school in Cadbury Falls. His wife had always been after him to get a job in the public schools "that paid". No teacher's salary was all that great, but the public school salary looked pretty cushy compared to the pittance he earned. The prep seminary, which was located in the suburbs, had a few more perks than St. Gen's did. Now he had to park on a city street and hope that a basketball from the playground didn't hit his car or, even worse, hope that he would find his car intact each day, not stripped bare.

So far, he'd been lucky. He'd only lost a battery the first year he taught there. The neighborhood apparently had a code that protected staff at St. Gen's. The nuns had a good reputation in the neighborhood; after all, they lived in the old convent next door to the school, which said something about solidarity with the urban poor, he guessed.

His digs weren't that much better. He lived just five blocks south of the downtown area, where the white niggers lived, he guessed. Yeah, that's what he was, that's all he amounted to! He'd had dreams of one day teaching at Harvard, but he'd never made enough to pursue his doctorate.

Some people had breaks and could speak so glibly about boot straps and the American dream, but John Hotchkiss always noticed that those people who spoke like that usually happened to be the successful rich! He hated them too. John finished his drink and filled it again without the soda. He stretched his legs out, failing to notice that the heel of his boot was pressed against the graded essays that had fallen to the floor.

John slouched in the worn, charcoal-gray, easy chair, resting his balding head against the back cushion. The heel of his cowboy boots, which he wore to give him more height, ground more deeply into the essays, the top two lifting their corners slightly as if to raise a protest, which remained unnoticed. John was only minimally aware that the hopelessness, which created such a growing inner pressure in him, required more and more alcohol to suppress it.

He swallowed another mouthful of the amber liquid and asked himself, "How could I already be at the end of the road when I'm only forty-two? How did it happen?" He had been a bright student in high school. "Shit, my own senior English teacher, let's see, yeah, Fr. Browning, told me I had real talent." John tended to talk aloud, addressing himself to the TV as the evening and the drinking wore on.

Had the old priest just lied to him? Or did he really have talent? Maybe he had talent for St. Regis High, but was he really talented at St. Benet's, the all-male college John had attended? No professor had singled him out there. He did get good grades, but no one told him he was talented. So maybe he was only talented for the kind of competition at St. Regis.

"That's how it is. You shine when you are in a small pond and think that means you're pretty special; then you test yourself in a bigger pond and find out your specialness is just ordinary. Then you go into a bigger pond, like when you go for your Master's, and then what happens? You become downright mediocre, that's what!" John's scowl deepened. He was glad the TV was still on because he didn't want to catch a glimpse of himself reflected back by a blank screen. When he shaved that morning, he had noticed how much he looked like his father. John hated his father.

John's thoughts skipped from his education to Sr. Rebecca's. She had asked to sit in on his senior English class next week when she had spring break. He had a suspicion that she would be replacing him at St. Gen's, and again he would find himself without a job just as when the seminary high school had closed. Yeah, that's how it worked with the Church; the layman was dispensable in the mission of the Church. Bright-eyed little nun Rebecca would be ousting him. He hated her too. He hated all nuns. The alcohol was having an effect, and John's unsteady hand did not coordinate well with his mouth, and the whisky dribbled down his shirt.

John brushed it off and looked for a Kleenex to wipe his hand. Nothing presented itself, so he reached down and picked up a paper that had lain next to the stack of essays on the floor. He wiped his hand on it, then wadded it and threw it toward a waste can next to the TV. He failed to notice that a penciled essay by Bob Murphy lay on the underside of the paper he had just tossed aside.

The night offered no release for John Hotchkiss, and he knew it.

Chapter 4

Fr. Ray Dunstan sat in his room, sketching out some ideas for his homily on Sunday. He glanced out the window and noticed the lights had gone off in the convent across the street. St. Genevieve Church and its rectory sat across Elias Street from the convent and high school.

The whole complex had once been such a bustling and promising parish. The Irish Catholics, who had once peopled its pews, had dwindled to a handful of families now, and their places in the pews were taken by a handful of Vietnamese refugees. Blacks had moved in too, but they didn't attend the Catholic churches. Most of the Irish had prospered and moved out to the suburbs, where they now mingled in parishes with the Germans their ancestors had refused to worship with at St. Hildegarde's, which sat a bit more than two blocks east of St. Genevieve's. St. Hildegarde's had the grade school to which St. Genevieve sent its youngsters. St. Hildegarde encouraged its students to enroll at St. Genevieve High. The Cadbury Falls diocese now heavily subsidized both parishes and their schools.

Gus, that is, Fr. Gus Spellinger, was pastor over there. Since both he and Ray were alone in their rectories, they traded off Thursday night dinners with one another. Usually, they would hit a restaurant uptown. It was nice to go into a plush or cozy place and forget the grinding poverty and constant scrabbling for money. Tonight, Gus had looked lower than usual. His boiler, as he had complained to Ray, was "busted but good." It was mid-March, but spring wasn't coming early this year, and they both had to keep heating their schools. Gus kept repeating, "Back in the seminary, they never told us it would be like this!"

It was true too. Sometimes, Ray wondered if he'd done something wrong. Had he inadvertently offended some Monsignor at the Chancery, and so they'd sent him, and others like him, to a dying parish? Ray scratched off the paragraph he'd just jotted down. He mused to himself that on Sundays, he'd be lucky if forty people showed for Mass. It was getting more difficult to bust his butt for a homily that echoed back at him in the huge vault of a church that he had been told to pastor.

Ray bent down to ruffle the head of his mutt. The dog had been an urban stray, left to rummage what scrap of garbage he could find. Ray had taken him in at a lonely time in his life, and it had been a good decision. With old Mack at his heels, the rectory hadn't echoed back so much when he walked from one room to another.

Mack looked up at him expectantly. "What's the matter, old fellow? You need a walk?"

Mack sat up and looked excitedly into Ray's face. He really wanted to bark his approval at the suggestion, but he knew he would be scolded and that would delay getting outside. It worked. Ray stood up and pulled on his heavy, gray pullover sweater. It would be enough for a quick walk up the block and back in the stiff March night.

As they stepped out into the night, Ray placed his jaunty tweed golfer's cap on. That hat was an anomaly because Ray never played golf. Gus had given it to him as a joke for his birthday last year. The street light always lit up the rectory entrance so Ray seldom turned on the porch light. He liked the idea of the city saving the parish a little money.

He and Mack began the nightly sojourn down the street, along the side of the church. As they reached the end of the block, Mack growled. Ray looked down the intersecting block and saw the dark figure move away from the church door. "What's up?" Ray called to the figure that was moving away from him, heading east down Mohammed Street.

The tall shadow stopped and turned. "Nothin', Father. I was just goin' to stop by the church, but it's locked."

Ray recognized the voice. He'd heard it often in confession as well as in his sacristy. It was Bob Murphy, the oldest son of one of the few Irish families that hadn't succeeded financially and moved to the suburbs. Bob's parents had emigrated in the fifties, but his father carried with him the scourge of the Irish. All of this information Ray called up to his consciousness from his brain's pastoral databank as he said, "I'll let you in, Bob."

"No, Father. Don't bother yourself." Ray had been taking steps toward Bob who remained standing where he'd stopped. Bob was wearing a worn navy pea coat. Ray figured that his mother had managed a good buy at the thrift shop down on Madison Ave. He was also wearing thin-soled sneakers that had a hole worn at each little toe. His long hair was unkempt.

"It's no bother, and I think the Lord would be upset with me if I didn't open up for someone who wants to come inside for a chat with him, don't you think, Bob?"

The boy couldn't refute the argument; now, he had to go inside whether that had been his intention or not. Ray couldn't help but wonder if the boy were trying to enter to steal the microphones. The most expensive items in the church were the mikes and amplifiers, more expensive than the chalice. Ray found that incongruous, but it was reality. He locked them up more carefully than he did his chalice, which his parents paid for and which he had used for his own first Mass fifteen years ago.

Bob followed him to the church door as Fr. Ray fished the key ring from under his sweater where it was tethered to his belt. The keys flashed a glint from the street light. "You go ahead in, Bob. I'll just walk Mack back to the rectory, and then I'll come back. Don't leave before I come back though. I wouldn't want to leave the place wide open. Some old guy might come in for the shelter, and I'd lock him in without realizing it. Some churches have burned down that way."

Bob shook his head and walked inside. Ray still couldn't decide if Bob was sincere about praying or not. When Ray returned, he saw Bob seated in a pew about a quarter of the way up the main aisle. The moonlight passed quietly through the window up ahead. It was a pretty sight and reminded Ray of the abbey seminary chapel where he had been educated for the priesthood. Those were his days of innocence when he wanted to do brave and wonderful things for people and for God. He hadn't known then how it would all boil down to dollars and cents.

As Ray's steps brought him closer, Bob became aware of the squeak in Ray's right shoe and slid himself a little further over in the pew to make room. Ray entered and sat next to him. They sat that way for a few more minutes. "I like it in here, Father. It's quiet, you know." Ray was aware that an ambulance was screaming down Madison Avenue, but for Bob, Ray knew, it was quiet. He had said nothing; he himself was feeling the peace that the moonlight brought to the interior of the cavernous church. Bob continued, apparently feeling that Ray needed more explanation. "It's hard with a TV blaring, and my old man swearing at Ma, you know. Jeremy and Sean are always fightin'. I don't know, but I just need to get out of there sometimes."

"I hear you, Bob. It's your age too. What are you now, sixteen?" Bob nodded in the affirmative. "When I was sixteen, I got restless too."

"Yeah?" Bob looked sideways for the first time. Ray no longer found it amusing that people thought a priest was a man without feelings, much less that he ever had the normal feelings of any young person.

"I think that the restlessness is good though, Bob. God has to get us ready to leave the nest, to go out and make it on our own. In a few short years, you'll be making your own "nest", and you wouldn't be doing it if you weren't restless. Once I watched a little fledgling trying to learn to fly. He sat, gripping the edge of the nest and flapping his wings." Ray tucked both hands into his armpits to simulate the bird as he flapped his bent arms. "Well, those flapping wings gave him lift, but he just clung to that nest. He nearly lost his balance."

Ray paused, wondering if a boy like Bob ever stopped and watched birds. His examples in his Sunday homilies were often drawn from his middle-class background and fell short in this inner-city area where few trees could be found. He pulled up and lifted his sagging torso; placing his arms out along the back of the pew, he raised his head and laughed briefly, saying, "I often wondered if that bird grew so big that he flew away with that nest he was clinging to."

Bob yawned next to him. "What time is it, Father?"

Ray pulled his sweater cuff back and turned the dial toward the moonlight. "It's half past ten, Bob. Think you better get home?"

"Yeah, I guess." Bob put his long arms on his knees and stretched his back. "Thanks for letting me in, Father. God will be happy with you, I guess."

They both genuflected, and Ray was aware that Bob used his left knee. He didn't bother to "teach" church etiquette just then because something inside him had sighed and said that it was no use. They walked down the aisle, and Ray noticed the squeak of his shoe in synch with the boy's soft pad. When they reached the outside, they parted with sparse words.

As Ray turned away to walk home, he noticed a light in one of the far windows of the high school. He reached for his keys again, the keys of the kingdom, he referred to them, knowing that if he didn't turn off that light, then it would burn the entire night and run up an already impossible electric bill.

Chapter 5

Detective Terrence Hogan was returning to the Madison Avenue precinct as he drove past St. Gen's. He saw the pastor and a young fellow parting company by the church. He automatically checked his watch. The boy had a half-hour to curfew. Terry figured the priest was sending the boy home with a view to the hour.

He stopped at the traffic sign at Mohammed and Elias, noticing the priest stopping and then heading across the street toward the school. Terry wondered if the priest was going over to check if anything was amiss at the school. Terry also had noticed the light shining from the second-story window of the school.

Terry drove across Elias and pulled to the curb, parking illegally against any oncoming traffic. He rolled his window down and yelled out at the priest. "Hey, Father, anything going on in school?" Terry's parents once lived in this area; he was glad they moved out to a safer neighborhood about fifteen years ago. Terry worked the old neighborhood with the homicide division. Business was increasing in that department almost week to week.

The priest stepped over warily. Terry was in an unmarked car. "I was just going to check on it. I'm Fr. Ray." He paused, waiting for the slightly overweight man with sandy hair to reciprocate.

"I'm Detective Hogan. Maybe I ought to go in with you, Father. Drugs are a problem in the neighborhood, and you never know if someone is looking for something to sell for a fix."

The priest looked at him and then at the upstairs window. "Well, I don't mind if you've got the time." Terry hefted himself out of the car. The patrol shift would recognize his car and not ticket it. He extended a hand to the priest.

"You can't be too careful anymore. Time was we didn't worry about that. Even priests aren't immune to violence these days, Father." The priest led him to a side entrance door and inserted a key. Terry had taken the time to grab his flashlight when he'd gotten out of his car. He snapped it on before the priest could find the light switch. "Better not turn the lights on, just in case." He felt the priest fall behind him, instinctively.

"Where are the stairs to the second floor?" Terry was thinking to himself that the place smelled like a school. Schools had a distinctive smell; maybe it was the chalk. It wasn't a people smell. Terry knew what people smells were: sweat, blood, urine, vomit.

"Just beyond those lockers." The priest's hand, gesturing toward the lockers, was suddenly illuminated by the beam of light from Terry's flashlight. It seemed detached from the rest of his body, which was enveloped in the darkness of the school and of his clothes. They walked forward. Terry saw the stairs, narrower in width than he expected. He leaned his shoulder against the wall and let the contour of the wall guide his ascent. He held his flashlight low to the floor, outlining the steps with a muted light.

When they reached the top of the landing, he snapped the light off. The offending light from the classroom lit the hallway from the point of origin all the way to the landing. They could hear a noise coming from the room. Terry looked at the priest and tried to sound as if he were making a suggestion, "Better let me go the rest of the way alone."

The priest nodded and stood shielded by the doorframe of the landing, but Terry knew that the priest's head was extended beyond, watching him as he walked quietly down the hall, his shoulder close to the wall. He passed two unlit classrooms and as he came closer, he could hear a man humming and then the sound of metal grating across the floor. He figured he was probably about to make a small-time drug bust. Some kid like the one he'd seen with the priest probably.

Then Terry placed his hand on the doorknob, his gun raised in position. Just like TV, he thought. He stepped quickly in and yelled, "Police!" A small, stocky man, apparently in the act of pushing a mop, stood still, his eyes growing bigger as he looked at Terry. Terry imagined the guy's heart was beating harder with each second. Looking at the mop, Terry knew the man's answer before he asked the question, but he asked anyhow. "What are you doing here?"

"I...uh...I...I...I work here." The man's mouth was a small oval but his eyes were, by comparison, much larger ovals. Terry almost wanted to laugh because the oval orifices reminded him of the cartoon of Little Orphan Annie. Wisps of hair seemed to shoot straight up from the man's balding pate, giving his appearance a further comical side. He was probably in his thirties. It was hard to tell, but judging by the fact that his cardigan was tattered and buttoned incorrectly, making it hang in a lop-sided way, Terry figured the guy was also mentally retarded.

"You work the night shift too?" Terry put his gun back and leaned out into the hall to beckon the priest forward.

"I didn't get my work done. I have to do my work, all of it, or God won't love me."

Terry looked back at the man. He was parroting something he'd been told which, in turn, confirmed Terry's impressions about the guy's mental ability. The priest came in just then.

"Duffy, why are you working now?"

"Sorry, Father. Got to finish now." The dumpy, little guy looked so serious.

"Duffy, it's alright. You don't have to finish. Tomorrow is another day." The priest looked at Terry. "Duffy helps out with the cleaning. He lives with his mother down on Grover." The priest lowered his voice. "She runs a pretty tight ship."

"No, Father, I got to finish. Jesus loves people when they do their job." Duffy had learned his lessons well, thought Terry.

The priest glanced at the detective. "Duffy, you can clean just this one room; then you must turn out the light and be sure to lock the door when you leave. Do you hear me?"

"Yes, Father. I clean this one room, just this one room. One room." Duffy turned and pushed the mop.

The priest shrugged his shoulders and left the room. Terry followed him out. He snapped on his flashlight when they came to the stairs. "Do you think he'll remember to lock the place up?"

"Yes, he's very conscientious that way. I gave him a key because he likes to open the school and greet the students when they arrive, and he does clean after school closes, so he usually locks up and leaves by the front door. Still, I'll check later on to make sure everything is secure."

Terry thought about the priest staying up later. He knew the bulletin board on Mohammed announced a 6:30 AM Mass. "You relax, Father. I'll have a patrol stop by and check the doors when they make their rounds."

"Thanks, Detective...Hogan, wasn't it?" The priest smiled wearily.

"That's right. I work the nights cleaning up after those sinners who don't get your message, Father. Rest well!" They parted then, Terry walking to his car, and the priest breaking into a trot across Elias to his rectory.

Chapter 6

Bob had noticed the car that slowed at the stop sign on Elias as he left the priest to return to his home. He knew it was a cop. He had been hanging out with Walter Atkins. Walter was a big black guy who lived in an apartment with his mother on Madison, not far from the precinct. Walter had studied the cops, and the unmarked cars they drove. He didn't have much else to do. He had dropped out of high school and was about twenty now. Walter had begun his "employment" as a lookout for the Madison Mandrakes, a street gang of toughs, as Bob's mother called them. And they were tough too.

Bob had met Walter in October when he had gone to the Madison Avenue thrift store at his mother's insistence. He had been told to return with a winter coat that would fit him. She had given Sean the coat he had been wearing. Bob liked it, but his mother didn't like the fact that his arms had outgrown the sleeves; at least, that's what she said, but Bob wasn't sure because his ma always favored Sean.

The problem had all started when Bob saw the pea coat. He liked it a lot because one day he planned to join the navy. If he could talk his folks into it, he wanted them to sign for him so he could join on his next birthday. Anyhow, he had looked at the price of the pea coat. His ma had told him to spend not more than 75 cents, and the coat was marked at $1.25. As he looked about, trying to figure what to do, he noticed this big nigger just milling around. The nigger glanced at Bob, and then, it seemed to Bob, the nigger suddenly was standing next to him. "You lik'at coat, white boy?"

Bob felt his throat go dry. He tensed for trouble. "Yeah."

"You gonna purchase dat coat?"

"I can't. I don't have the money." Bob felt the sting of his poverty as he heard his own words.

"Dat's right, white boy. You don't purchase no coat; you take dat coat if'n you want dat coat."

Bob looked quickly at the thin young man who stood a head or more taller than himself. "You want me to steal it?" Bob had stolen small items before but never anything as bulky as a coat. He hadn't a clue how to do that. You couldn't slip a coat into a pocket and walk nonchalantly out of the store.

"You chicken?" The fellow looked down at him with amusement and mischief dancing together in his dark eyes.

"No. I just never took anything like this before." Bob didn't want to seem like a complete neophyte in this rough neighborhood.

"Tell y'what, whitey, I'll do it for you. How dat be? Den you give me the money you got."

Bob thought about the proposition. After all, he would be paying for it that way. It wasn't as if the store would be out. Someone donated the coat in the first place. "Okay. But you have to show me how you do it; in case, I need to use the skills again." Bob figured he would get the most bang for his buck or, more accurately, the three quarters in his pocket.

"Deal." The nigger raised his hand for a high five. After Bob had raised his hand to return the salute, the tall boy leaned over. "Y'go ovah to the othah side of da store. You be lookin' pale t'me, so you go ovah and fall 'ginst dat rack dere. Dey gonna come runnin', and you be ackin' like you faintin'. Kinda roll yo' eyes upatop yo' head." He drew the last word out, motioning upward with his own head. "Den come out of it and giv'em a line about havin' fits, y'know, eplepsy or sumpin'. I meetcha on Downer Street by the ol' pickle factory. You ready?"

Bob had the feeling he was dealing with a professional. He also felt he had to show this guy just how good he was at acting like an epileptic. He nodded and flashed a rueful grin at the tall boy. As he slowly stepped away, he noticed his accomplice removing the coat from its hanger to examine it. He also noticed that one of the volunteers who ran the place was watching the nigger nervously. Bob knew he would have to be very convincing.

He had stopped by a bin of shoes and hunched down on it, rubbing his temples. He hoped that his new mentor was watching his performance. Then without looking in the direction of the black boy, although he wanted to, Bob stood up and walked with uncertain steps, staring straight ahead. He could only hope that this was what an epileptic did. He had no idea since he'd never seen anyone who was having a seizure.

Finally, he stood at the appointed rack. He reached out for some article of clothing, blinking his eyes, and moving his head as if trying to shake something off. Then he fell forward, toppling the rack with him. He heard the woman shriek. He held his jaws rigid and kept grinding his teeth, trying to make his eyes roll back. He succeeded only in seeing the lights on the ceiling, but with his chin resting on his chest, he hoped his eyes were rolling backward. Two other women from nowhere had joined the original. They were talking at once, and one was commanding the others to call 911. Then they all shouted 911, but no one was moving to make the call.

With a grunt, Bob let his eyes drop, but he kept focusing in the distance, presuming this would give a kind of eyes-open-but-unconscious look. One of the ladies finally hefted herself from her kneeling position and declared, "I'll call the police." Bob then realized how dangerous that would be. They would be able to spot a fake. His mentor hadn't told him what to do in that case. Suddenly Bob was ready to come out of his fit, coat or no coat.

"Where, where am I?" He tried to say the words slowly, but his panic was causing his pulse to race, and he feared his words followed in like manner.

"Take it easy," assured one of the kindly women whose reassuring smile contrasted with the fear in her eyes.

"Oh, I'm alright. I have these little spells. They pass." He moved to stand, and the women immediately grabbed his arms.

"Maybe you should sit down." The fat woman to his left called to the one who had intended to put in a call. "Jeannette, call the police. Tell them we might need an ambulance."

"No!" Bob realized he sounded too strong. "I have these spells all the time. They pass as quickly as they come on. Honest, I'm just fine now." He smiled at them.

The women looked doubtfully at one another. "Well, I don't know much about epilepsy although my dog has had some seizures, and it's true that as soon as the seizure is over, you'd never know he had one." Jeannette was culling through her canine experiences as they looked at one another doubtfully. They looked back at Bob. He felt reassured by Jeanette's account of canine seizures.

"Thank you, ladies. I'll just go home now and get some medicine if you don't mind." They watched him as he left.

When Bob reached the sidewalk, he tore off running for his rendezvous with Walter at Grover and Stanton. Within a block, Bob was panting and had to run in shorter spurts the rest of the way. He saw Walter waiting for him with a grin on his face, his lips showing red and his teeth a bright white against his dark skin.

"Good show, my man!"

"Thanks! I didn't see you leave. That was good."

"Walter's my name. What's yours?"

"Bob." Bob felt his status change as they gave out their names. Now they were on a personal basis because he had won the other's respect. "Can I have my coat?"

"Sure, Bob. All you be needin' is some cash."

"Oh, yeah. I almost forgot." Bob dug into his pocket and pulled out the coins. "It's what my ma gave me for the coat."

Walter looked into his hand and shook his head. "Not 'nuff, Bob."

"What d'ya mean? You told me you'd steal the coat, and I'd pay you."

"I know, man. Take it easy. Look at it dis way. Didn't I just risk jail for yo' coat, Bob? I been in juvey three times, man. I'm old enough to do hard time now, and I risked everything, so's you could get dat coat. Hear me, man?"

Walter was right. Bob didn't like it, but he couldn't refute it either. "Look, Walter, I want to give you more. You're right about deserving more, but I don't have more. If I did, I'd give it to you." As he fished in his pocket on the off chance that he was carrying more, he felt his half-finished pack of cigarettes. "Here, I'll throw these into the bargain."

"Dat's real sweet, Bob." Walter's look turned sinister. "But, Bob, a pack of stale cigs don't cut it. Know what I mean?"

Bob looked around nervously. He was not in safe territory, and he suddenly realized it. "What do you want from me?"

Walter smiled appreciatively at his coming to his senses. "Bob, I be wantin' sumpun like a favor now and den. Not too much. In fack, I be wantin' you to make a little money here and dere. You be wantin' money too, don't cha, little Bobby?" Walter placed a firm hand on Bob's shoulder and looked questioningly into Bob's eyes.

Bob felt the little sick feeling he'd had a moment ago increasing. Maybe he should just walk away. He could just tell his ma that he couldn't find anything his size. He'd give her the money back and tell her to find him one. He never wanted to go near Madison Avenue again. Then he realized that he would not be able to walk away with his money. Walter continued to look into his eyes. Bob looked away.

"C'mon, Bobby. You goin' do me a favor?"

"What are my options!" Bob said with sarcasm and sadness.

"That's my man!" Walter stepped away and placing his fingers in his mouth let out a piercing whistle. Then Bob saw six other boys around his age appear from various hiding places. "Jo-Jo, let me present to you my man heah, Bob. He wants to help us out." Walter was apparently addressing a thin, wiry, short boy with a navy blue stocking cap covering his head. The tip of his earlobe revealed a small gold earring. He kept sniffing his nose, and Bob wondered if he had a cold. The scar on Jo-Jo's cheek made the uneasy Bob even more so.

"Good! Bob, I'm glad to have you with us." He glanced around, gesturing toward the others. They looked somberly at Bob. "Why, Bob, you are our very first white boy. You are one lucky motha-fuckah!" The other boys all laughed. "C'mon in, Bob. You lookin' like you be needin' to sit down." Jo-Jo led the way down Grover to the side of the old, abandoned pickle factory. He came to a busted-out basement window and slid through and down to the floor with ease. Walter pushed Bob toward the window. Bob slid through without Jo-Jo's facility. The rest slid through with an agility that reminded Bob of firemen descending the firehouse pole in a movie he'd seen.

"Let's sit." Jo-Jo sat down cross-legged on the floor. The rest followed Jo-Jo's lead. The fellow who sat across from Bob unzipped his jacket, and Bob saw a huge, mean-looking revolver shoved in his belt. Bob licked his lips; his mouth had gone very dry. "Now, Bob, I believe you owe us a favor. Is that right?" Bob noticed that Jo-Jo's English was not unfamiliar to him. Jo-Jo must have a mother like his own, always correcting his grammar.

"I owe Walter some money for a jacket which I don't have." Bob glanced at the coat, which Walter had laid across his lap.

"If you owe Walter, you owe all of us. Ain't dat right, brothers?" They all murmured their assent. Bob could see the look of hatred in their eyes. He wondered if he would die in this vacant old building.

"Well, that's a right nice coat, Bob. That's worth plenty, wouldn't you say?"

"They were selling it for $1.25." Bob was trying to sound brave, but he felt the urge to pee.

Jo-Jo didn't miss anything. "Hey, Bob, you go over to that wall and piss. Then we goin' ta talk business."

Bob was horribly embarrassed, and he again felt their scorn. Still, he had to go so badly that he stood up. His legs felt shaky under him. He reached the wall and unzipped his pants. He tried to keep his private parts out of their view.

When he returned to the circle, he noticed the boy with the revolver, leaning back on his hands, his long arms extended out behind him and his long legs now sprawled in front of him. The effect was that the revolver was more ominously in view, the butt hanging forward over his belt. Bob sat down, but now he was fighting that feeling of nausea again.

Jo-Jo leaned forward. "Bob, you an intellectual, aren't you? I mean, you goin' ta that nice school up on Elias, gettin' a good edication?" Jo-Jo was putting out questions, but Bob knew he wasn't asking from a need for the information.

"Yeah." Bob was trying to meet Jo-Jo's eyes.

"Good. Bob, my man, we in de bizness of sellin' a commodity. You look like a real good salesman, Bob. I want yo' ta learn a trade that can make you a rich man. You won't be wearin' old pea coat no mo' if yo' be learnin' yo' trade good." Bob wondered why Jo-Jo kept wondering in and out of good English and nigger talk. He thought maybe when Jo-Jo looked at his followers, he slipped into their lingo, but when he spoke looking at Bob, he spoke regular English. It scared Bob even more since he felt he was seeing a human chameleon who effortlessly changed from one person to another. Nothing was steady or recognizable for Bob, and this disorientation was unnerving.

"Bob, pay attention! Look up here at me!" Bob's head jerked up. He hadn't realized that he had dropped his head. "My commodity is coke. Your little classmates are bored in that classroom, Bob. They need some relief. They be glad for some. You gonna provide dat relief!" Jo-Jo's cadence was reminiscent of a preacher that Bob had seen on television. "Bob, I gonna give you some now, just so you know what kind of relief I be talkin' about."

One of the boys produced a bag of white powder. They proceeded to show him what to do. Bob had never been so frightened in his life. He tried not to sniff deeply, but they insisted he do so until the white powder had disappeared. Very shortly, Bob felt euphoric release. He had never known euphoria before, but he believed that must be what he was feeling. He didn't feel afraid anymore. He found himself laughing with these menacing types. Time passed without his awareness although he saw that it had grown darker in the room. But Bob was enjoying himself. He felt camaraderie with these guys, a feeling he liked although he was pretty much a loner at school. Why did his father think they were just "dumb niggers?" He liked them. In fact, he liked the whole world, and he liked liking the whole world.

Then, he heard Jo-Jo addressing him. "Here, Bob, you stand up now." Two boys lifted him, and, at first, he felt he would float. "You take this coat, Bob. Den you come back here in a couple days, Bob. We talk business den, and maybe we'll have some more fun too."

Bob was happy and giggled as they pushed him out the window. He walked taller than he'd ever walked down Stanton and back down Madison, past the little thrift shop. He found himself sneering over at the police station. Pigs, he thought. He was proud of his coat. He was proud of his new friends. He had even hugged Walter before he'd left and thanked him.

As Bob had entered the house, his father was at the door. His ma was standing a distance behind with a worried look on her face. "Where have you been?" Before he could speak, his father leaned forward to smell his breath. "He ain't been drinkin'." His father had spoken the words over his shoulder, apparently meaning them for his wife. "You get yourself upstairs and do your school work, hear me? You're grounded for a week. Scarin' your ma like that!"

That's how he came to this night, Bob thought, as he looked up at the moon and wondered if his father would ground him again for being out so late tonight. His dad wouldn't believe that he'd been to church, praying for God to release him from his need for the stupid drug!

Bob was right. His dad met him at the door, followed him to the bedroom he'd ordered him to, and beat him with his belt. The physical pain was almost a relief from the inner turmoil Bob Murphy was suffering.

Chapter 7

Duffy finished his work that night. He went to his janitorial closet on the first floor and put the mop in its place. He stuck his head back out and looked up and down the hall to make sure he was alone. He could barely reach the top shelf above the deep sink, but standing on his toes, he stretched until his fingers met the curled edges of the magazine. He inched it forward. Finally, the edge protruded over the shelf where he could grab hold. He removed the magazine and then walked stealthily to the men's room. If he turned on a light there, no one would see because the bathroom had no windows. He would not have to worry about the policeman or Fr. Ray there.

Sr. Gretchen had given him the magazine. She had done a locker search and discovered the "filthy thing" and told Duffy to "dispose of it". Duffy wasn't sure what all the words meant. He seldom did, and so he had decided to put it aside. He would look at it and try to decide what to do with it later. Now, it was later, and none of the boys were around, and neither was Sr. Gretchen. Duffy feared her as much as he feared his mother.

He began to look at the magazine. There was a pretty girl on the front page who smiled alluringly at him. She was glancing over her shoulder. Duffy felt uncomfortable. He didn't like it when a woman looked at him. That's why when one of the sisters spoke to him, he always looked away. They always looked at him, straight in his eyes. He didn't like that.

Duffy turned the page and looked at some words he couldn't understand with numbers written next to the words. He knew what the number 2 looked like. He could always recognize that because it looked like a bent little man. That's what his mother had told him. He could never remember what she told him about the other numbers though, just the bent little man.

Duffy turned another page. He saw a woman's breasts. He'd never really seen them before. Well, he looked at some of the girls in the school sometimes, but they always had sweaters and blouses covering them. He only imagined what they looked like. He never knew until now. Well, not really, but this was the only time he dared to just look at them. Once he'd seen a naked woman on a television movie, but his mother had slapped him for looking. He liked looking at them. He raised the page to his face. He wished they were real. He wondered what they felt like.

Duffy turned another page. Another pretty woman was looking at him. It was a scornful look, and Duffy quickly turned to another page. There on the sand was a beautiful woman with her arms stretched out, lifting her bare breasts higher to meet his eyes. Her own eyes were closed. Duffy liked that. He felt very aroused. He kept staring. He began to stroke the body in the picture, and she kept her eyes closed. Duffy liked the feelings he was having. He put the magazine on the floor and lay down next to it. He felt all kinds of sensations that he never had before. He decided that Sr. Gretchen was right. The magazine was filthy. All except this picture.

He leaned forward and tore it carefully from the magazine. Then he folded it just as carefully and returned to the janitor's closet. He looked around for a place to put his picture. It would be too difficult to reach it on the top shelf. He saw the bag of rags that hung from a nail on the wall. He slipped the picture deep into the bag. Then he took the magazine and held it with the cover underneath so that he wouldn't see that woman looking at him and threw it into the trash can in the front office.

Duffy left through the front door and carefully locked it. He liked carrying the key to that door. He envied Fr. Ray's big key ring that he wore on his belt. Fr. Ray was important. He was the boss, and even Sr. Gretchen knew that. He wanted to be like Fr. Ray and make women not boss him. If he could get enough keys, maybe he could be like Fr. Ray.

Duffy padded down the sidewalk and continued down Mohammed to Madison. This was the part of his journey to his home that he didn't like. He had to cross Madison and continue down Mohammed to get to his mother's apartment on Grover. At the corner, he nearly always encountered the black boys. They always made fun of him. One of them, a tall boy they called Walter would walk like an ape behind him for half a block. He didn't like that. Tonight, he saw that there were three of them. Walter was not among them. Maybe they wouldn't notice him.

"Yo, man! What's up?" One of them yelled at him as he approached the curb. Duffy kept his head down and walked with determination. As he tried to pass, the one who'd called to him, caught him and held him. "Hey, man, you hear me?"

"LeRoy, leave him be. He's a fruitcake." Duffy turned to look at the speaker. He had a dark blue cap on and an ugly scar on his face. LeRoy released him. Duffy stood there, not knowing what to do. "Go on, whitey, git!" The scarface pushed him with a foot to his behind. Duffy scuttled forward and kept going. He heard the laughter behind him.

When he entered the apartment, his mother was sitting in a sheer nightdress, watching TV. Duffy averted his eyes as he pulled off his coat. "Where the hell you been?" She glanced toward Duffy. "Oh, my gawd! You filthy thing! Get those pants off. I'm ashamed of you! You get any girl pregnant, and that's it for you. They'll ship you off to a looney farm for sure. I won't be able to do anything about it, you hear me?"

Duffy turned and walked into the room behind him, pulling the little curtain behind him. His mother continued to rant for a few more minutes. He didn't understand what she was saying. Why was she so upset? He never could understand why she screamed at him when he came home.

She often threatened him with being shipped off. He vaguely understood that it meant separation from her, but sometimes he wanted to be separated. It was hard to understand if that was a good thing or a bad thing. Duffy dutifully pulled his pants off and noticed that they were wet near the crotch. Maybe when LeRoy grabbed him, the scarface had thrown water on him. Duffy sat on his bed, wishing he could understand all the things he couldn't seem to understand. He reached in his pants' pocket and pulled out the key. It made him feel better.

Chapter 8

"So early, Bob?" His mother had just entered the kitchen where he was eating a slice of bread heavily smeared with peanut butter. "I can fix you a proper breakfast. School doesn't start for another hour, does it?"

"No, Ma, I have a meeting before school. I belong to that new club, remember?" Bob crammed the rest of the bread into his mouth.

"Now, that's no way to eat!" His ma was always trying to teach him to be a lace-curtain Irishman. No chance, thought Bob.

"Bye, Ma," Bob kissed her soft cheek. His mother had no kind of life. Her husband was a drunk who couldn't hold a job for long, which left her valiantly trying to cadge the little money she pried out of him to take care of the three boys he'd generously given her.

Bob walked down the street, torn as he always was. He was on his way for his "fix" as Walter called it. It would get him through Hotchkiss's boring English class and Sr. Maria's choral practice. He walked with determination but with his head down. He was meeting with Walter twice a week now. It had started out as a weekly meeting on Fridays. He would give Walter the money from the previous week's order for the kids at St. Gen's. Then for his pay, Walter would give Bob his snort of coke. Bob never saw any money.

Walter had told him that he used his pay up, buying his snort. Bob was so eager to get the coke for himself that he didn't care about the figures, but about midweek, his head would clear, and he'd feel he was being cheated. He was doing some risky business after all.

It had been difficult to get started. There was a little Vietnamese girl, a freshman. He called her Lily because she seemed so fragile to him. Her real name was Liu or something like that. Anyhow, she liked him. For himself, he didn't much care one way or the other nowadays. Jo-Jo had told him he'd "loan" some coke to Bob to help him get started in the business.

So, he asked Lily for a date. She seemed so happy. He was taking her to the dance that the upper class at St. Gen's held once a month to raise money for a prom. They danced for awhile, but the white powder in the little baggy deep in his pocket was constantly on his mind. It was the only thing that released him from the agony of his life at home, at school, everywhere.

"We go now? Why so soon?" Lily looked crushed as he pulled her toward the exit.

"I thought we'd just go for a walk. It's too hot in here." Bob led her by the hand out of the cafeteria-turned-dance-hall. Her hand felt so small, like a child's. Sometimes she had to run to keep up with his stride; that's how small she was. They went out to the alley behind the school.

"I good girl, Bob," Lily said. Bob knew she was protesting for her virginity.

"Sure, you are, Lily. I won't hurt you. I just want to share something I found. It's helped me a lot. I get pretty depressed and sad a lot of the time."

"I know what you mean," Lily's small voice indicated that she felt the same way; her little face was sad at the moment.

"See this?" Bob pulled the baggy out and held it close between them. Anybody observing them would have thought a young couple was out in the alley, trying to neck.

"What that?" Lily, who had carefully maneuvered her mouth to make the "th" sound of English, looked up at Bob, puzzled.

"It's medicine for sadness." Bob was getting more eager to have some. "Here, I'll show you what it will do for me. Then, I'll let you try it too."

"I don't know, Bob. Maybe not good to take other people's medicine." Lily's forehead had little furrows across it.

"No, Lily. This is a universal medicine. It makes everybody happy who takes it. Watch." He couldn't wait any longer. He prepared and sniffed deeply. It wouldn't be long before the euphoria would come. "This is so great, Lily! Now, you take some." Bob prepared it for her, but she backed off a step.

"I not know, Bob."

"Lily, do you want to be my girlfriend?"

Lily needed a boyfriend. Her father had died last year, and while her mother worked hard, they never got ahead. Her brother, a senior at the public school several blocks away, would come home to the empty little apartment to find his only amusement, abusing poor Lily. She hated being alone at home with him. Since she was disgraced and no longer a virgin, Liu wondered if she would ever get a boyfriend. But, she reasoned, if she could get a boyfriend, one as tall and strong as Bob, then perhaps her brother would leave her alone. She felt so afraid and depressed most of the time. Maybe Bob was right. He was smiling and moving back and forth like she did when she got that A on her composition from old, mean Mr. Hotchkiss. "You be my boyfriend, Bob?"

"You bet," Bob found it hard to focus on her words.

"What I do, Bob?" She was dutifully instructed. From Lily, Bob's list grew to include her brother and slowly some others in Lily's class of freshmen. However, Bob found that the depression and sadness of his daily life had begun to increase. One time a week was not enough anymore. The good feeling was so quickly gone. So Bob reasoned that his list of customers had grown enough to merit a visit to the ol' pickle factory at least twice a week.

As he neared said factory last week, he had seen Walter turn and head for the entrance window that Bob had learned to master as well as Jo-Jo and the rest. When he slid in, he high-fived Walter who asked, "Hey, man, where's the money?"

Bob, already pulling it out, had been growing ever more eager to get his portion of the coke. Walter had insisted on counting the money lately. Bob hated that; it slowed things down.

"What's the order?"

"Same."

"That be three weeks now. Ain't you increasin' yo' share of the market? Gotta do bettah dan dat, man!"

Bob's ache was nearly intolerable. "Let me have it, man. I got to have it now."

Walter smiled at him and held a little baggy up. Bob lunged for it, but Walter merely held it higher. "Now, Bobby, my man. You gonna work harder?"

"Yes! Please!" Walter handed him the baggy, and Bob rushed to set up his snort. He sat still for awhile, waiting for his release. Walter had turned to leave. "Wait," Bob called out. He'd almost forgotten about Wednesdays.

Walter turned back and stood over him. "Whachu want, little whitey?"

"If I get more on the list, can I have a hit on Wednesdays too?" Bob knew his voice sounded pleading, but he couldn't help it.

"If....hmm. Dat's a big if, Bob. If'n y'double yo' list, den, sho, Bobby. But, Bobby, lissen to Walter." Walter grabbed Bob's face in his hands and looked menacingly at him. "I be here on Wednesdays, but you bettah show me green if'n y'want my stuff. So, don't be wastin' my time!" Walter released Bob's face and hoisted himself deftly out the window. Bob sat enveloped in his smog of happiness.

Bob had trouble adding to his list. He had to be very careful since the anti-drug message was so heavy at the school. Squealers were everywhere. Lily's brother and a friend of his also wanted a Wednesday hit, but that wasn't enough money to provide for Bob's extra hit. On Tuesday, Bob had decided to ransack the girls' purses when they were at gym. Usually, they left them on top of their books just outside the entrance area to the cafeteria-turned-gymnasium since going to one's locker other than at the beginning and conclusion of school was forbidden. It was one way to control the use of drugs, but Bob decided it might help his use. He managed to scrape together from those purses what he thought would satisfy Walter. It was a good-will offering.

As it turned out, Walter, who seemed to have no good will lately, gave him less than his usual dose because there hadn't been enough money. That frustration had led him to the church last night. He'd hoped that some door would have remained open. He had never tried to visit in the church other than for going to Sunday Mass, so he had no idea that churches were locked up. He intended to take anything to barter with Walter. As it turned out, Fr. Ray had caught him, and he ended up praying for God to release him from this need for the drug that he couldn't stop.

Today he had the money to turn over for his Friday fix, but he knew that he needed to start working to find money for next Wednesday. His world was so small: church, school, family. The church was locked up, his family was broke, and that left the school.

That was already difficult in any case. He had narrowly escaped when he stole money from the girls' purses. It had created a big stir in the school. He had simply skipped the rest of his classes and headed out after he'd stolen the money. Apparently, Sr. Gretchen held a locker search after the girls reported the ransacking of their purses. It was kind of amusing because when he had ransacked the purses, he'd found condoms in some of them. He was willing to bet no one had claimed them when they found them scattered on the floor outside the gym. In fact, Bob figured they had probably been left to lie on the gym floor like pariahs. Wonder if Sr. Gretchen told old Duffy to go pick 'em up. Duffy wouldn't know what they were.

As it turned out, old Gretch had found a stash of money in one of the lockers. Joe Hennessey had been running a crap game down on Stanton, close to Madison. His old man did numbers, so it was in his genes, thought Bob. Whatever, Joe didn't own up to the gambling, so he was accused of stealing from the girls. Hell, thought Bob, anybody could have known Joe didn't take that much from the girls. They probably made all kinds of false claims and dumb old Gretch had handed Joe's money out to them.

Still, Bob's problems were increasing, and the only outlet was his fix. For a little bit of heaven, Bob was sure living a lot of hell, he considered. Then he saw Walter standing, waiting for him, and he quickened his step.

Chapter 9

Detective Hogan was spinning the wheel of his unmarked car to make a right turn up Stanton from Madison. He was setting out for a call on Fenton Place, a little half street that dead-ended on Grover near Stanton. A dead woman had been found in an alley just off Fenton Place. That's when he spotted the lanky, white boy coming from the direction of the old, abandoned building. He checked his watch and smiled. The boy had about 10 minutes to get to St. Gen's or 20 minutes to get to Orrin Hatch High if that was his destination. At any rate, if he hoofed it, he'd be all right. Judging from his pace, he would. Something about the boy wanted to connect with some storage file in Hogan's head. He tried to ignore it though since he had to concentrate on a crime scene.

It was a frosty morning, and the murder was the reason for having to put in overtime. The night had been relatively quiet for homicide. The cold night had kept most of the action inside, but that's usually when the homicides occurred. People crowded inside, starting to fight and letting it accelerate until it got out of hand. Usually one party was drunk or drugged in some way. It was a disgusting world that Terry Hogan saw during his watch.

A cop had a hard time seeing the bright side to this world, he said to himself as he settled back. He saw the boy bobbing along in his rear view mirror, getting smaller as Hogan accelerated in the opposite direction. He could only see the pea coat moving up and down as the boy walked down the sidewalk, having passed the peak of its arch as it descended down Stanton Street. Pea coat! That boy at the church last night had a pea coat. Couldn't be the same one though, Hogan shook his head, because that boy had walked away from Madison, down Mohammed, on his way home. All the same, Hogan decided to keep a sharp eye out for boys wearing pea coats. Leather substitutes were the in thing around the neighborhood at the moment anyhow, so a pea coat wouldn't be hard to spot.

Hogan was pressing the accelerator too heavily, he warned himself. He spotted another juvenile. Kids on their way to school; *I got to slow down.* He grabbed a sip from his coffee mug. The thermos from which he'd filled it rolled around aimlessly on the floor. *Millie still makes the best coffee,* he thought, *even if she's no beauty anymore.*

He remembered that first shock when he found himself going to bed with a bunch of wire curlers and a greasy face. It wasn't easy to make love that way. They never showed that in the movies where the girl's hair was so fine and her skin so soft. Millie was a grease pit, and he had learned not to get too close to her wire curlers. One time, he got nicked, and the guys at work had commented on it, but he'd told them he'd nicked himself shaving. They must have thought he was out of it because the nick was above his beard on the high side of his cheekbone. Aside from that, he couldn't complain about Millie.

He was no great catch either. He was a steady income, and he tried to be a good father, but he wasn't kidding himself. Being a cop meant he wasn't there for the family. People didn't kill at his convenience. On top of that, his family had to put up with what they called his "suspicious mind." Over the years, Detective Hogan had grown in his mistrust of the human being. Sometimes that spilled out to his family. It was inevitable.

Jody, his 14-year-old, had wanted to go on a date last week. He had been investigating a death of a kid her age at the time. The prime suspect was a boy who apparently had tried to rape the girl because he didn't take no for an answer. Jody got so mad at Terry when he kept asking her questions about this boy. She probably didn't know the answer to his questions about this boy she was dating because she was so naive she couldn't even have thought to ask them herself.

She couldn't understand that all people were capable of homicide. When he heard someone say, "How can people do something like that?" he was suspicious that was the person most capable of doing something like that. People who were out of touch with their underside were more apt to snap and do some crazy thing, something they were so sure they were incapable of.

He learned that early when he was on the beat. He always felt he was pretty laid back and had good negotiating skills. Then he was called to check a domestic at a house on his beat. The guy had bashed the woman's face in. She had a broken jaw, and he was higher'n a kite. He'd listened to the guy's alibi. When the woman started to speak up, the guy swung at her. That's when Hogan's baton came down on the guy's wrist with a fury he wasn't aware he had.

Later, he'd talked with his police chaplain about it. The priest had told him to stay in touch with his anger. As they talked, he had realized that his father had hit his own mother once. There, lurking in his heart was a little boy waiting to grow strong enough to defend his mother. Maybe that's why he was a cop in the first place.

Terence Hogan spun the wheel to the left as he came to the alley on Fenton Place. He got out and walked up to the uniformed officer, who stood guarding the crime scene. "What we got, Jones?"

"It's a woman, young, maybe in her early thirties. She's Asian." Officer Jones opened the woman's billfold. "The identification is a green card. There's a picture of a young girl and a boy. School pictures. The girl's wearing a uniform--St. Gen's." Hogan took the billfold and studied the pictures. Jones' voice was more distant. He was leaning over the corpse. "She's beat pretty badly. They bashed in her skull."

Hogan shook his head. "Probably drugs. These druggies are so violent, you know." Hogan looked at the thin face of the little girl in St. Gen's uniform. He wondered if she had a father or if she was an orphan now. "They come to this country, expecting they'll be as rich as the GI's they knew. Hell, it's not just the language they don't know; it's the streets, they don't know. She probably stumbled into some guy needing a fix, you know." Hogan handed the documents back to Jones after making some notations in his small notebook. He stepped forward to do what he always hated, viewing the smashed body of the victim. It could still turn his stomach, but Hogan always did his duty.

The scene was very ugly. She had tried to fight, he was sure. She was no match though. One shoe had come off her foot and the other lay almost perpendicular to her foot, her toes still stuffed into the upper part of the shoe. They were inadequate footwear. Somebody's pumps, a satin-like covering, the kind you'd wear to a fancy dance. She'd probably bought them at the thrift store near the precinct. From the looks of it, it was possible that as she fought, the perp had lifted her off the ground and then thrown her down. The weapon. Hmm. He looked around. "Did you find a weapon, Jones?"

"No, sir." The courteous Officer Jones was a tall, black man. He lived in the neighborhood and his color might be of help in turning up any witness. "Sir?"

"Yeah?" Hogan looked back quickly at Jones.

"I think it might have been the butt of a gun. Come over here; see that."

Hogan observed the area by the temple that might be an indentation caused by the handle of a gun. The guy might have hit her at first to knock her senseless, and then, as usual in the case of drugs, he just went wild, beating her to a pulp. It would make sense since the blows seemed to fall chaotically. Her eye was smashed and so was her jaw and nose--repeated, hammering blows.

Hogan finished making notes. "Got any witnesses?"

"No, sir. I can keep at it though. Someone may remember, but they are pretty scared around here of the gangs that are starting."

"Who owns this territory?"

"Mandrakes. I can identify some of them."

"Good. Let's get some in for questioning. Sometimes that shakes them up, and once in awhile, we even get some good tips. Thanks, Jones. Go ahead and let 'em clean up here as soon as forensics gets done."

Hogan left to go home after that. He slept for about 3 hours and then awoke with a start. He knew sleep was over. He got

up and dressed. His wife was at work, so he left a note. It wasn't
uncommon for him to work for days at a stretch. He arrived back at
the precinct just after lunch and found the report on the victim on
his desk. He also found the box of donuts. Apparently the day guys
used his desk as a buffet table! He pitched the box into the waste can
while one of the uniforms cried in protest.

"It's all yours, Mike." He lifted the waste can and offered it
to Mike who took it and looked down into the interior with disgust.
Terry sat down and read: Dha Ling. He smiled sadly, poor, little
dah-ling. She had two children and a husband. The report didn't
contain much more information than he had gleaned at the site
itself. He looked at his watch and decided to check St. Gen's to see
if they would recognize the girl and provide more information. A
small private school might know more family details than the larger
public school.

He walked into the front office at St. Genevieve High School
during some sort of hubbub. An older woman, the secretary, was
holding a trashcan toward a nun. "I just found it there, Sister. It's
a disgrace."

"It looks like the same filthy thing I gave Duffy. Either that
or Kim Phong has plastered the school with this smut." Neither
seemed aware of his presence. "It's 2:00 o'clock now. He should
come shortly. We have parent-teacher conferences tonight, so he
will come early to start cleaning. His ears will burn plenty good if
this is his doing!" At that moment, the nun realized that Hogan
was standing in the doorway. "Oh! Excuse me. May I help you?"
She shifted gears easily, thought Hogan. Even her red face drained
quickly and showed the cordiality that he associated with nuns.

"I'm Detective Hogan, Sister." Her eyebrows raised slightly.
He saw the alarm in her eyes. "May I have a word alone with you?"
He sensed that the secretary was eager to hear what he had to say.
She'd probably be on the telephone to a friend the instant they
disappeared into the nun's office.

The nun stepped behind her desk and remained standing.
Etiquette told him that he was to remain standing until she sat, but
she was ramrod straight and looked as though she were holding her
breath. "Please, Sister, sit down. It's a picture I want to show you. I

need a little information." He leaned over and handed her the girl's picture.

"My, God, it's Liu." She slumped into the big chair. "What's wrong? She's a quiet student." She moved some papers about on her desk with a frantic air. "I think she's here today. Yes, she's not on the absence list."

"It's not about her, Sister. I'm glad she's here. It's a woman I believe is her mother, a Dha Ling. Can you give me any information?"

"Mrs. Ling. Yes, they're Vietnamese refugees. They have been here just two years. Liu is a freshman. I think Mrs. Ling also has a son, but he doesn't attend St. Genevieve's. Her husband died last year."

Hogan's heart sank. He'd have to get word to the agency. "Is she alright? Has she been taken ill?" The nun's questions were rapid fire.

"She's dead, Sister. Someone murdered her. Did she have a job?"

"Murdered! Merciful heavens!" The nun seemed to gasp the latter words, and Hogan thought of them as both a half-prayer and a half-oath, if there were any such thing.

"Yes, Sister. I need your help. Did she work anywhere?"

The nun jumped up and walked to a file cabinet. "Let's see." She was thumbing through file folders. She pulled one out that satisfied her. "Yes. She worked at the Helpin Laundromat on the corner of Grover and Stanton. Here's the telephone number for emergencies." As she reached across the desk to hand the entire folder over to him, some slip of paper fell to the floor.

Hogan took down the name and number and then the current address of the deceased. "I take it you might have met this lady, Sister. Was there anything you noticed about her?"

"Yes. No. I mean, yes, I've met her, and no, nothing unusual. Her English wasn't all that good, of course."

"Was she what you'd think of as an interested mother?"

"Oh, yes, officer." He ignored her failure to get his rank right.

"Well, when you spoke, even though her English was not good, did she seem coherent. No mental problems?"

"She was a fine woman, I'm sure. No, no, quite concerned about Liu and eager for her daughter to be in a private school for her safety."

Hogan smiled at the incongruity. This mother should have been more concerned about her own safety. "Thank you, Sister. And, please behave as though nothing of this is known. A social worker will go to the home this afternoon and break the news and take care of the children. Liu may not be in school here again, but they'll let you know." Hogan stood and the nun shot up from her chair. She didn't seem happy with what he'd told her about keeping the information sealed.

"May I tell Fr. Dunstan? He's the pastor and the administrator here at the school?"

"Yes, Sister, but tell him to wait for the social worker before he contacts them. Oh, Sister, I was just wondering. Have you ever heard the word 'Mandrakes' before?"

"Mandrakes? I take it you don't want the definition?"

He looked at her. Maybe she was more savvy than he thought. "No."

"I saw some graffiti down on Madison once. I was with a senior student, and he told me that was the name of a street gang: the Madison Mandrakes."

"Thanks again, Sister. Oh, just a personal concern of mine. Any drug problems here at the school?"

She laughed slightly. "Right now, I'm just struggling with pornography. But now that you mention it, we did have an incident. A student went through the purses of some girls while they were at gym and stole money. I always suspect the person steals for drug money nowadays. We found the student and suspended him. Knock on wood, but that's all we have experienced so far."

"That's good, Sister. I'll be on my way now." He found himself bowing toward her and wondered where that had come from. He couldn't help but think she was a little less savvy about drugs in her school than about gangs on the streets though.

As he stepped out of her office, he saw a balding, middle-aged man in a rumpled suit and tie standing with a student in tow. The guy looked very angry, but what caught his attention was the pea coat the student was wearing.

Back in his car, Hogan made a call into the station to get the ball rolling with the social services and sat waiting for school to let out. He wondered how popular pea coats were. The students peeled out of the building, and most were wearing fake leather jackets. Those who weren't were wearing cheap cloth coats and the few who could afford them were wearing jackets with a team logo blazoned across their backs or chests. "Very interesting!" he said as he drove back to the station.

Chapter 10

After the policeman left, Sr. Gretchen's head was pulsing with the beginnings of a headache. She was rummaging in her drawer for some aspirin, when Hotchkiss knocked. Bob Murphy was with him, shackled by Hotchkiss's hand, which firmly grasped the thinly padded shoulder of his worn coat.

She could read the teacher's face. It couldn't wait. If she even suggested it, Hotchkiss would look aggrieved. She also needed him here tonight and sober enough to deal with parents. He was not an easy man to work with, and she understood why Margie had divorced him. Margie, his ex-wife, had been a classmate of Gretchen's back in the novitiate. She doubted the egocentric Hotchkiss even knew that about his wife. Poor Margie left the novitiate to find her true love. She had such a romantic notion, and it probably blinded her when it came to choosing a mate.

"Yes?" Gretchen tried to shift gears again. This was definitely a day from hell!

"This boy (he spit the word out, making it sound like something contemptuous) has called me a liar in front of my class!" Hotchkiss's face reddened from scarlet to a purplish hue. Gretchen didn't want a heart attack on her hands.

"Come in and close the door please. I'm sure we'll straighten this out."

They stepped in. Bob looked nearly as surly as Hotchkiss, so Gretchen felt her words only bespoke her hope, not her belief. "Now, I want each of you to tell me about your perspective on this matter, but only one at a time. No interruption of one another.

45

Clear?" She assumed her authoritarian pose, fixing each of them in turn with her stern look. She was glad she was wearing her brown suit today. The brown of her suit brought out the dark color of her hazel eyes. When she wanted to look softer, she wore her blue suit, which made her eyes seem bluer and lighter. They both nodded. Hotchkiss pulled at his collar. To Gretchen, his shirt collar seemed to be yellowing. Surely the man does his laundry, she thought. "Mr. Hotchkiss, may I hear your perspective?"

Hotchkiss had been scowling threateningly at Bob Murphy and seemed to turn his eyes toward her with reluctance. "I returned some essays during my class. We were doing quite fine in class, discussing how to improve our writing when Mr. Murphy interrupted and told me I had failed to return his essay. I told him that he had not turned in an essay or, obviously, I would have returned it."

Hotchkiss paused and Gretchen wondered if that was all. "You said that he called you a liar?"

"Yes! In front of the entire class. Most disrespectfully." Hotchkiss had paused because he had to deal with a spasm of hatred. He was having to talk to this woman in such proper language. He had to choose his words carefully. A woman, his boss! A woman, his judge! A woman, pretending to be clear-headed and fair! A nun, waiting to hear him slip up on his syntax or his facts. God, how he hated them!

"What you've said thus far only indicates that he asked about his essay, Mr. Hotchkiss. Is there anything else?"

See, she did it. She pounced on him and belittled him. "There's more. He stood up without my permission to leave his desk and told me that he had turned in the essay with the others. He accused me of losing it and, worse, of being biased and deliberately destroying it. He made quite a scene. I had to threaten the rest with bloody murder just to be able to bring him down here. It's the last hour on a Friday, you know." Hotchkiss was satisfied that he had let her know what pains he'd taken to preserve a little discipline around there!

"I see. And Robert, what have you to say?"

Robert slunk sullenly in his chair. Why try? They were in cahoots anyhow.

"Please, Robert. I want to hear your perspective too."

"I did turn it in. We wrote it in class, for Christsake!"

"Robert, no profanity!"

"Sorry," he shifted and with a side movement of his head tried to fling his long hair back. He wound up pushing it back over his ear with his hand. He wished one day to get a gold earring like Jo-Jo to wear in that ear. He felt a new flush of anger.

"Did you confront Mr. Hotchkiss as he said?"

"Maybe."

"Not maybe, not perhaps. Did you do as he said?"

"Yes, Sister." Bob had mumbled the words as he looked down at the hole in the side of his right sneaker.

"Robert, there are better ways to settle a dispute. I must suspend you for a day. I want you to consider how you might have handled this dispute in a better way. I expect to see you here on Tuesday morning with your answer written in essay form. Is that clear?"

"Yes, Sister."

"Good. I do think an apology is in order."

Hotchkiss swelled. His swagger made Gretchen wish she could have found in Robert Murphy's favor. Hotchkiss was not a good winner, but then Robert was not a noble loser either. His apology lacked sincerity and suggested a good deal of anger, but she would let it rest and not push him further. She sent them off.

She needed to see Duffy about the pornography and Fr. Ray. That poor child, Liu Ling, going home to such news. Her life suddenly torn out from under her! Tears misted in her eyes. She prioritized Fr. Ray and hastily tried to make her desk neat as she left to walk across the street.

Chapter 11

"Hey, Terry, I got a couple of guys for you. Jones just rounded them up for you. Let's see. One's called LeRoy Parsons. Here's his rap sheet. He also got a guy he believes is a ringleader of some renown. He's a mean sonabitch. He's spent a lot of time in juvey and should graduate shortly to the big time." Mike glanced down at a paper he was holding. "He's known as Jo-Jo something."

Hogan had just returned from his visit to the school, and Mike was calling out to him while he held the telephone receiver he was talking on at the end of his extended arm away from his mouth.

"Okay. Hey, get Henderson for me, will you?" Terry called to Tom Delaney who was headed back to the snack machines. Terry knew that Henderson, who would be playing bad cop during the questioning to Terry's good cop, could be found at the coffee machine. In the meantime, he looked over the rap sheets that Mike had handed him. The typical stuff--shop lifting, car theft, destruction of property. He studied the demographics of the criminal activity. All the crimes had occurred on Madison or west of it except the destruction of property which had taken place along Mohammed. He was about to check dates when Henderson walked up.

"Here's your bad guy!" Henderson announced himself and then sipped from his steaming coffee. Hogan, who carried a thermos of his wife's coffee to work, found himself wondering why coffee that hot didn't melt the Styrofoam cup, which Henderson was holding somewhat gingerly, thumb at the top and a little finger

48

at the bottom. Henderson had picked up the rap sheet on LeRoy Parsons. Then, he tossed it down. "Ready? Who's first?"

"You take LeRoy," Hogan rose from his chair, taking a last drag from his cigarette. This past week, he was smoking again after quitting six months ago. He knew he was overworking again, but the murders were up this week, and he was going nowhere fast in making any arrests.

As he stepped into Jo-Jo's presence, he sensed the defiance. The guy sported an ugly scar that seemed to be his badge of courage. Apparently he liked displaying that side of his face, like a scorpion, raising its tail to warn an intruder not to mess with it.

"Hello, Jo-Jo."

"Ain't talkin' without representation." He slid further down into the chair, arms folded.

"You got representation?" Hogan looked around the room mockingly. "C'mon, Jo-Jo. You aren't accused of anything. In fact, a little guy like you couldn't do much harm to anyone over five feet, I figure."

"Who say? I can handle myself."

"Oh, no doubt about that. I figure you could defend yourself all right. Look at that mean scar there. Bet you managed that dude."

"Sure did. Damn motherfucker! He was fucking with the wrong nigger that time."

"Why'd he want to do that?" Hogan had the guy talking now by using the ego-trap.

"He my momma's boyfrien'. He was plannin' to knife her when I walk in. Then he turn on me--which is what I wanted." Jo-Jo realized that the cop might think Jo-Jo had not been entirely in control of the situation, so he added that to make sure there was no mistake. "He come at me, see, but I duck." Jo-Jo was demonstrating his quick move from his seated position. Hogan thought of a snake's movement as it strikes a victim. "Then I bash his balls in." Jo-Jo was reliving the scene with obvious delight. He laughed aloud, emitting jerky sounds. Hogan figured the boy seldom had cause to laugh and was out of practice.

"I like that. A boy stickin' up for his mother." Hogan brought out his pack of cigarettes, tapped one out of the pack about a half inch and offered it to the young man sitting across from him, all the while thinking about how his father had hit his own mother. He hadn't been able to take on his old man as directly as this young punk, and his own father had not been armed with a lethal weapon. His praise rang with sincerity, and Jo-Jo, sensing that, warned himself to be wary.

Hogan continued after stretching across the table to light the cigarette for Jo-Jo. "Guy like yourself would probably never hurt a woman, not like that motherfucker you were talking about."

"Maybe not." Jo-Jo blew the smoke in his direction, creating a very real smoke screen to hide behind. Hogan knew that he'd lost him somewhere in the last few seconds. He glanced at his watch: four o'clock. "Well, Jo-Jo, you'll have to excuse me. I have to make a phone call, but you stay here. I'll be back as soon as I can."

He stepped to the next interrogation room and made a single tap on the door. He could hear the roar of Henderson's voice although it was muffled by the soundproofing. In a couple of minutes, the door swung open and Henderson stepped out, his face still red from the exertion of his yelling. "He's a hardened criminal, Terry, but I got him to sweat a little. He slipped and told me he 'didn't kill no Chinese woman.'"

"Good work!" Hogan clapped his hand on Henderson's shoulder. No one had mentioned that the murdered woman was oriental. "Jo-Jo will be even harder to deal with. I thought I was getting somewhere in there, but maybe I admired him too much. He drew back. Hammer him about his size; it might work." Hogan stepped into the room.

The young black male sat picking at the skin on his hand. He glanced up, knowing that the next cop would be the friendly cop. He stopped picking on his hand, crossed his arms over his chest and slid further down in his chair, sighing.

"Hello, LeRoy." The boy did not return his greeting, but he did look at Hogan. "Say, you want some coffee?"

The boy looked at him skeptically at first. Hogan held his gaze and continued to look innocent. LeRoy let out another sigh, "O.K. Sure." Hogan left and got a Styrofoam cup of murky, steaming liquid. As he passed his desk, he took another gulp of his wife's home-brewed coffee. Nothing like it, he said to himself.

"Here you are, LeRoy." He almost said, "It's black," but stopped himself in time. His lack of sleep was catching up with him, he warned himself silently. "Now, LeRoy, you been in a heap of trouble, haven't you?"

"You tell me, Cop!" LeRoy said after taking a drink of the coffee. Terry joked to himself that either the coffee was really bad today or LeRoy was a belligerent son of a gun.

"I was reading your rap sheet, LeRoy. Looks like the trouble you've gotten into gets worse and worse, like you are caught in some downward spiral, you know. I'm the guy who works homicide here, and I got to tell you, LeRoy, that someone with your kind of rap sheet...well, it's only a matter of time before I find them committing murder."

"I didn't kill that Chinese lady, man. Y'ain't pinnin' that'n on me. No way. I tol' that other dude too."

"Chinese? What you mean, LeRoy? I didn't say anything about a Chinese lady."

LeRoy looked confused. He realized that he'd made some kind of mistake, but he hadn't yet realized if it was fatal.

"LeRoy, for the life of me, I hope that you haven't crossed that line. What you've just said is that you know something about the death of a woman down near Stanton and Madison." Hogan deliberately misnamed the location.

"Stanton and....no, no way. Who be killed down there?" LeRoy was fumbling now.

"The lady you mentioned."

"No way, man. Dat's our turf. No dude kill no lady on Stanton."

"Who you talking about then?"

"Dat lady dey found off Grover. There on Fenton. What's amattah, homicide man, you forgettin' yer job?"

"Look, LeRoy, I want to play it straight with you. You have just implicated yourself in the death of this woman. It doesn't look good for you."

"I didn't kill her!"

"I want to believe you, LeRoy, but you know a lot about this lady. You know what she looked like and you know where she was killed, don't you? And I have to tell you that judging by the rap sheet you have, well, it isn't unusual for a guy like you to turn to violent crime."

LeRoy was beginning to sweat for real now. "I told you I didn't kill her. Maybe I heard some talk, that's all."

"What kind of talk, LeRoy?" Hogan looked up at the ceiling as though he didn't think LeRoy could tell him anything.

"One of the guys talked about meeting a woman. He needed some money for a fix, so he hustled her. She wouldn't give him her purse and kept yammerin' in Chinese. He just wanted to knock her out so he could look in her purse, man. Dat's not murder."

"You know a lot, LeRoy. That either makes you the killer or it makes you an accomplice. Now, how am I to decide which you are?"

LeRoy's eyes dropped. Hogan was feeling good. For once, he was closing in on a murder fast, might set some kind of record. Maybe he would be home in time for supper. He glanced at his watch.

"I can't say who it was. It was just talk."

"Who was talking to you?"

"Look, if I tell, it ain't becuz he did it. I don't know, y'unnerstan'?" LeRoy's brows arched upward, pulling at the flesh between them at the top of his nose. Another tough guy looking like a plea bargainer thought Hogan.

"We need to know the name of this guy, LeRoy. Maybe he's our killer and maybe he's not, but we have to question him. I know how to pick him up without implicating you. I'll never mention your name to him."

Hogan studied LeRoy's face. He was neither as hardened nor as well schooled in survival as Jo-Jo. LeRoy was simply a pretense, but pretense on the streets around Madison was dangerous and often led to precipitous actions as a way of covering itself; still Hogan didn't think LeRoy was tall enough to raise Dah Ling off the ground. It took a tall, strong male, one on drugs. LeRoy had already indicated that his "talker" was on drugs; now, a name and a little more were all Hogan needed, and then he could go home and crash!

"Walter." He was barely audible.

"Who did you say?"

"Walter." He came louder.

Hogan reached to his shirt pocket and flipped open his small note pad and then reached for a Bic pen in the same location. He pulled the cap off with his teeth. He made it all into a longer-than-necessary ritual. He wrote the name on a clean page; then he looked over at LeRoy, who was sitting stiff and uncomfortable in his chair.

"Does Walter have a last name?"

"Yeah. Atkins." LeRoy glanced down at his hands. He was not a happy camper.

"I appreciate this opportunity to clear your name. If Walter can help us find the killer; well, LeRoy, you are off the hook. I guess you won't be a suspect anymore."

LeRoy didn't look at him, but his face relaxed slightly. No honor among thieves, thought Hogan. He folded his pad, recapped the pen and stuffed them back into his shirt pocket. He rose, and as if suddenly remembering, he leaned on his hands, which he had placed flat on the table.

"Oh, LeRoy. I forgot. How will I know this Walter? I mean what does he look like?"

"He be tall; 'bout six foot, more probly." LeRoy was not bright or he would have told the cop he knew where to find his rap sheets. The wind had gone out of LeRoy's sails. Hogan was smiling and saying to himself, Bingo!

"I'm a big man, but I wonder if Walter is bigger than me. Maybe not so heavy though. I need to know because a dude on drugs can be pretty strong."

"He taller than you. Not as fat though." Terry's eyes expressed the slightest merriment. "But he strong. He can be mean, but not like Jo-Jo."

"Thanks, LeRoy. I think you've been helpful, and if Walter can verify your story, then I won't have to see you again. Let's hope you told me the truth."

"I didn't kill her. I mean it."

As they left the room, Hogan knew he would see LeRoy again, either dead or as a live witness. Hogan rapped on the door loudly, signifying to Henderson that he could release Jo-Jo. Then he went to his desk to fill out papers to start the search for Walter Atkins. Hogan felt absolutely bone-tired.

Chapter 12

Gretchen told the secretary to let anyone who might drop into the office know that she had left for the day. The secretary who had, all the while, sat there hoping that Gretchen would confide what the policeman wanted, now had to work hard not to look disappointed. Gretchen stopped at the office door, and the secretary immediately perked up, her hopes of being confided in renewed. Gretchen, however, merely added that Duffy was to be reminded to clean all homerooms first, and only then should he begin on other classrooms. She would probably be back around 5:30PM to open up for the parent-teacher conferences. Duffy should leave the building by that time, she had told the secretary, and return tomorrow to complete the classrooms. Then she headed out the door, leaving the secretary as curious as ever.

The wind picked up as she stepped onto the broad sidewalk beyond the school's front door. Instinctively, she reached down and clutched the side of her skirt so that it wouldn't follow the wind's direction. Her left hand reached to keep her hair in place, but that was in vain. She then used that hand to wipe at her eye which had a particle of fine dirt blown into it from the gutters of Elias Street. She paused until a car passed and then darted across the street in diagonal fashion so that she arrived closer to the rectory entrance.

She rang the doorbell and waited, wondering if Fr. Ray were home. Perhaps the detective had already spoken to him. She rang again as she glanced down the street where an old man leaned unsteadily against the wall of the church, having just peed the pint of whiskey he'd ingested less than an hour before. She looked away in distaste just as the door opened.

When Fr. Ray saw who was standing at his door, he tensed. Gretch was so capable a leader that she seldom came to see him. When she did, it was something of major proportions. "Hi, Gretchen, come in." He led her to a parlor, of which there were two. To parishioners, they looked like two large living rooms, with comfortable easy chairs but no television set. Across the hall from these two large rooms was a dining room. It was seldom used now, but in its day, it had provided for gatherings of priests from all over the central deanery. Wonderful meals had been served to these gatherings of brother priests, occasioned by deanery meetings and Forty Hours Devotions.

The Forty Hours had dropped out of existence and most deanery meetings skipped the neighborhood because some of the priests didn't feel safe parking their cars there. Consequently, Ray used the massive dining table for parish council meetings where coffee was served. When the trustees counted the change after Sunday Masses from the collection boxes, the nearest repast with a dim resemblance to the feasts of old that the dining room had seen was of coffee and donuts.

Ray turned as he stepped into the parlor, gesturing to an easy chair. Gretchen sat down stiffly. She wasn't used to easy chairs. All the chairs in the convent that she had occasion to use were sturdy straight backs. She pulled at her skirt on both sides and carefully tucked the folds under her thighs. Nice girls do not show their underpants! She always remembered her grandmother's caution every time she sat down. She had been all of five years of age when she heard that warning the first time.

Ray was still standing. "Can I get you something? Coffee or a coke or something?"

Gretchen's first impulse was to decline, but she relented. She'd been going at a clip all day and tonight promised no reprieve. She needed to slow down. "Any chance of tea, Father?"

"Sure, Gretch. Be back in a second." He turned and left the room. She noticed the squeak in his shoe as he walked down the tiled hallway. She also wished he wouldn't use that dreadful nickname. She knew students used it, but they had nicknames for everyone. One time she heard someone call him Radial Ray, but that was after he'd gotten a new set of tires. At least, that's what she thought was the basis for that tag.

Gretchen yawned. They called Hotchkiss, Scotchkiss or Hoochkiss, and she feared that students smelled the stale alcohol from his weekend benders, precipitating that particular epithet. Unfortunately, she had found a rumpled note once, written by a student she had just suspended, in which the student had called her Gretch the Wretch. So, she did not take kindly to any of the faculty using any of the students' nicknames for them. Fr. Ray had even attended the faculty meeting wherein Gretchen had made a point about the need for modeling respect. He apparently missed the point!

Gretchen leaned back into the chair finally. It felt good to relax and with the noisy shoe announcing his return, she would have time to sit up correctly. If she weren't careful though, she might drowse. She could feel the muscles in her arms beginning to relax. She lived her life with tension. Even in sleep. Sometimes, she would jump with a start, just when she would begin to relax and slip into a light slumber. She ground her teeth in her sleep too, and the dentist had recommended a bite plate. That was far too expensive though.

Gretchen had talked to Suzanne about some meditative relaxation techniques, but she really couldn't get the hang of all that controlled breathing. She'd breathe in, hold, and then breathe out, but she began concentrating so much on doing it right that she found herself tensing up all over again. Nothing was ever simple in life!

She glanced out the window and saw the convent across the street. She noted the second story window of Mechtilde's bedroom. Now, there was a woman who seemed to be always relaxed. Gretchen often found herself studying her in chapel or at the dining room table. Such serenity. Probably born with it, Gretchen reassured herself. Still, if she herself ended up having to spend her days sitting in a chair, she would go mad!

Gretchen heard the squeak of Fr. Ray's shoe and began rearranging herself in a more upright position. The fabric of her skirt didn't slide on the fabric of the chair, so that when she pushed forward, her slip was exposed about three inches. She had to stand to let the skirt fall down and then took her seat again.

As Ray entered with the tray, he noticed Gretch sitting down again. He wondered if she had been pacing. "I couldn't remember if you take cream, so I brought some along. Well, how about milk?" He smiled as he confessed.

"Just tea." She extended her hand as he handed her the cup.

"No sugar either?"

"None. Thank you." She stirred the tea with a spoon, allowing the metal to absorb the heat from the tea, which Gretchen always found was served too hot for her taste. When Gretchen looked at a cup of tea, she was reminded that this drink presented the easiest way to burn one's tongue. She didn't want to spend the night with parents, distracted by a raw tongue, seared by tea that was too hot.

Ray leaned back in his chair comfortably, crossing one leg over the other, making a four pattern with his legs as seen from Gretchen's view. He appeared absolutely relaxed, she thought, a gift he had. Inwardly though, Ray was just as tense as Gretchen. "It's good to see you, Gretchen. We don't sit down enough like this. It's my fault, but you do such a good job over there that I get lax and let you carry the load."

Ray was worried that one day Gretchen would quit on him. It had to be taking its toll on her. He could see how tense and rigid she was just from how she was sitting there, balancing the cup and saucer in her hand just about six inches from her knee. He had to worry about her because there was no way he could handle both sides of the street!

"Thank you, Father." Gretchen's answer was matter of fact. She took the first tentative sip of her tea, noting the tinge of peppermint. "A matter has come up that I need to tell you about." Gretchen put the cup down on its saucer and then carefully, using both hands, replaced them on the tray that sat on the coffee table between the two occupied chairs.

Ray's glance followed her movement. She had delicate fingers. However, he wasn't cognizant of the beauty of her hands because he was wondering why she had signaled the end of a cup of tea before she'd had more than a sip. Should he set his cup down?

Did she expect that? He sat with his cup poised for a drink, finally deciding to take one last swallow. He sat his cup down on the saucer that had remained on the tray. He raised himself back up to listen.

"Do you remember the little freshman Vietnamese girl, Liu Ling?" Gretchen waited for some sign of recognition. Ray ruffled through his memory as someone might a file drawer. Gretchen suspected he wouldn't have a specific name for a face. They were just a Communion line, after all, and Fr. Ray taught religion only to the seniors. "They live over on south Hobson."

"Ling! Didn't I have a funeral last year? Yeah, the father?" Ray was not good at details, but something was emerging from his mental filing system.

"That's right, Father." Gretchen was impressed that Ray had made a connection. "Well, this afternoon, a policeman came with the terrible news that Mrs. Ling has been murdered."

"God!" Ray always recoiled at the thought of violence in the neighborhood. It worried him when it fell so close to his world, south of Madison, the parish boundary. "My, God," Ray repeated and shook his head. "How did it happen? Did he say?"

"Apparently, she was apprehended when she got off work. She works...worked at the Helpin Laundry down on Stanton, near Grover."

"Down by the old pickle factory!" Ray was placing the laundromat. "Probably some of those creeps down there. I've seen them hanging on the street corners. I wish the cops would break it up. How was she killed?"

Gretchen suddenly realized that she had no details. The policeman had somehow skillfully extracted information without giving her much. "I don't know the details, but the policeman, a Mr. Hogan, told me that I shouldn't mention this matter. He needed to send someone from Social Services to the home. I made certain that he knew you, as pastor, should be informed, but he told me to tell you to delay until someone from the agency got to the home."

"Hummm." The name of the policeman sounded familiar to Ray, but he couldn't place it. "When's that going to happen? If the mother's been murdered, won't those kids be wondering where Mom is?"

"That's right! Poor Liu spent all day in school wondering where her mother was. She didn't come home last night and wasn't there for their rising. That poor child." Gretchen felt such pangs. A frail girl like Liu going through the motions of following her academic schedule, wondering the whole day if her mother had run away or been hurt. How many students did she see during any given school day who had such hidden pain, and Gretchen never noticed?

Guilt washed over her as she saw herself just that day dispersing students, lingering after the bell for first class. Now she recalled how Liu and that Bob Murphy had been among them. She'd thought they were just getting one last peck in before going their separate ways. She'd begun to see that regularly on Friday mornings now that she was piecing it together. A group of freshmen mostly, hanging around by the lockers. Bob Murphy was the only upperclassman among them. Maybe that was his problem; he wasn't socially at the age he should be, hanging around freshmen as he did. Gretchen was lost in her replay of Friday morning.

Ray looked at his watch and then at Gretchen who was staring hard at the tray on the table. She didn't seem to be blinking even. It was probably also hard for Gretch to hear about violence being so close, touching their lives. "Well, Gretch, I'm sorry he swore you to secrecy, but I want you to be able to talk about this with someone, maybe the sisters."

"Oh, no. I can't. We have conferences tonight, and I don't want them upset."

"Well, I'll head over to the Ling home and check out the situation. I don't want those kids to be alone. But, I think it would be good for you to be able to talk to someone, especially since you have to see so many people with their complaints and questions tonight." Ray stood because he was anxious to get to his parishioners on Hobson.

Ray's movement seemed to drag Gretchen from her stare down with the tray. "Oh, yes, Father. You need to go now." She stood, and as she walked across the room, she smoothed her skirt in front and hoped that static cling had not hiked her skirt in the back, but she couldn't bring herself to run her hand along her fanny to check, not with Fr. Ray walking behind her.

At the door, she remembered, "Oh, Father, under the circumstances, I don't expect you tonight."

"Thanks, Sister." He hadn't remembered about the conferences even though she'd reminded him three times during the week after morning Mass. "Take care of yourself, Gretch."

Ray hastened up the stairs to his bedroom. This call required his collar. Mack looked up at him as he fastened it and fed the black dickey down under his sweater. As he reached under his sweater in back to tie the bottom, Mack cocked his head in that cute way dogs have. "O.K., so I don't wear it much! Ya gotta make a comment? I think you're a snitch for the bishop, that's what!" Ray bent to ruffle Mack's furry head and grabbed his car keys off the bureau as he headed downstairs.

Chapter 13

Suzanne was whipping along I-35. She was getting closer to the exit for Cadbury Falls. She had told Gretchen that she had a meeting at the motherhouse, but it was a lie. No one could catch her in it though since the superior general could not reveal who was seeing her. Suzanne had been engaging in this little deception once a month now for over a year.

Only Maria knew about her affair. That sounded so tawdry. It wasn't, but that is what Maria insisted on calling it. Suzanne was in love with Gus Spellinger. Whenever she thought of him, she felt herself growing lustful. That was another word that Maria insisted on using.

Maria and she went back to the novitiate together. Maria seemed like such an artistic flake, but she was also seriously spiritual. Music was her connection to God, and she really took her teaching at St. Gen's seriously. She felt that if these kids could hear real music, they would connect with God. Maria hated their loud music with its insipid lyrics. She often made fun of the latter. She would have Suzanne in hysterics when she would imitate some of those songs.

But the way Suzanne felt about Gus made some of those songs real for her. She had no intention of leaving the convent, but she also believed that God had sent this man into her life for a reason. Maybe he was the guy she was supposed to marry; like destiny had meant them for one another. Maria scoffed at that and said it was just scent-titillation. Maria had a theory that unconsciously people were attracted to the chemical scent emitted by the other. She'd read an article or heard something about it. Maria told her that

62

she'd watched from her bedroom window and thought it was true. For example, she'd seen Mack hike his leg and hit a utility pole along Elias on a walk with Fr. Ray. Within ten minutes, an old drunk had come along, unzipped and unloaded on the same pole. "Phernomes!" she'd say.

Whatever it was, when Gus was near her, Suzanne felt shimmers go through her. Just the sound of his voice could do it. Once, when she taught at St. Hildegarde's, she was in the faculty room eating lunch when she heard his voice in the back room. That's where the smokers gathered. Anyhow, she was sitting there listening to the horrors of the classroom being recounted by the third-grade teacher when she'd heard his voice. She had the awfullest time listening to the teacher. She had managed to laugh at all the right places, but she sounded hollow, fakey. She just wanted to go plaster herself against Gus.

It had started innocently enough. He was pastor at St. Hildegarde's and came into the classroom to teach religion once a week. Something had clicked with them the first time he came to her classroom, and he smiled easily at her. Then about mid-way through the year, she had been teaching the exciting triple-digit with decimals division and had turned toward the doorway where she saw him standing in the hall, just watching her. He beckoned for her to come out. She had felt uncomfortable, actually had blushed a little, she guessed.

He just smiled at her when she stepped out, closing the door after warning the sixth graders to remain in their seats and work quietly until she returned. He had made up some pretext, some discussion about one of the students, and they had both pretended the matter was serious and had prolonged the discussion. Finally, she knew she had to get back to prevent a riot breaking out, but she felt a happiness she hadn't had before she'd stepped out into the hall.

Suzanne checked her watch. It was 3:00. She'd speed over to the motherhouse, whip through so that some of the sisters would see her, pick up any mail or circulars from her leadership and head for Gus's place. His school would be out by then, and they'd have the rectory for themselves. Then around nine-ish, she'd drive over to St. Gen's. She'd park in the alley on the side of the school and go to the side door.

That was a departure from the usual routine. Usually, she'd go over to St. Gen's by 4:00 and slip by to see Maria who would be waiting for her in the music room, playing some good music on the ancient record player or at the piano. Maria insisted on Suzanne checking in with her. She thought she could keep Suzanne from going too far with Gus. But they had crossed that line ages ago.

Suzanne was happy that she and Gus would have a longer time tonight since St. Gen's was having the parent conferences. Maria was tied up until 9:00 with parents. Maria always left the side door to the school unlocked for her by placing a piece of tape across the latch. Duffy, the janitor, checked the door before he went upstairs to clean but always went out by the front door when he left.

Maria simply waited for him to go upstairs, and then she would tape the door latch. Suzanne would remove the tape as she let herself in, and all was well. Then she would go up to Maria's music classroom, where they'd talk old times at first. Suzanne always knew that there would be the "lecture" part too. Maria really didn't like what Suzanne was doing, but she just didn't understand it.

It had happened when dear Gus had come one Saturday when Suzanne had gone to school to work on grades. No one else was there, not even a janitor. Suzanne didn't like to admit it, but she had parked on the side of the lot nearest the rectory, just in case Gus might see her car was there.

He had. She had heard a lock turn on the big steel doors at the entrance of the school. Then she heard him clear his throat, maybe self-consciously as he walked down to the office where she was. She'd kept the office door open out into the hall, like a giant flag for him as to her whereabouts. Then suddenly there he was, smiling at her. "What a pleasant surprise," he'd said.

They'd been so self-conscious about one another. Really klutzy at first. Then, after they talked about nothing much for most of the morning, he'd asked if she'd like some lunch. She thought he meant to go out for some fast food, but he'd taken her over to the rectory. On Saturdays, he had no one in to do any cooking.

They'd made some sandwiches and taken them to the parlor, sitting together on a couch.

She felt so hot and couldn't really eat. Finally, he just put his sandwich down and kissed her. She'd surprised herself how quickly she'd responded to that. It was a long, long kiss. They came up for breath and immediately went for it again. She didn't want it to stop. They kissed and petted and came so close to going all the way. She was in love!

They began to meet whenever they could. She stayed later after school. It was hard finding time for one another. Suzanne had to learn the art of telling a believable lie back at the convent. She and Gus lived in a constant state of distraction, longing only to be in one another's arms.

Finally, he told her that he had the use of another priest's cabin out in the woods, about 50 miles from Cadbury Falls. He would get someone to cover for his Sunday Masses. They'd not have school since it was Thanksgiving weekend. That had been a year ago last November. She would never forget it! She'd told everyone that she was visiting her family and had actually spent Thanksgiving with them, but then told her family that she wanted to get back and visit with some of the sisters at the motherhouse. Instead, that evening, she had driven to the cabin. It was glorious the whole time. She loved making love with Gus.

One time, Maria had asked her if she thought she was addicted to sex. Suzanne was startled. Maria had been reading some article again. Suzanne told her that she would not be able to dream of doing it with anyone else except Gus. She kept trying to get Maria to understand that this relationship was meant to be from all eternity. Everyone has someone meant just for her. It's just that sometimes God also gives some people a vocation to be a priest or nun and so.

"And so?" Maria had asked.

"So, when they meet, then they are not always able to resist the forces of fate. They, she and Gus, were like that. They were spiritually married, but were also being faithful to their vows to God."

Maria had scoffed at the idea. "I guess as the population increases, the chance of meeting your one great love decreases exponentially. Aren't you the lucky one?"

Suzanne always loved sparring with Maria because she never knew what twist or turn Maria would take in the argument. "Well," Maria sighed and with a *voce sotto,* she had said as if acceding to Suzanne's logic, "that must explain why there are so many unhappy marriages today. It's that darned population increase."

Suzanne had replied, with a charming smile, "At least, Gus and I won't be adding to future unhappy marriages by adding to the population!"

"Are you sure about that?" Maria had added quietly and seriously.

Once the craziness for one another's body lightened a little, Suzanne had given thought to that possibility. Suzanne had begun to watch her cycle more carefully. In truth, Maria had brought Suzanne's lurking fear to light. She definitely didn't want a scandal, nor did she want the agony of causing Gus to leave the priesthood. He was happy being a priest, but she never doubted that he would go with her if she needed that.

That's when Suzanne had gone to the other side of town, incognito. The Family Planning Center told her how to use the birth control pills and the happy percentages in its prevention record. She felt the Church was totally unreasonable anyhow about birth control. God gave mankind the ability to crack nature's codes. The Church didn't object to that God-given ability when it came to the calcium she took, so what the heck!

Besides, she knew too well that many of the kids she taught were unwanted. The parents would comment right in front of their kid: "He's an accident, Sister." God, she hated that phrase, but what could the good Catholic parent do? They relied on an unreliable method because the Church wouldn't allow them any other.

When she told Gus that she was on the pill, he looked relieved and began undressing her right away. They'd laughed, and she did have more freedom to enjoy their sex than she had before, something she would never have thought possible. Maria would have been shocked if she'd known that her question had started them into more sex, more often.

The motherhouse was just ahead. She parked near the entrance. She didn't want to take long because she couldn't wait to see Gus. Thinking about their relationship had made her body ache for him. She slipped through the large glass doors and stepped inside. One of the nuns was just crossing the lobby, carrying some letters for the mailbox. She looked through thick glasses, blankly at Suzanne.

"Hi, Sr. Jeannine!"

"Now, who is this?" smiled the otherwise stern-looking nun.

"Suzanne."

"Suzanne? Suz....oh, Sr. Suzanne." It was her indirect way of correcting Suzanne's failure to use her title. Jeannine was the most passive-aggressive woman Suzanne had ever met. Inwardly, she felt herself fume.

"Now, you're at...?"

Everyone was known by her geographic assignment. That was lucky for Jeannine who would then key into a place and sap the visitor for gossip about everyone else from the same location.

"I live alone, Sister. Out in the woods."

"Oh, yes! Our hermit. Well, have you had any visions yet?"

The woman dripped animosity, but it was always cloaked in charity. "No, I leave those visions to you, Jeannine. You're holy enough for them, not me." Suzanne mentally kicked herself for descending to Jeannine's level. Before Jeannine could detain her further, she continued, "I'm just here to pick up my mail. It's been good seeing you."

Jeannine had stood there in the lobby for a few seconds after Suzanne had departed, trying to remember what she had been doing before that young nun had breezed in. They are hellbent to get somewhere, she thought. Everyone was these days.

Suzanne was in and out in less than ten minutes. She spun her rear wheels as she fled the parking lot, rushing to her lover's arms. But, by God, she was a hermit too! She had not only fallen in love with Gus that Thanksgiving weekend, but she had fallen in love with being in nature. Gus had always slept longer than she after a night filled with love-making. She would rise early. Her body was happy, sated with Gus.

She would lean lazily with a mug of hot chocolate against the huge plate windows that looked out on the valley that expanded across to the hills maybe five miles away. There was nothing but God's beautiful earth. It was so peaceful. She loved God in those moments. After the hot chocolate was finished, she put her heavy jacket on, tied the hood close around her head and walked out. So refreshing! Her body came alive; it definitely woke up out there.

When she would return from her walk, Gus was standing there in his briefs, the Miraculous Medal hanging from a chain around his neck, resting on his hairy chest. She would take off her coat, and he would hold her while he rubbed against her. Then, they'd go back to the unmade bed and begin again. They'd laughed about how the bed was never made that entire weekend, and that if they were married, there'd never be a made bed in their house.

Still that time had awakened in her a desire to be alone, living in nature, close to God. God was real for her out there, and that is why she would not allow Gus to come to her cottage in the woods. He had told her it would be perfect. No chance of being caught or of talk starting, but that was God's place not Gus's, she'd insisted.

Suzanne was stopped at a light. Another fifteen minutes and she'd be in his unmade bed at the rectory. Oh, God, she couldn't wait another minute. She rapped her fingers on the steering wheel. "Finally!" She muttered to herself, and off she sped. "Lover, come home to me," sang the falsetto voice over her car radio.

Chapter 14

Mrs. Murphy had just stepped out on her front porch. It was misting and the skies were slate gray. She hoped it wouldn't snow. She felt stiffness in her wrist and elbow and decided that the weather was probably taking a turn for the worst. Spring seemed to be taking its good time coming this year. She just then caught a glimpse of Fr. Dunstan driving by. And whom might he be visiting over here, she wondered. It was news when the priest came. It meant someone was dying or someone was in trouble. She counted it a blessing that he hadn't yet been under the roof of her house. That priest before him, though, he'd come.

That was when Jim was drinking more heavily. Well, maybe it was when it started to get so bad. He swore at her and took his belt to the boys sometimes 'til they bled. She feared for Bob's life at such times and couldn't stand it when he hit sweet Jeremy. She'd tried to interfere when he lit on Jeremy once. That was the time he hit her so hard she had a black eye. She had to miss Sunday Mass because of it, and that is why the priest had come 'round. It was simply that she couldn't go because if anyone had seen her, the talk would have begun. The worst thing Betty Murphy could imagine was being the prime piece of gossip up and down the street.

She might be poor, but when they buried her they'd say she was a faithful wife, a good mother, and she kept a clean house too. She did that, she did. Wasn't she just now shaking out the rugs from the boys' bedroom? She wondered if the priest had noticed. Well, someone in the neighborhood would surely coach him on what to say when he buried her.

She took a step down and leaned forward to follow the priest's progress down Hobson. She saw his brake lights go on as he neared the end of the block, just where Hobson crossed Stanton. As she stepped a little further out, she noticed Mrs. Sweeney from across the street, looking in the same direction.

Mrs. Sweeney had her arms wrapped in her apron. Her kitchen faced the street, and she had been peeling potatoes when she saw the priest's car go by. "Wasn't that the priest from St. Gen's?"

"Yes, I believe it was," answered Mrs. Murphy. She didn't want to seem to know for sure, for she didn't want to have seemed overly curious. Certainly, she didn't want them saying she was a gossip when they waked her. That they could surely say about Doris Sweeney!

"What do you s'pose is happening down there?"

"I don't know, but I hope no one is dying." Mrs. Murphy crossed herself just in case.

Doris Sweeney called out in a screeching voice, "Johnny! Johnny!" The second time she had called the name, she aimed her face toward the house. Finally, her fourteen-year-old son came sullenly out of the house. "Johnny, you go down the block to where the priest's car is parked. Find out what's going on." He hunched past her along the small sidewalk. Then for Mrs. Murphy's benefit, she added, "And if it's someone dying, hurry back and tell us so's we can pray for the poor soul!"

Mrs. Murphy crossed over the street to Mrs. Sweeney's barren front yard. She had a better view from there since cars were not allowed to park on that side of the street. When she arrived, Mrs. Sweeney was shivering. "Sakes alive, you need a coat, dear." She at once felt she'd made a faux pas. One could not presume any more that a housewife owned a coat. Mrs. Sweeney was raising her son without the benefit of a husband. The no-account drunk had up and left her several years ago. Women like that were apt to put any available money into clothing their children and often went without what some would think of as essentials.

"Yes, my, I'm cold." She checked Johnny's progress down the street and noticed that others were peeking from their doors, hoping to make something out. She felt she could trust that Johnny would scoop up what he could, even if it was only hearsay. When she wasn't watching her soap opera on television, she was gathering the material from the one playing in the neighborhood.

Next door, for example, big Tim Herrington could be counted on to swear nightly in his drunkenness. He usually railed at Sean, his oldest boy. Poor Theresa, his wife, was one of those women who seldom knew a non-pregnant state. They had six children now, and she was pregnant again. Yes, Hobson was a place that sometimes proved a rival for what those people on television were doing. "Let's go in. There's a few minutes left before supper. Unless you're expectin' your man soon?"

Mrs. Murphy's stomach twinged. She knew Mrs. Sweeney was well aware that her husband wouldn't be home until late. He always stopped off at that saloon on Stanton, just below the church. He always came staggering home though. At least, she had a husband come home faithfully, which was more than Mrs. Sweeney could say. They stepped inside.

Mrs. Sweeney's home was a mess. She switched off the television, which usually ran non-stop from the time the family rose until they went to bed late at night. She picked some rumpled clothes off the floor and removed a pile of books and papers from a chair at the kitchen table. "There you are, dear. Just sit down while I get some tea. The water's still hot, so it won't be a wait."

If Mrs. Sweeney hadn't been so cold, she would never have invited Mrs. Murphy into her house with it looking as it did. Everyone knew Mrs. Murphy cleaned clean floors. Such a prude she was. No wonder her man didn't come home until late. She and Theresa Herrington had just laughed over tea yesterday, saying that Murphy wouldn't be able to sit in a room without Mrs. Murphy yelling, "Raise your feet," as she vacuumed under him.

Yes, thought Doris Sweeney as she poured generous cups of tea into her cracked and chipped mugs, better to have no husband than the drunken pigs the two of them put up with. "Here, you are, darlin'." Doris Sweeney smiled very sweetly as she placed the cup graced with a primitive yellow flower design on the table before her guest.

"Will you be goin' to the school meetin' tonight, Doris?" Mrs. Murphy's pinkie was extended as she raised her cup. She felt it was an elegant thing to do.

"Oh, I guess we have no choice. I skipped such a meeting once and that principal, what's her name?" Mrs. Sweeney stopped, stumped to think of the nun's name.

"Well, now..." Mrs. Murphy scratched the side of her head, pretending to be stuck. She knew full well the principal's name at St. Gen's, but out of politeness, she thought she should seem just as forgetful. "Oh, yes, it's Gretchen, it is."

"Yes, I believe you're right. Well, that Sr. Gretchen, she caught me after Sunday Mass and took me over to the convent for a talk about my Johnny there."

"Oh, yes. She's a hard one. She cracks the whip, I tell you. I think my Bob is scared of her."

"Yes, well, that's as it should be. Lord knows that Johnny ain't afraid of me." Mrs. Sweeney shook her head woefully and noticed a tea leaf slowly descending to the bottom of her mug after she'd taken another drink of her tea and rested her dull, brown mug on the table.

"No. It's the truth. Bob's father has to take a belt to him sometimes. He's getting so big; I can't do much with him. But lately, he's got a better attitude, I think."

"Really?" Mrs. Sweeney was partly envious and partly suspicious about any change of attitude a teen-ager might exhibit.

"Well, he's joined a club up at the school, you see. He attends regularly, twice a week, which is more than he goes to church, it is." Mrs. Murphy laughed a bit.

"A club? Well, what kind of club is that?"

"Oh, something about foreign missions, I suppose. Bob told me I wouldn't understand. I think it might have something to do with medicine too. Maybe it's medicine in the foreign missions. It's hard to follow what they say nowadays. He's never taken chemistry, but I was thinkin' maybe my Bob will become a doctor or study for the priesthood." Mrs. Murphy liked to dream for her boys since they seemed so aimless themselves.

"You don't say! Why I thought he had a girlfriend." Mrs. Sweeney had been impressed by Bob's lofty goals. She began to wonder what she was doing wrong with her Johnny.

"He does?" Mrs. Murphy certainly didn't know anything about a girlfriend. Bob never seemed to take an interest in any girl. Then she realized what she had revealed. "Well, I mean, I certainly expect Bob to be a normal boy for his age, but it doesn't mean he can't give it up. Bob is a smart boy, you see. I expect he hasn't failed but one class in all his three years up at St. Gen's."

"Is that so? My goodness, you have reason to be proud. I'm glad of it for Bob, but I truly thought that little Chink girl down the street was going to drag him down."

"A Chink girl? No, you must be mistaken." Mrs. Murphy couldn't suffer such a blow. Her mind had reeled at the word.

"Well, now, Johnny said that Bob is sweet on some little Chink girl, took her to the dance up there one night. Johnny sneaked into the dance. He's big for his age and they passed him in, taking him for a junior. Anyhow, Johnny said that Bob was there with a Chink but he left with her early."

Oh, God, she cried to herself. Bob out fornicating with a Chink. Oh, dear, and this despised woman throwing it in her face. Mrs. Murphy suddenly wanted out of the woman's lair. However, she kept an outward composure, mostly by lifting the mug to cover her face as she pretended to be draining the last drop, which she had managed to do already two minutes before.

As she sat the mug down firmly on the rickety table, she said with a firmness about her lips, "Well, if indeed your Johnny is correct, then my Bob will have a backside to favor for a week to come, I'll tell you that. Mr. Murphy will see to it!" Let old Mrs. Sweeney talk; Betty Murphy would straighten her son out; every last one of them would be bound for heaven and not hellbent like Mrs. Sweeney and her lot! "I better be going now."

Just as she stood, Johnny came in, slamming the door. His sleeves, though frayed, were long enough to reach the length of his long arms, but he had scrunched his hands up into his sleeves, so that he looked as though he had no hands. He walked into the kitchen, placed a sleeve on the lid of a kettle, and looked under and saw to his satisfaction that it held the night's stew. Mrs. Sweeney looked at him while Mrs. Murphy stood, not willing to leave until she'd heard the news.

Quickly, Mrs. Sweeney grew impatient. Johnny produced a hand from his sleeve, dipped his finger in the stew, and slurped it from his finger. She strode over to the stove and slapped the boy's face. He recoiled at the slap but never raised a hand to her. "Ouch! What'dya do that for?"

"Your mother sent you to find out something. When you come into her house, you tell her right away. Now keep your dirty fingers out of my supper!"

Mrs. Murphy's eyebrows inched upward. Mrs. Sweeney, she saw, knew how to do a man's job with her boy. Mrs. Sweeney continued, "Now, what did you find out?" She stood back, a potholder had appeared mysteriously in her hand.

"A Chink lady got killed last night."

Both women emitted a sound of shock. "Jaysus, right here on this block? My Gawd in heaven!"

"No, Ma, not here. Down where she works."

"And where is that?"

"At the laundromat down by Grover."

Mrs. Sweeney looked at Mrs. Murphy for confirmation, "Is there a laundromat down there?" It was difficult for housewives to imagine doing laundry in any place but the privacy of their own homes. In fact, one of the greatest joys for Mrs. Sweeney was checking laundry that was hanging out to dry. She could get a fair fix on the economic advantages of her neighbors that way. Anyone who could afford new underwear was starting to make some advances. Right now, she knew Johnny didn't have any on because she'd already overmended what he had and couldn't buy any thing until her check came the first of the month.

"Yes, I've heard of one down there. They employ the Chinks." Mrs. Murphy had heard tell about a Chinese laundry down Stanton somewhere, but her memory was vague because, now that she thought of it, it was Jim who told her, and he was drunk at the time.

"How about that! Dead, murdered in cold blood, she was." Mrs. Sweeney was letting the scene take shape when Johnny looked over at Mrs. Murphy.

"It was Bob's girlfriend. I mean her mother."

Mrs. Murphy hated to hear him refer to a Chink girl as Bob's girlfriend.

"Ah, then, that's a blessing in disguise, it is," said Mrs. Sweeney in sympathetic tones. "Why, that's an end to that romance, don't you see? The girl and that rough brother of hers that goes to the public school will be taken off somewheres."

Mrs. Murphy signed herself automatically. Her head had begun to hurt, and she wasn't sure where the devil was but that he might be in this house on the instant. "I've overstayed myself, Mrs. Sweeney. I best be gettin' my own supper ready and be off to that meetin' at school. Thank you for the tea." With that, Mrs. Murphy raced from the house to the safety of her own.

Chapter 15

After returning from seeing Fr. Ray, Gretchen went into the chapel located on the first floor of the convent, next to the large parlor, which had been the chapel for the large community of nuns who had once lived there. She sank into the kneeler and leaned heavily on the pew in front of her. She couldn't get her mind to work. She would need to contact someone at the school office to send someone for counseling. There'd be the funeral. The school would attend and needed to take part in the liturgy. But she couldn't get herself to plan it out. She was just tired, that's all. She kept trying to get herself to buck up. Just as she tried to exert the effort required to do that, she found her spirits sag again. She glanced at her watch.

Everyone would be gathering for supper soon. She mustn't appear unduly strained. It was important to keep everyone on the mark. Parents needed to know about their children. No distractions! Besides, Maria was always willing to listen to people go on and on. She said she was just being compassionate, but Gretchen told her she was just commiserating, which, to her, meant that Maria was just being miserable with them. Gretchen believed in keeping a professional distance. People could not be raised up by wallowing in their pity with them.

Finally, Gretchen sat down and tried to do the breathing exercises Suzanne had taught her but which she'd abandoned some time ago. There was this terrible void in the middle of her, the pit of her stomach. She hoped she wasn't developing an ulcer! Finally, she reached for her rosary. Maybe the repetition would calm her. At least, she'd be praying. Yes, she could pray the rosary for that poor woman and her children.

Gretchen managed to get through four decades when she heard the bell indicating that Rebecca had supper ready. Gretchen rose, genuflected rigidly, and passed from the chapel, still lecturing herself. As she entered the dining room, she noticed Maria giving a hug to Rebecca and smiling happily. She hoped she wouldn't spoil the joy, but she felt anger rising in her throat that she had these burdens to carry while Maria only had to teach people to sing and, if she was lucky, to read music. Maria never had days from hell like Gretchen's as far as she could tell. Rebecca was still too young to have been tested, and Mechtilde, well, she was so old, she'd probably forgotten half her life.

"Gretchen, Becky passed her exam! Isn't it wonderful? Now she can relax this weekend." Maria still displayed a broad smile.

"Of course. I'm glad you can rest this weekend. I wish we all could, but our week is not over yet. Shall we get started?" With that she began the grace before the meal.

Becky had felt reproached. Was she supposed to feel guilty because Gretch and Maria had conferences in school tonight? She felt her eyes burn, but she would never let herself cry in front of that awful Gretch. She glanced up and saw Maria smiling sweetly at her.

Becky smiled amiably as they sat down at the table and continued, "Well, I'm going to pop some popcorn tonight and watch some awful television program. I have no idea what's on. Do you want to watch with me, Mechtilde?"

Mechtilde looked up. Her eyes always seemed to express love when they looked at someone who had addressed her. She did the same with all of them, including Gretchen, but Gretchen never seemed to notice. Becky always melted. "Why, Becky, I might, but not that shooting and killing."

"Great! We'll just watch the ones where there's love-making!" teased Becky. Mechtilde gave her a look that seemed to express surprised disapproval, but it was in jest. "We'll celebrate again when you guys come home," Becky added with a feeling of guilt.

"It's good of you to include us," said Maria, "but we only finish at 9:00 if we're lucky." Maria knew that afterward, she'd be meeting with Suzie in the music room.

"Hey, I thought Suzanne was coming tonight," Becky looked from Gretchen to Maria.

Gretchen looked as though she had forgotten about Suzanne's coming and looked at Maria to see if she knew where the absent Suzanne was.

Maria spoke more quietly, the exuberance suddenly evaporating, "Oh, she thought she'd get in late. I guess she figured we'd be busy in school, and so she's probably spending a little more time at the motherhouse." She began stabbing at several green beans in her plate.

"That's a good idea. I sometimes wonder if being off on her own won't weaken her connection with the rest of us. She needs to spend time with those sisters at the motherhouse, if not for herself, then for their benefit. They don't understand anyone wanting to go off into the woods to be a hermit," said Gretchen.

"You know, I think that's strange, don't you?" Becky was thoughtful.

"That she's a hermit?" Maria looked up from her new activity, rearranging the green beans into three piles on her plate, next to the over-baked fish filet.

"No, not that. I think it's strange for nuns not to understand being called to be a hermit. Isn't that how religious life began? How we are today simply grew out of those original hermits. It's like we don't know our own roots." Becky forked a mouthful of mashed potatoes into her mouth.

"You have a point, Becky. That's why I love history so much. If we lose touch with our foundations, we become unrooted, to use your words. If a plant is uprooted, we know what happens to it. I believe the same is true with humans." Mechtilde had not said so much in one sitting for a long time. Becky had strummed a cord deep within her.

"You think we religious communities will die?" Maria had given her full attention to Mechtilde.

"Civilizations do, cultures do. Religious life is a subculture of sorts within the auspices of religion. I think these can all die if they do not remain rooted."

"But we have to adapt, don't we?" Maria seemed really concerned that Mechtilde explain this to her.

"Of course, we must. I suppose science can explain that, " she said, nodding and glancing toward Gretchen who had been a science teacher before being assigned as an administrator. "If one doesn't adapt, then one becomes withered." She laughed lightly and then explaining her levity, she added, "I'm withering, so I guess I'm not adapting." Mechtilde held up her arm for all to see the sagging flesh.

"Tilly, you are not! You have the clearest mind of all of us, I think." Becky was adamant that Mechtilde not put herself down. As far as she was concerned, Mechtilde was the soul of the community at St. Gen's.

"Well, the body loses its ability to adapt eventually. Perhaps, like plants, we wither when we've sucked all the nutrients we can possibly hold from the environment in which we're placed."

"God help us if that's the case," Gretchen spoke so suddenly that they all turned as one to look at her. "I was only thinking of this neighborhood and how little nutrition for life can be found here. Not even a tree along Elias. I doubt a tree could live in the city air." Gretchen wondered why she felt she needed to explain herself.

"You make it sound so hopeless!" Becky suddenly felt drained. She had a difficult time living in the neighborhood where she didn't feel safe walking along the street. The only place she felt safe walking was on the campus. She was glad the university was located in the suburbs.

"You speak truth, Gretchen. There is a hopelessness about the neighborhood. I watch from my window and notice how people don't even look up when they walk down the street. Everything is in decay. People don't find much that is life-giving around them any more." Maria was looking long and hard at Mechtilde, amazed that she was so talkative but more that she spoke as pessimistically as Gretchen did.

Gretchen had paused with her fork lightly resting on her plate herself, looking long at Mechtilde. She too was puzzled that Mechtilde should share an opinion of hers. She was also acutely aware that while the shared opinion had the effect of depressing her, it didn't seem to distress Mechtilde at all. She was still sitting there, serene as ever.

"So, Mechtilde, does that mean there's no hope?" Becky was getting concerned, as if her moorings were being loosened by the one person she had counted on for security.

"What are our roots, Becky?" Mechtilde tilted her head.

Becky sat thinking. "The Garden of Eden?" she asked doubtfully.

"That is true, but I think the garden is where things started to go sour. Think further back than that," Mechtilde had their undivided attention.

"Yes!" Maria had suddenly found the answer. "God blew his breath into the clay."

"I think so. We must never stray far from the clay, from the dust. We are so mortal, but we spend most of our days trying to avoid that reality. Here we are in Lent, eating our Friday fish, but the message of Lent is that we are dust and will return to dust. We have to make peace with that, but I don't think many do."

"As in being busy about success?" Maria was into this discussion wholeheartedly.

"Yes. We deaden the message of mortality in so many ways. We worship the body and do all sorts of things to keep it looking young, and some others, fearing and dreading the mortality we carry about, drug themselves. Drugs make us feel immortal, I suppose. Look at all the pills the doctor forces on me to keep me alive. My!" Mechtilde held up one of the pills she took.

"But death is hard to think about," ventured Becky for the defense. She'd been horrified by a gray hair she'd found that morning as she dried her hair.

"Oh, yes, it is. I think that is the cross everyone must submit to. Didn't God's own son have to?"

For the first time, Gretchen had forgotten her burdens from the day. She was enthralled. Why was Mechtilde going on so about death? Was God using Mechtilde to send a message to Gretchen to let go the stress of Mrs. Ling's death and of Hotchkiss's drinking? She'd talked about drugs as an escape from the pain of mortality. "You know, Mechtilde, on a bad day, I've even thought of death as an escape from the misery of everything that seems so impossible."

Becky nearly gasped. She'd never known Gretchen to be so transparent.

"Me, too," admitted Maria.

"Oh, yes! I suppose it can seem sweet when we have so much pain. I wonder why we recoil from pain so much that we could see death as a deliverance?" Mechtilde had posed another question, and Becky felt she needed to search for the answer. If Tilly kept this up, Becky would never get her chance to unwind in front of the television.

"I think there's another side we must look at--about our roots, I mean." Maria was thoughtful again. She'd stopped picking at the green beans some time ago. "I think Gerard Manley Hopkins speaks about how we've smeared and bleared the earth. We don't touch it anymore. He writes how we walk with our feet shod so we don't come in contact with it. Maybe that's about avoiding mortality again, but maybe it's also simply trying to lose contact with the earth. Creation--of our creaturehood!"

"Yes," smiled Mechtilde with delight in her eyes. "But not just that--but with other creatures. I think your key word is creaturehood. Remember that it was God who blew into the clay. That's an important root. We come from God and that is our source of life and nourishment."

"Of course, religion!" Becky smiled sheepishly.

"No, not religion, Becky." Becky was startled. She felt another tether loosening from her moorings. Mechtilde continued, "God. Religions are the result of groups of people who try to define God and pattern lives according to that understanding. They are mostly harmless, not always though. History reveals that certainly. Perhaps the word I want is spirituality. Staying rooted in one's relationship with God so that God can continue to breathe into us the life we need."

Gretchen was resting her chin on her hand when she heard the chime in the hall indicate it was nearly six. She had deliberately set the clock forward ten minutes so that Maria, who perpetually ran late, would be on time for prayers and meals. "Goodness! Maria, we have to get to school."

"Okay, I'll do everyone's dishes," Becky raised her arms as though on a cross in a gesture of her mock martyrdom.

Maria dabbed a napkin to her mouth. "I'll just go comb my hair and be over in a jiffy."

Gretchen knew hers needed combing too, but she headed to the door because she had to unlock the front door of the school.

Chapter 16

Detective Terence Hogan could see the dining room lights on as he pulled into his driveway. Finally, he said to himself, I'm going to sit down to dinner with my family. Gee, I might actually have a normal weekend at home. As he walked up the flagstone path to his front door, he noticed that the weeping willow was beginning to have an indistinct look about its branches, a sure sign that spring was coming in spite of all the dark, dank cold of the day.

As he stepped inside, he pulled off his jacket and hung it on the hall tree. He heard the scrape of the chair and saw his beloved Millie looking around the door of the dining room. "Oh, my goodness! Will wonders never cease?" Her smile lit up his heart. "Jody, set the table for your father."

"Dad?" He heard his daughter's high voice question his appearance.

He entered the room with an arm draped around his wife's shoulder. "Wow, what's for supper? It smells great." He sat at his usual place at the head of the dining room table. Millie was seated opposite to Terry with Jody and Brad sitting opposite each other at the sides. The kids joked that there was no head of the table because everyone was the head of the table, depending where one began the count.

Jody placed the silverware next to the plate she set before him. He smiled up at her. She was young and healthy looking, her long blonde hair shining in the light of the chandelier above the table. He couldn't help thinking of the sweet young girl, whose picture he had seen earlier, who had lost her mother to senseless violence. Brad passed the platter of roast beef, which swam in heavy gravy.

He glanced at Millie who was looking at Brad. "Tell Dad about your good news, Bradley."

His son glanced at his mother, but he seemed shy about speaking. Terry urged his son, "Hey, sport, don't hold out on the old man."

"I made the cross country varsity cut today."

"Hey, no kidding! That's great. I'm proud of you, Brad. You are blessed with fleet feet!"

Brad groaned, but he lifted his water glass to return his father's tribute. "A toast, a toast!" It was an old joke. They waited for his punch line.

"Whatsamatter, no bread?"

Terry tried to eat as a man who truly relishes his wife's cooking, but he overplayed the compliments that belied his reality. Terry was too tired to be hungry. He found himself feasting more with his eyes. It was so rare that he sat down at table with his family. His kids were good-looking and healthy. Their eyes were clear. They were not at all like the sort of kids he dealt with down at the station, and his heart was full. If he had cried, they could not have understood why, but he felt like breaking down and sobbing. That didn't help his appetite either.

The girls cleaned up after the meal. Brad had sauntered into the living room to watch some TV. "Finished with your homework already?" Terry had followed him into the room.

"Yeah. I did it at school. Mom picked us up late so I could wait to see the posting about cross-country."

"That's great, Brad. I like that you know how to use pockets of dead time like that. Very constructive."

"Thanks, Dad. You want this?" He offered Terry what they called the "surf board".

"No, son. You go ahead and pick the show. It's your night."

Brad picked a show with several breasty babes. Everyone had clever one-liners. Terry wondered if the cast was capable of memorizing more than one line at a time. He reached in his pocket for his pack of cigarettes.

"Not in here, Dad," his son warned him of the recent non-smoking areas they had declared in his own house. "Passive smoke is dangerous," he added when his father looked with displeasure at his son's invocation of a family prohibition. He sat with the pack in his hand, not willing wholly to concede his compliance by re-pocketing the cigarettes.

The next show was a police drama. Terry hated them, but the first scene showed a successful drug bust. He was just about to get up to leave when the commercial took over. His son had muted the commercial and looking at his father, asked, "I'm gonna get something to drink. You want anything?"

"Yeah, maybe a 7-UP." The carbonation might help his gas pains, Terry thought. He lifted the pack to his nose and smelled the cigarettes and then heaved himself out of the comfortable chair to step outside for a quick one.

As he blew the smoke upwards, he noticed the stars were bright. That's good, no clouds tomorrow. We could use a little sunshine down here. Terry reflected on his thoughts and wondered whom he was addressing. Maybe he prayed more than he thought. He was a church-goer on Sundays, but more because it was an early habit engrained in him by his Irish parents. He wasn't exactly a religious man and often wondered if God hadn't abandoned the world that he had created.

One time he had told the chaplain down at the station that from all he could see, God didn't have the balls to stand up to Satan. How else could you explain the evil the cops like him had to encounter day after day! Terry dropped his cigarette and slightly twisted his foot as he pressed the cigarette against the cement step. He left it there, a small, rebellious objection to being forced to smoke outside his own home.

When he came back into the living room, he saw that Millie was still in the kitchen. He sat down heavily. He would wait to go up to bed with her. If he went early, he might fall asleep and tonight, he felt some passion awakening in him. Maybe it was from watching all those busty girls on TV. He wondered what effect they had on his hormonal son. Brad's eyes did not stray from the show. A cop was being laid out by the captain for some oversight--or for thinking for himself. Terry knew that the script would eventually link some politician who was in control of the police commissioner but who also was the real drug kingpin in the city. Whatever! He took a deep drink of his 7-UP.

Suddenly Brad muted the screen. Terry couldn't tell where the commercials began and the show ended. He glanced over at Brad. "You know, Brad, I was wondering. Are there any gangs at Peter Claver?"

"No, not really." His son's answer was matter-of-fact and his eyes were still captivated by the screen. Terry glanced up, as a woman seemed to writhe on the hood of a luxury car.

"What's that 'not really?'"

Brad looked at his father then. "Oh, Dad. Peter Claver isn't St. Gen's or wherever." His attitude was patronizing if it was possible for a kid to patronize his father.

"Don't give me that. Gangs are growing everywhere. The suburbs aren't immune."

"O.K. I think there's a small group of guys that hang around together. They have some hand signals, and if you mess with anyone of them, they all get together and take care of the offender."

"So, are they dealing?"

"Dad." Brad's look was mixed with pity and patience, the kind of look Brad might more appropriately give Terry in a few decades as he sat in some wheelchair in some nursing home.

Terry cleared his throat to prevent the wrong words from coming out. "So, is drug use pretty wide spread then?" This was a private Catholic high school, for Christ's sake, Terry thought. Where could his son and daughter find a safe environment for an education if not there?

"Look, Dad. I don't use the stuff and neither does Jody. It's there, but you always say that life is full of decisions. That's just one of them. Don't get wild on this, OK?"

Terry hated it when his children treated him as if he were out of control. They didn't know just how dangerous their world was. If they did, then he could calm down. Just then, Millie stepped into the room. She probably heard them and was running interference between the two male rams, as she called them. "I'm going up now. Terry, will you check the doors?" She bent to kiss her son's cheek.

"'Night, Mom." He glanced up at her with a remarkable tenderness. Terry even resented Brad's look, perhaps because he never saw any such tender look directed toward him.

"I think I'll call it a day too, Brad." Terry pushed from the chair again to right himself. He needed to eat regularly and then he'd lose some of this excess spare tire. The life he led caused him to eat when he could and sometimes he was overhungry and over did it, especially with all the wrong foods. Still, if he was home more, would he just have to put up more with these kids talking down to him? He rubbed his eyes as he stood there.

"Don't worry so much about us, Dad." Brad's voice had a softer quality to it. Terry glanced at his son. His large brown eyes had a softness to them, but only for an instant.

"That's what Dad's do best, I guess, Brad. Goodnight, Son." Terry checked the door at the entry and the one in the kitchen. Next he checked the one that led into the garage. That was the hot spot because it was seldom used. The garage was a catchall and although it was a two-car garage, only his wife's Ford Escort could fit. Mostly, they parked their cars on the driveway. Because the garage was seldom used, the door was often forgotten and could go unlocked for days. No one listened to his admonitions about that door. Brad had said that the electric door to the garage was locked, so why worry. They always had an answer. That was it, the real danger; they felt secure in an insecure world.

Terry stripped off his outer clothes and slid in beside his wife in his boxer shorts and tee shirt. He lay close to her and began to feel more aroused. She turned over on her back and touched his cheek gently. "Hard day?" She asked.

He felt some anger. Why did she think he wanted her because it had been a hard day? Did their sex have to get complicated too, damn it? He bent to kiss her lips and raised his hand to catch her breast.

Afterward, he felt he'd been a little too rough, and he definitely rushed her. She hadn't reached an orgasm, but he felt a lot better when his came. Now, he lay there, wanting a cigarette, but she strictly enforced the "no-smoking-in-the-house" rule. He leaned over her and whispered, "I'm gonna go down and have a cigarette."

"You never answered. Did you have a bad day, Terry?"

"If I answer, can I have a cigarette here?"

"O.K., but just this once."

Terry was surprised, but he jumped out of bed and hopped over his shoes to find his shirt pocket. Then he fumbled in his pants pocket for his lighter. He didn't want her changing her mind. He inhaled deeply. This cigarette was the best he'd had all day. When he got in bed, he saw that she had raised up and supported her head on her hand elevated by her bent elbow.

"My life consists of murder and mayhem, Millie. Sometimes, it's not so bad, but other times, it gets to me. Today, I got a mother whose face was smashed in. Her husband's dead and now her two kids are orphaned. They're Vietnamese. Her little girl, she's so fragile looking. She's Jody's age. Her brother is about Brad's age. Why is the mother dead? It's all about drugs and gangs of boys selling the stuff and getting strung out on it themselves." He glanced at Millie and saw her pained expression. She had probably uttered something, but he hadn't paid attention. He just kept puffing on his cigarette, inhaling as deeply as he could and holding the smoke in his lungs longer than usual.

"You know, Millie, our kids don't understand the real danger. They don't use drugs yet because they know that we wouldn't approve. They need to know where it all leads. They don't know that. It just occurred to me that I should take them on the job with me. Just one day. That would be enough."

"Terence Hogan!" Millie sat up, twisting to look him in the eye. "Under no circumstances!"

"I wouldn't endanger them. I just want to let them see things."

"I will not have my children viewing cadavers whose heads are beaten in. What are you thinking?" Her whisper was reaching audible levels. He knew the kids would hear her if he didn't calm her. Just then the phone rang on the stand by his side of the bed.

"Damn," he said aloud as he glanced at the alarm clock that stared back: "11:00" in laser-red lettering. "Hogan here." Millie noticed that for the last year, her husband answered the telephone in their home as he did his desk phone at the office. It made her wonder if he ever really came home.

"Jesus! Of course, I'll come in. My God!"

Terry got up then and walked to the bathroom to douse his cigarette in the toilet and to take a leak. He heard Millie asking him what it was, but he ignored her. His mind was already racing ahead of the rest of him. As he pulled his pants up, he realized that his penis was hanging out of his shorts still. He shoved it back in and zipped up, feeling a momentary regret at his inability to have given Millie some pleasure. That was out of the question now. As he buttoned his shirt cuffs, he bent down and kissed her goodnight. "Naivete is a dangerous thing, Babe. Just think about it. I love you."

Terry left in a hurry. He put his light on the roof of his unmarked car and sped to the scene of yet another murder, but this one had roused even more indignation in him.

Chapter 17

"There you are, Duffy," Gretchen could see Duffy's legs emerging from the janitorial closet. The rest of Duffy was bent forward as he rummaged in the bag of rags that hung from a nail in the closet's interior wall. "I'm sorry; I didn't mean to startle you."

Duffy had jumped at the sound of her voice. He stood now in front of her, looking down as he always did. He always reminded her of a little boy being chastised. The thought of the pornography had fled her brain when Terence Hogan had appeared in her office that afternoon and now her mind was on the order of the homerooms.

"I trust that you've cleaned the bathrooms and made sure that all the homerooms are in order?" He nodded his assent but kept his head down. "If there's any classroom cleaning to be done, then take care of that, but I want you out of the school no later than ten." Gretchen could see that Duffy would not be vacating the building until the job was completed regardless of her admonition that he leave while the parents were meeting with the individual teachers. She checked her watch. It was ten after nine. The crowds, if one could be permitted to use that term for the number of parents who had shown up, had come early and only a few stragglers were milling through by eight. The place could have closed at 8:30, but she kept the faculty until the agreed upon hour of nine. Duffy only nodded his assent.

Gretchen had decided to give herself a reprieve and leave ten minutes early and walked out the school entrance, locking the door behind her. The cold night air felt good to her. She knew that the factories released toxins from their smokestacks at night, but regardless of the pollution, the coldness against her cheeks made her feel liberated as though she had been suffering from some sort of confinement.

She looked down Elias to make sure that no one would be walking behind her and then headed to the convent. She saw lights in the rectory and knew that Fr. Ray had returned. She did not envy his priestly ministry. She was not an emotional woman and believed that any emotions she did feel should be kept reined in. No use unloading one's burden on another soul. A priest had to deal with people who lived and believed differently. He had to bear too many burdens that belonged to people who could not manage their own affairs.

By now, she reached the door and inserted her key. She stopped to get one last breath of the "fresh" air. She had been amazed at how many of the residents along Hobart had already heard about the murder. It was difficult to keep people moving along to their conferences since they would see someone who lived elsewhere in the neighborhood and would stop to pass along the awful information.

That Mrs. Sweeney, ever the busybody anyhow, had been holding up quite a gaggle of people earlier in the evening. Gretchen had to run interference to "encourage" everyone to keep to the schedule as the teachers were waiting in their homerooms. That crazy woman actually had turned to her and said, "But have you heard, Sister, about the murder on our street? Cold-blooded, it was. They say someone strangled her and raped her right there in broad daylight. Imagine!"

The detective hadn't said anything about rape. It had truly bothered Gretchen to think of such a thing happening. Even if it was down on that rougher side, down past Madison, this one touched home. She wondered what was left of the body. That poor child. Still Gretchen had pretended to know everything about Mrs. Ling's death and hurried the people to their appointments with the faculty. If it wasn't Mrs. Sweeney, then it was Mrs. Murphy or some other Hobart resident.

That Mrs. Murphy had said something strange. What was it? Oh, yes, something about a missionary club. That was it, she was so glad that we had a foreign mission club. Bob was so excited about it that he couldn't wait to attend the meetings. Gretchen was upstairs in her bedroom now, changing into her pink flannel pajamas. She had brushed her suit and hung it carefully in the closet, noticing that a button was coming lose. She made a mental note to sew it on again.

She padded into her bathroom and began brushing her teeth, glancing at herself in the mirror. She could see the crow's feet around her eyes. Well, she was fifty-two, what could she expect? After rinsing, she reached for her floss. She tugged at the string and found that the spool unwound an unsatisfactory length. Empty! She looked at both the string and the dispenser and sighed aloud: "Murphy's Law!" Then she tossed them both into the wastebasket, bared her teeth for a thorough examination, turned, and flicked the light off as she returned to her bedroom.

A sudden gust of wind blew against her window and rattled it. She shivered. The floor was cold and her feet adjusted to the temperature of her body's sensors, sending goose pimples along her arms. She moved quickly to her bed and set the alarm, noting it was already 9:45. She hadn't heard Maria come in; perhaps she had left before she did herself, Gretchen thought. She yawned, flicked out her light, and lay her head on the pillow. With her eyes shut, the images of the evening played against her eyelids. There was Duffy jumping upright from the closet. Such a pathetic figure! She would have to get down to that business about the pornography on Monday somehow.

First thing in the morning though, she would have to try to contact the school office. She would have to finagle a home phone number for the superintendent since tomorrow was Saturday. That would not be easy. Weekends were so inconvenient; they interrupted the flow of work. Of ministry, she corrected herself. Gretchen turned over. It would be the beginning of her tossing and turning. She wished she could turn it off, but she couldn't. Foreign missions, indeed! St. Gen's didn't have a foreign mission club; it was a foreign mission club itself.

Agnes, the Superior General of Gretchen's religious order, was always trying to establish a foreign mission for the congregation. Her main reasoning, Gretchen knew, was that other congregations were doing it, so they needed to jump on the bandwagon too. Monkey see, monkey do as her grandmother used to say. Gretchen had a meeting last summer with Agnes regarding her reassignment to St. Gen's. Gretchen could speak French fluently; she had a knack for languages. Agnes was suggesting that should Gretchen want to escape St. Gen's, she would be happy to have her lead a group of sisters to Rwanda in Africa. It had been a French colony, and her language abilities would be an asset.

Gretchen had told Agnes that St. Gen's was a foreign mission. "What on earth do you mean?" Agnes's blue eyes had looked wide in bewilderment.

"First of all," Gretchen had used her graceful fingers to count off each point, we have Vietnamese students, who make up nearly 58% of our enrollment. They have to adjust to American culture, but before we can help them do that, we have to understand their culture. My French comes in handy with them since Vietnam was also a French colony at one time.

"Secondly," she had continued, noting that Agnes had blinked her baby blues, indicating that Gretchen had already scored big time, "we live with left-over Irish who feel besieged, bewildered, and very threatened. While these Irish have been here a generation or two, they are still very unwilling to "mix" with the other populations. That's much like these African nations who have borders that include various tribes which now find themselves split, so that some parts of the tribe are themselves in a minority in one country and a majority in another. I deal with the minority who feels dispossessed. I work for peace every day at St. Gen's among the quarreling factions."

"Finally," Gretchen's three fingers stood upright, so that she looked as though she were giving a papal blessing. Gretchen had glanced at her fingers then and had been also reminded of statues of saints with these three fingers raised. Gretchen rolled over again. She was grinding her teeth already. She let her final point with Agnes drain away.

Rape! Good grief. Wasn't it bad enough to lose your life without them raping as well? I could have told Agnes that our people are pillaged and sacked, much as any third world country. I am in the foreign missions. A tear leaked from the corner of one of Gretchen's closed eyes. With the tip of her finger, she brushed it across her cheek.   Another followed and then Gretchen fell asleep. She did not hear Mack bark as Fr. Ray walked his faithful stray down the side of the Church along Elias Street. It was just ten o'clock, earlier than usual for Gretchen to slip into a deep sleep.

Chapter 18

Maria had watched Duffy check the lock of the side door and then ascend those narrow steps to the second floor. She stepped from the shadows under the stair well when she could no longer hear him. Opening the door quietly, she took the piece of duct tape that she held in her hand and placed it carefully over the latch of the door. The door closed noiselessly.

Maria moved her head from side to the side, stretching her neck muscles. She had heard some awful news about Mrs. Ling from Mrs. Sweeney during their conference. Mrs. Sweeney kept talking about the death, probably to keep Maria from discussing Johnny, whose music and religion grades were in the "terlet" as Doris Sweeney responded when Maria had finally gotten two words in about Johnny.

She'd leaned forward to look at the grades, looked back at Maria, sniffed, and said, "Unsatisfactory, you say. I say them grades is in the terlet, that's what I say. Well, pardon me, Sister, but his sorry ass is going to be sorrier when I'll be getting home."

Maria really loved the woman's colorful language. "She was of the earth, she was in truth," said Maria softly to herself as she walked up the side stairs to the second floor. When she reached the top, she began to hum "The Rain in Spain" from *My Fair Lady*. The only difficulty for Maria that night had not been with any parent, that would be the expected, but instead it had been with John Hotchkiss.

She had noticed how argumentative he had been with Mrs. Murphy, something about not being responsible for Bob being suspended. He had been so loud that she had stepped into his room to see what the matter was after Mrs. Murphy had left. She caught him drinking from a pint bottle, which he'd taken from his desk drawer. She knew she'd have to talk to Gretchen about that, and he knew too. He had started yelling some irrational things at her about being so holier than thou. It had been quite upsetting, a hard conclusion to her day since it had happened at the end of her last conference.

Well, now she would go to her music room where she would wait for Suzie, hoping that she had not violated her vows again. She knew she wanted to share with Suzie what Tilly had talked about at supper. Suzie was in the woods as a hermit, and she should have been closer to God, but if Suzie was not letting God's breath into her life, then she would go on filling the void with Gus.

Maria had always thought of herself as being faithful, but after listening to Tilly, she felt a renewed sense of call. She wanted more than ever to belong to God, fervently, wholly, completely. Her heart had been yearning ever since supper, right through all the Mrs. Sweeneys and Mr. Hotchkisses.

In fact, at one point that night, she thought she'd seen a movement in her classroom. She had just greeted the first parent of the evening, walking her into her room, when out of the corner of her eye she had sensed a blur of movement. Kind of like when a mouse moves; it's so quick that you wonder if you did see something. Since she had been thinking about how much she wanted to belong to God at that same moment, she wondered if perhaps the spirit world had stirred as she experienced that longing. Maybe so!

Maria turned into her music room, not the homeroom where she talked with parents. That room abutted the alcove at the back of the music room. The music room was her refuge. She loved to play the piano here. Maria walked to the piano and picked up the matches from within the seat, and then lit her candle. She was always amazed at how much light one candle in a dark room could make. She sang the words: "What a bright world this could be!"

As she held the last note, she heard something around the corner. The room was in an L-shape, creating the small cubbyhole or alcove where she stored some instruments and sheet music.

Maybe her earlier vision had been a mouse after all. She walked back, carrying her candle.

"Oh!" Maria was shocked. "What are you doing here?" His back was turned to her and his hand was in her little cabinet, the one that held her little cask where she deposited the nickels she charged for various infractions in her classroom--chewing gum, passing notes, not having homework. The money would be sent to the foreign missions at the end of the year.

The money jar was really a heavy old metal cask, resembling a small barrel. On its side, three x's were stamped to suggest it held moonshine, but Maria always said that the x's meant kisses and that the contributing students were sending their love to the missionaries.

"What on earth are you doing in here?" She looked more sternly now that her initial fright was over. "Are you stealing my money?" She stepped toward him. As she did, she saw the wild-eyed look he had. She could not know that he had taken Liu Ling's cocaine as well as his own that day or that Walter had inadvertently laced it with angel dust. Liu Ling had been too upset about her mother, and Gretchen had broken them up before he could pass it to her so he had used it to steel his nerves as he waited for the parents to clear the school that night.

His heart was pounding as though it would come through his chest. He tore his hand, still lodged inside the cask, away from the drawer where it rested. She came at him. The candle seemed like a torch. He swung his arm in a backhanded fashion and although she raised her right arm to thwart the blow, she was too slow. He hit her across the forehead and she fell backward.

Bob's heart continued to pound fiercely. He looked down at her. She was unconscious. It didn't matter; he was in for it now. He couldn't think. His heart was pounding in his ears now. He couldn't make it stop. He leapt over her, slid a little. Someone must have spilt something.

He ran down the hall, toward the main stairs. He stopped, remembering that he couldn't go out the main door, which was locked and did not have a panic bar. No. He turned and ran back down the hall to the side steps just past the music room. He descended the steps two and three at a time. As he felt for the door, he dropped the cask. It was too dark to see where it had rolled. He didn't care. He flung the door open; it flew wide before it swung back. It didn't click. Maybe it was broken. He was in too much of a hurry.

Maybe he could find Walter. He needed some help. He needed something to clear his head, to make his heart stop beating like this. He ran all the way down Mohammed to Madison. Walter lived near the precinct. People would know where he was.

Duffy had been busy, pushing desks into alignment. He had just finished a room and had stepped out into the hall. He could hardly wait to get back downstairs where he could take his picture to the bathroom and have that feeling he liked so much. That's when he heard the soft but rapid padding of someone down the adjacent hall. He glanced down the hall and from the glow of the exit light at the main stairwell, he saw a figure in a dark coat quickly disappearing around the corner.

Duffy was puzzled. How could anyone be in the school? He was about to go down to the janitorial closet to get his picture. He had to be alone or someone would tell on him. They might take his picture away. He took some steps down the hall. When he came as far as the music room, he noticed a light that seemed to go off and then back on. He looked in. The light flicked on, off, and then on again. He walked toward the back of the room where the strange light was. He saw the candle on the floor, the small flame dancing back and forth along the spilled wax. He moved a desk and stepped toward the wall. The little room had a light switch that would help him clean up the candle mess. As he stepped forward, the candlelight went out and the room was total darkness.

Duffy stumbled over something in the dark, and then while regaining his balance, he slid on something. Finally, he felt the wall, found the opening to the alcove, and then located the switch. He flipped it on and turned around. Then he saw her, lying on the floor. She had her eyes closed, but the light shone on her hair. Her face was turned to one side, but Duffy could see her quiet profile. He was sure that this was the girl in his picture. She had come upstairs for him. Sr. Gretchen had stopped him earlier from checking on his pretty lady, but his pretty lady wouldn't be stopped.

Duffy reached out and touched her, fearful that she would awaken. She did not move. She was so pretty this way. He touched her hair. That thrill ran through him again. Her eyes remained shut in sleep. He reached down and touched her face. Oh, she was so quiet. Was it possible?

He reached for the top button of her blouse. Something was urging him to hurry. His stubby fingers were awkward; his breathing was hard. Finally, the button gave way. She remained still, letting him do whatever he wanted. Tears came to his eyes. This woman wanted Duffy to touch her. She wouldn't laugh at him or hurt his feelings. He took the blouse in both his hands and pulled hard. It gave way. He pulled away the garments that covered the treasure. He held her breasts in his hands. He lay down and kissed them, sucked at them.

His hand reached under her skirt. He hardly knew what he was doing, but the fire in him led the way. He only followed and as he followed, the fire grew more intense. He pulled her legs apart and poked and poked until he found the place of least resistance. Duffy had never known such pleasure. It was so painful, he cried out.

Only when his body stopped its rhythmic movement, did Duffy come back to the room. He thought Sr. Gretchen might come and check on him. He got up and turned the light out. The lady disappeared and Duffy felt sad. He took a step forward and tripped over his pants, which were down around his ankles. He pulled them up and walked slowly against the wall, once again slipping on something.

Then he heard a loud clanking sound. Someone must be coming. Maybe his mother or maybe Sr. Gretchen. He would come back tomorrow and clean up the spilled candle wax. Now, he should go because Sr. Gretchen told him to leave by ten, and she must be coming to check on him. Duffy could not tell time, but he felt that he had been gone a long time.

Duffy felt good though in spite of his fears. As he passed the piano, he saw some keys on the piano bench, reflecting the exit light, which glowed just a few feet down from the music room door. Duffy smiled and picked up the keys. Being with the lady that way made him feel he had earned more keys. Maybe that's how Fr. Ray got all his keys, thought Duffy. Now he knew the secret.

When Duffy left the school, he carefully locked the front door and walked down Mohammed toward Madison, holding himself more erect than he ever had. He breathed in the cold night air and felt that he wouldn't even be afraid of those guys who might be on the corner, waiting to make fun of him.

Chapter 19

"Oh, God, what time is it?" Suzanne had fallen asleep in Gus's arms.

He squinted toward the alarm dial. "Nine thirty five." He yawned and felt the warmth of her body being removed as she rolled away. He liked the pressure of her body against his. Instinctively, he reached out and held her. She stopped and looked over her shoulder. Immediately, he became aroused. "You might as well stay the night. Better yet, spend the weekend with me."

"My car on your parking lot the whole weekend? I thought you were afraid of the talk." She was reminding him of his insistence that he come to her hermitage in the woods because he had overheard some old biddies talking after Mass last month. One had asked about a strange car parked on the church lot. It had happened after their last liaison.

He was nibbling at her breast again. A thrill went through her. Then she thought of Maria. "I can't, Gus. She's waiting for me. I have to sneak into the convent so that I can appear in the morning because I have been there all night." It was difficult for her to refuse him. She never did, but some inexplicable uneasiness was taking over just now.

"C'mon. Just one more time." Gus was not being helpful. He was working his tongue over her nipple.

She pushed his head away as her back arched in pleasure. "I can't. I'm late already, and Maria is probably still waiting." This time she rolled further away until she could sit up on the side of the bed. She dared not look back. If she saw him sitting there, pouting, she couldn't leave. She craved him as much as he did her. She pulled on her jeans, dancing precariously on one foot and then the other. Fully clothed, she glanced at Gus, smiled and said simply, "'Bye," and ran down the stairs to retrieve her car coat and purse.

But she was thinking of Gus upstairs, sitting there, cross-legged in the bed. She sighed and glanced at her watch. She could be at the school in five minutes. She walked briskly to her car at the side of the rectory, got in and glanced up at the bedroom window and saw Gus in the window watching her. It was getting harder to leave him, but when she was in the woods, she didn't even think that much about him.

She inserted the key in the ignition. She had the right kind of life, she decided. God had her a whole month at a time; Gus had her only for short, brief encounters. This time, though, she sensed that he was dissatisfied with her arrangement. He wanted more time, more regularly. Things were coming to a head, and she was not happy with the prospects.

She sped down the streets, feeling safe to do so at that time of night. She took a left onto Mohammed and crossed over Hobson, her thoughts turning to Maria.

Maria wouldn't be able to help her with what looked like a new dilemma, she knew that, but Maria would give her one of her lectures, and Suzanne would feel better afterward. Knowing that someone else knew her secret and could and would keep it brought some measure of relief. She didn't have to carry her burden alone.

As she neared St. Gen's, she saw Ray with his dog. She sped across Elias and continued down to Madison, not wanting Ray to see her stop near the school. He might investigate what a woman was doing alone in this neighborhood, lurking around his school at that time of night, and that would not be cool. She looked in her rearview mirror. Ray was looking down at the sidewalk, but the dog was looking in her direction and barking. Dogs have super senses; he probably recognized the smell of her car. Thank God, Ray was into some deep thinking; he hadn't seen her.

She turned right onto Madison. It was a creepy part of town. Some black guys were standing on the corner at Mohammed and Madison. They were up to no good. She pulled into a small parking lot next to the thrift store to turn around. Her headlights picked up a small black kid with a dark stocking cap covering his head.

He was talking to another black guy who had his hands raised, palms upward. He apparently was excited and looked like someone who was pleading his case. The little guy had a boom box that was on loud enough to invade her car with the beat. She quickly spun the wheel as well as her tires as she exited left from the parking lot. Neither boy attempted to walk toward her. They seemed so surprised when she'd turned in but her lights probably blinded them so they couldn't see that she was a lone woman.

She passed back down Madison. She saw a car stop next to the boys on the corner. Something passed between them. Drugs, she thought. Addictions are so stupid. Then she thought of Maria asking her if she thought she had an addiction to sex. Actually, when it came down to it, Suzie didn't really understand addiction. Gus smoked and he couldn't go long without a cigarette. Was that how she was with sex? Wasn't that different? The body was made for sex, so naturally, it craved sex. That couldn't be an addiction.

Finally, the light changed, and she took a left onto Mohammed. As soon as she turned and started down the street, she saw this white kid running for all he was worth. He looked strung out about something. I guess some whites still live on that side of Mohammed, she thought, as she saw the turn into the alley where she would park near the side entrance to the school.

As she turned to get her purse from the seat next to her, she noted the time on the dashboard clock--10:00. Well, a half hour late wasn't that bad. She closed the car door and pushed her body against it so that it shut quietly. Then she walked quickly, her car keys held between her fingers just in case she met up with someone hiding in the shadows. If the side door were locked, then she would know that Maria had given up on her. Well, she could always go back to Gus. It would definitely be fun to spend the night with him.

Still, she was relieved to find the door with the tape still holding it open. It would mean fewer lies to tell if she was at breakfast in the convent tomorrow. She peeled the tape back and carefully closed the door behind her. The place was so dark. Fortunately, the exit sign dimly lighted the upper part of the landing. She always navigated the lower part of the flight by memory--nine steps. She was about to begin when her foot hit something hard and it skittered across the floor, banging against the wall and rolling around until it finally came to a stop. It was a terrible racket. She stood still, wondering what it was. It sounded metallic and heavy.

She found herself forgetting to breathe. Then she thought Maria would probably have been alerted by the noise to her coming and call down any minute to tell her she'd made enough noise to wake the dead. Suzie immediately felt lighter. She went back to her count. Let's see, was that two or three. She took the steps very carefully and when she got to the ninth step and reached the landing she was relieved because the exit light in the hall gave her enough light to see the end of the next flight of stairs.

Her eyes had already adjusted to the dark of the interior and, once in the hall, with the light from the exit sign, she walked briskly to the music room door. Then she was distracted by a movement at the end of the hall, but that part of the hall was too dark to see clearly. Yet she was sure that something had moved at the place where the hall intersected with the main hall. It had been so quick; something dark moving swiftly in more dark. Get a grip, she told herself. She wasn't usually this jumpy.

She wondered why the light wasn't on in the music room. Funny. She whispered, "Maria." She waited and then called in a hoarse whisper, "Maria, where are you?" There was no answer. Maybe Maria was the shadow she'd seen. But she wouldn't have used the main stairs if she'd given up and left. She would have gone down the side steps to fix the door there.

Oh, well, she thought. I'll just go down along the side of the wall and flip the light on in the alcove. Since the music room faced the alley, a light could not have been noticed by Fr. Ray in his rectory or anyone in the convent. Even so, she and Maria always took the precaution of turning on the little alcove light. It was always wonderful to watch Maria playing at the piano, the low light from the alcove sometimes causing her hair to glisten as her head moved to the music.

Suzie inched down the dark aisle next to the wall. As she came close to the alcove, she skidded on something. Strange to find a slick spot. Maybe Duffy waxed the floors for a change, she thought as she groped around the corner for the light switch. She flipped on the light and turned around. She looked at the front of the room. The piano stood open. The only part missing was Maria sitting there playing. Then she glanced down.

Her face froze in its half-smile. She was about to call Maria's name, but it never came. There Maria lay, her clothing in disarray. Had she fallen? Suzie could see the pool of blood that had oozed out across the floor. Maria's lifeblood! Suzie knelt down and reached for Maria's wrist. She didn't need to take the pulse; she knew. She began to cry, "My God, no!"

Then she stopped. The shadow--the killer. Had he seen her? Was she in danger too? My God! She stood up and flicked out the light. She could hear herself breathing and wished she could quiet it. She knew how. Deep breath, hold it, let it out slowly. Now hold on without taking a breath for a bit; then breathe again. All she could manage was to let the inhaled air out jerkily, and when she tried not to breathe again right away, she found herself gulping for air. She wanted to cry, but she couldn't let herself. The killer might still be there.

Let's see. I have to get out of here. She began to inch down the wall, her left shoulder heavily rubbing against the surface. Her right shoulder was rigid and held back as though her body was trying to warp itself into one dimension. When she reached the door, she stopped. What if someone waited just outside the door for her? She held her fist to her mouth, trying to suppress the sobs she felt surging up from her solar plexus. She feared the killer was standing there just outside the doorway. She had no choice; she had to get out.

She stepped out. No one grabbed her. She forced herself to look down the hall where the shadow had been. Nothing. Maybe she was safe. But what if he was downstairs waiting for her? Had he heard that noise she'd made? God help me, she said and then repeated it as a prayer, adding the word please this time.

Her eyes were so used to the dark now that she felt that the exit sign glared and lit up the entire stairwell. As she approached the top step, she leaned over the railing to see if a shadow lurked below. She couldn't see anything. She began her descent, walking carefully. When she reached the landing, she leaned down again and saw nothing in her limited line of vision.

If she could reach the door, she'd be able to scream and be heard if someone attacked. Could she scream? She'd never been attacked; she couldn't be sure how she would react. Then she remembered her car keys. She'd pocketed them and left her purse locked in the car. She pulled the car keys out and placed them between each of her fingers. Anybody attack me, and I'll maul your damn eyes, she said with all the bravado she could muster.

She reached the bottom step, and no attacker presented himself. Her heart was pounding as though she'd run five miles. Her knees were weak, and the muscles in her legs were spasming. She hit the door, and it flung open. She stepped out and the cold air hit her full force. She must have been feverish because she began to shiver in the cold.

She ran erratically toward her car, hearing herself sobbing. She got in, fumbled with the keys and drove the short spurt down the alley and out onto Stanton. She drove up onto the sidewalk by the convent where she lurched to a stop. She couldn't control the amount of pressure her leg delivered to the brake. She turned the key off and managed to pull it out of the ignition with uncontrollable hands.

She half ran to the convent entrance, her side aching. She stood under the porchlight, trying to identify the key. She tried one, but it didn't go into the lock. "Oh, God!" She fumbled some more and found another. She tried it and it worked. The door hit the wall and bounced back. She didn't bother closing it but made for the stairs.

The first door at the top of the stairs would be Gretchen's. She flung the door open. Gretchen bolted upright in bed. "It's me, Gretchen."

"Stay where you are!" Gretchen hadn't a clue who was breaking in, but she did know it was a woman. Could it be Becky? She fumbled for her table lamp and knocked off the alarm clock. Finally, she got hold of the lamp switch and turned it. The light nearly blinded her, but through her squint, she tried to identify the person who had entered her room. Whoever it was stood with her arms up and her head held sideways, blocking the piercing light from her eyes. Slowly, she lowered her arms. It was Suzanne.

"What the devil?" exclaimed Gretchen. She glanced at the clock, which lay face up on the floor; it was 10:25.

Suzanne took two steps toward her and then sank to her knees and began bawling. Gretchen was fighting a wild feeling inside. Her mouth felt dry and her jaws hurt. She'd been clenching her teeth again. She moved to get out of bed. As her feet hit the floor, she felt she'd stepped on an ice block, and the thought flicked through her mind that if hell would ever freeze over, it wouldn't be any colder than her floor.

She knelt down by Suzanne, putting her arms stiffly around her. She had to get her quiet before she woke the others. Fortunately, the room next to hers was unoccupied, as was the one across the hall. Mechtilde was a little deaf, so she probably couldn't hear--yet. "Calm down, Suzanne. I can't understand what you are saying." Suzanne sobbed unabated.

Obviously, Gretchen's technique wasn't working. She stood up and closed her door. Too late. Becky was just arriving from down the hall, tying her robe and looking very sleepy-eyed. Gretchen admitted her and then closed the door.

"Suzie?" Becky was on the floor immediately, but she sat and brought Suzanne against her chest so that Becky cradled her. Suzanne finally began to sob intermittently but still seemed unable to speak coherently. She had assumed a near fetal position. It was a bit too much for Gretchen; she needed to know what was going on. Had Suzanne had an accident, she asked as she walked nearer. She couldn't bring herself to get back down on the cold floor; instead she carefully lifted her desk chair and brought it close to the two of them and sat, cupping the elbows of her crossed arms with her hands to hold in what little heat her body had.

Suzanne shook her head no. "Look, Suzanne. It's late. I can't play guessing games. You have to find your voice and tell us what's wrong."

Suzanne looked at her and formed a single word and burst into tears again.

"Maria?" Gretchen knew the flood had to abate again before she would understand anything about Maria, but she felt her inward panic rising.

Becky cradled her head and patted her back as she began to rock Suzanne gently.

Although Becky was feeling panic-stricken too, she began to experience herself as a person who tended to the external crisis before dealing with her own feelings and impulses. Being the oldest of six children counted for something, she thought, as she rocked Suzie. She could feel the effects of her gentleness on Suzie who had returned to sobbing intermittently.

Becky spoke softly, "We want to help, Suzie. Can you tell me about Maria?" She felt her question to be odd since Maria was back in bed, sound asleep. Becky and Tilly had given up on television after they'd watched one sitcom. They'd retired early, and Becky hadn't heard either teacher return from school but had presumed they had.

"She's dead." Suzie's breath came in little jerks that were interspersed with her words. "In school." Becky went cold, and Gretchen stood up so quickly that the chair tipped over.

Gretchen fled the room to get to the telephone. But she stopped in the hall and walked carefully down to Maria's room. She had to check. She opened the door and switched on the light. Her heart sank. The bed was untouched. "Dear God in heaven!"

She turned quickly and raced for the telephone room and dialed 911. She heard the sirens from the Madison precinct just as she reentered her bedroom. She was awake now; she had to take command again. "Becky, take Suzanne downstairs and give her some coffee; she's shaking so. I'll get dressed and meet the police and take them to the school."

Becky stood and helped Suzanne up. They left with lowered eyes. They were in a state of shock. Gretchen walked to her closet and looked at her clothes. She chose her black suit. Ray called it her power suit. When things seemed to spin out of control, she always reached for that suit.

Chapter 20

As Terry Hogan sped along, his light flashing, he could feel the blood pressure in his carotid artery rising to beat the steady rhythm of his pulse against his shirt collar. He glanced at his watch. It was nearly 11:30 now. This was turning out to be the week from hell. It would take that bent, just when he was counting on a weekend as a family man. Up ahead, he saw two cruisers with lights flashing. Neighbors were standing on their porches in nightclothes, holding their pajama collars or coat lapels close around their necks. It was a cold night. Would spring ever come?

Terry nosed his car to the curb, next to one of the cruisers, and yanked on his parking brake. He strode rapidly to the main door of the school. A patrolman, setting up crime scene tape, pointed toward the stairs, wearily. Terry didn't break stride. He reached the second floor and found another patrol pointing down the hall. "Take a left at the end of the hall."

Terry continued his rushed walk. The walls were not covered with graffiti. They were just blank. He hoped this was not an omen suggesting that they would hit a blank wall in this heinous murder. A mother with kids one night and now a nun, for God's sake. This world was getting too crazy. For the first time, Terry thought about retirement, even though it was years away.

As he turned the corner, he saw Herrington, a small guy, a graying fringe along the sides of his head with a shining pate on top. The light in the hall was acting like a spotlight on his bald spot. The guy oughta wear a hat, thought Terry. Herrington was very near retirement--a month or two away. Herrington looked at him as Terry continued to walk toward him with his longest possible stride.

"You're out of breath, Terry. Better watch that weight."

"Where is she?"

"Inside, in the back. I got guys checking blood trails on the floor so be careful and use the middle of the room to approach."

Terry went in and the guy taking pictures stepped away. Terry stood there looking down at her, but he was viewing her upside down. He stepped around and looked at her as her assailant must have seen her. She seemed so peaceful. A quiet look on her face. She was getting into middle age, but the slender build and long, blonde hair made her seem younger. The pool of blood to the right of her head was dark and hardening at the edges. The blow struck her right temple. Her arm, bent at a 45-degree angle seemed to suggest someone saluting, but Terry knew that she had tried to fend off the blow that killed her. She wasn't beaten to a pulp, but a heavy object must have been used to cause such a depression on her right temple.

Terry's professional eye was taking in all the details he needed, but something in his mind kept locking into the gentle, quiet presence she presented. She didn't look like a victim of a violent act. If it weren't for the blood and the location, he would have thought she was just lying down, peacefully sleeping even.

An evidence man was taking a sample of blood from a smear along the floor. There were several such smears between the wall and the body. Was there more than one assailant? Could be gangs again; maybe it was an initiation rite. Kill a nun! Jeez! Terry lifted his hand to scratch his thumb across his forehead. He glanced down at her once more and turned to leave. He felt the impulse to lift this hand again to make the sign of the cross and caught himself; he pretended that he was just scratching his forehead again. "Jeez!" He uttered again, although aloud this time. "O.K., Herrington, what do you have so far?"

"The guys have the murder weapon." Herrington reached his gloved hand into a large canvas bag and pulled out a large, clear, plastic bag. It contained a large cask, but one end was cut to provide an opening for a lid, which now was in another bag. The cask had blood on it. The lab would later find blonde hair as well as Sr. Maria's skin.

"I guess we've seen murder every which way. Her clothes suggest rape."

"Yeah, and the lab will get the samples. We'll know a lot more tomorrow."

"How many do you think were involved? It looks like they were taking turns skating on the blood spill in there."

"Joe's not sure. This is the interesting part. He checked tracks going two ways. One goes down the main hall and probably out the main door. I hope we haven't screwed the microscopic details because we all used that door to get in here. He thinks there were at least two different shoes that went down the side stairs."

"Maybe a gang, but why a nun?" Terry looked at Herrington who was giving him a raised eyebrow.

"They could've been looking for a virgin."

"It gets uglier all the time, doesn't it? Who found her?"

"That's where your work begins. I'll handle these details. I haven't got that part straight. One of the other nuns found her, but apparently it wasn't the one who met us at the door."

"Where are they?"

"In the convent. I have Quent over there holding them. They all seemed pretty scared. The priest is also with them. He doesn't look any better off."

"O.K." Terry took a few steps and looked back at Herrington. "I want this to crack. I want these guys bad."

"Me too," Herrington nodded. "My wife's family used to belong to this parish."

Terry left the school, noting that his earlier path was now cordoned off; he noticed some bloody footprints on the other side of the tape. Lab guys were beginning to show up in stronger force. He reached his car and noted that the crowds on the porches across the street had thinned. Tomorrow or the next day, patrol officers would be knocking at their doors, looking for anyone who saw any activity that night.

Terry started his car, forgetting to release the parking break until the drag of his car backing up made him aware. He released the parking brake and drove around the other cruiser, taking a right up Elias and another at Stanton where the entrance to the convent was. He noticed the car that had jumped the curb and was standing on the pavement with one wheel on the lawn. Terry parked at the curb and got out. He rang the doorbell, and Officer James Quentin III opened the door before it finished ringing. "The sisters are in the parlor over there," he said as he nodded the direction.

The room reminded him of an old Victorian parlor, seldom used except for company. Every lamp in the room was lit, but the people in it were pale and looked shell-shocked. Everyone but a very old nun who sat hunched in a chair, a large quilt stuffed around her lap and falling to the floor around her legs. She had a rosary in her hand, and her eyes were closed. A handkerchief was balled in the other hand, which lay by her side.

Two younger-looking nuns were sitting beside one another on a sofa, holding hands but not looking at one another. They had both turned to look at him as he entered. He nodded a silent greeting to them. A priest, who had been sitting with his elbows resting on his knees, had risen and was approaching Terry. It was the priest he had gone into the school with just a night or so ago.

Just beyond the priest was the nun, the principal he had spoken to about the little Vietnamese girl. He deliberately cocked his head to look past the on-coming priest to nod at her, but she was looking at the two younger nuns.

"I'm Fr. Ray, pastor here and administrator of the school." The priest held his hand out.

Terry shook his hand and felt how cold it was. "I think we met the other night, Father."

The priest looked closer at the man and a dim recognition registered in his eyes. "Oh, yes, I remember. The light in the school."

"Could you tell me which of the sisters found the victim?"

Fr. Ray turned and looked at Sr. Gretchen. She stood and walked toward them. Terry felt she was willing her legs to move in his direction. He reached out to her. "I'm sorry, very sorry about this, Sister."

"Thank you, officer," she said somewhat distractedly.

Terry remembered that she had made the same mistake about his rank in her office. She seemed so distraught that his heart went out to her. "I know that this is a very difficult time, more so for you."

She glanced at him with a questioning look.

"You found Sister's body?"

"Oh." She looked at the priest and then back at him. "No, not the first time."

"The first time?"

"Sr. Suzanne found Sr. Maria. I took the police in." She turned toward the two younger nuns. "Suzanne."

Terry took a quick look at the old nun in the quilt; she was the same as when he came in, only now he noticed that her lips were moving as she prayed the rosary. He glanced toward the other two. One looked startled and had a pained expression, like a kid being called to come into the dentist's office. The other nun reached a hand to her shoulder and encouraged her to move.

"She was quite shaken up, Mr....." The principal was explaining the slow response.

"Hogan. I understand, Sister." Terry walked toward Suzanne. "Stay there, Sister. I'll come to you." The nun settled back as though she were taking a seat again. She hadn't really done more than shift her body.

Terry reached out and pulled a chair toward the sofa. "My name is Terry Hogan, Sister."

She looked at him with very tired, swollen eyes. "Suzanne," she said and then looked down at her hands.

"May I ask a few questions, Sister? If you get too tired to answer, just tell me. It's just that the more you can tell me, the sooner I can get to work on this."

She nodded but her eyes seemed too heavy to lift. She continued to look at her hands.

Terry looked out of the corner of his eyes at the other nun who seemed to be a caretaker for this Suzanne. "Can you tell me what happened?"

Suzanne looked up at him, "I found her."

"Yes, Sister, but could you tell me how that happened?"

"I went to the music room, but it was dark. I went in and turned the alcove light on and there she was." As she said this, her eyes moved away from him and brimmed with tears.

Terry bowed his head and waited for a second. Then he asked as gently as he could, "What time was this?"

He could almost see her pulling her thoughts together. After a trauma, people's thoughts just scattered in random fashion; it was hard for them to think straight. "I arrived at 10:00. I know because I was half an hour late."

"Late?" He thought of nuns as being in bed early and rising at the crack of dawn. Ten o'clock in a deserted school?

"Yes." She apparently saw no incongruity. "I went to turn the light on in the back and then I found her."

"Sister, why were you in the school to meet her, may I ask?"

"I always get together with Maria. We were classmates. Well, she was two years ahead of me in formation, but we were close friends."

Terry was having trouble following. "Excuse me, Sister. You live here; yet you meet her over there?"

The other nun intervened. "No, Suzie lives out in the country. She came in for the weekend and was meeting with Maria before spending the night and the weekend here. The teachers had a meeting, a parent-thing, over in the school that ended at nine o'clock."

Terry began to understand why Herrington had given him the nuns to work with. "I see. You had a pretty long drive then to get in so late."

"She visits the motherhouse first and then comes here." He noticed Suzanne tense up. He looked at her.

"Yes," she said too quickly. "I knew about the conferences in the school, and that's why I came later." Her eyes grew bright and had darted from the other nun back to him. The sudden animation disturbed him. She had actually shifted her position and crossed one leg over the other. He saw the red blood traces that remained in the spaces between the ridges of her white Nikes as she turned her foot up, stretching her ankle. He made a quick note about that observation. One less gang member.

"O.K., Sister, let's get back to Sr. Maria. Can you remember any other details; anything, even if it seems insignificant to you now, may be of immense help to us.

She sat for what seemed an eternity, replaying everything in her head. "I parked the car and entered the side entrance. I knew Maria was still in the school because the tape was still on the door."

"She taped the door open?" Terry wanted to shake his head in protest at naiveté that was so dangerous. When he got home again, he'd use this to make a point to Millie about the kids and that garage door.

"Yes. That's how I could get in. I don't have a school key." She trailed off then but lifted her eyes back to him. "The noise. I bumped into something metal. It rolled around with such a loud clatter. It was awful." Suzanne was remembering her thought about raising the dead and her body shuddered.

Terry made another note in his book and underlined the word cask. "Anything else?"

"I walked up the stairs. It was hard to see, but at the top, in the hall, I think I saw the murderer."

With those words, Terry felt that the priest and the principal had moved closer behind him.

"You saw him, Suzie?" The youngish nun was hearing this for the first time, as were the two behind him, Terry suspected. He also feared that this was going to become a free-for-all rather than a police interview.

"Excuse me, Sister," he said to the youngish nun. "Sister Suzanne, can you describe what you saw?"

"A shadow." The nun looked at him and realized that her words were disappointing. In better times, Terry thought, she was probably a pretty good-looking woman. Her eyes could be particularly attractive if they were bright with happiness. They were dull-looking at the moment. She continued, "I had just come into the hall, but I thought I saw a shadow moving down at the end, going down the main hall. After I found Maria, I was sure that it was the murderer and that he was still there somewhere. He could have heard the noise I made on the stairwell. Maybe I scared him off...only it was too late." Her eyes filled with tears.

Terry knew he wouldn't get anything more from her for now. "Thanks, Sister, you've been very helpful. May I ask that you not leave town after the weekend? That's just so I can contact you if I need you to answer more questions or if you remember anything." Terry fished in his pocket and pulled out a white card, "Here's my name and number to call just in case you remember anything else.

Terry stood and turned toward the principal and the priest who were not a foot from his chair. The priest had to step back when Terry gave the chair a little push backward. "I know it's not a very good night for sleeping, but I suggest that all of you try. I'll ask Officer Quentin to remain the night for your protection, but I honestly don't expect any more trouble. The assailant has long ago fled into the night." His last words reminded Suzie of the young kid whom she'd seen racing down Mohammed earlier that night but she made no connection.

"I'll stay here too, Gretch," the priest said.

"No, Fr. Ray. If the policeman stays, we'll be alright."

"Sr. Gretch? Is that right?" Terry asked. It seemed a funny name to him, but nuns always had funny names.

The nun looked horrified. "Gretchen, Gretchen, " she repeated.

"Excuse me." He had caught a slight smile on the priest's face. "Sr. Gretchen, I'll come back tomorrow to see how you are, and if I may, I'd like to ask some questions. We'll need to know if any property is missing from the school for one thing. Perhaps you've had some trouble in the school or know someone who is a troublemaker. Perhaps when I come tomorrow, I'll have some additional information or some questions that you can help me with."

Gretchen nodded, and Terry dipped his head as he thanked them all. As he passed the very old nun-in-quilt, he glanced down and saw her looking up at him. He stopped, bent down, and intended to comfort her, but instead he remained locked in her gaze. He'd never looked into eyes like hers. They were like oceans of kindness, of wisdom, of some kind of power that Terry had never encountered before. They held his attention so long that the others became uncomfortable. They were probably asking themselves what he was doing. Terry had no words, for once. He simply nodded, pulled his eyes away and walked out.

"Quent, you're detailed here for the night. Enjoy the digs!"

Chapter 21

Everyone had a sleepless night at St. Gen's Convent, all except Officer Quentin who slept in spite of the lumpy couch in the parlor. The next morning, Becky, Suzie, and Officer Quentin had coffee together around the kitchen table. Quentin had some cereal with his coffee and followed that with some bacon wrapped in a thickly buttered slice of toast. Becky had fried the bacon while he made toast. Suzie seemed edgy and non-communicative. Once she got up from the table to make a phone call but came back quickly and said something about Gretch being on the phone.

In fact, Gretchen had called Agnes at the motherhouse. She got hold of her secretary, Sr. Vincentina, who understood the matter was utterly and absolutely urgent. Vincentina assured Gretchen that Sr. Agnes would call at her very earliest opportunity. Then Gretchen called the chancery to find a number for the school superintendent. When she'd informed the secretary that a faculty member had been murdered in the school, she finally got some action.

The superintendent was roused from bed by his wife. He had scowled at his wife for not fielding the call and answered grumpily. He certainly woke up and changed his tune when Gretchen told him the news. He suggested that Gretchen cancel school on Monday so that the school office could coordinate counselors and get them to the school on Tuesday and Wednesday. This was Holy Week, so school would not be held Holy Thursday or Good Friday.

Gretchen then called Fr. Ray, who was still trying to get hold of the bishop. Apparently, he was at a meeting in New York City, but Fr. Ray had reached the hotel where the bishop was staying. He was waiting for a return call too. They both knew that Maria's funeral would probably be Monday at the motherhouse, but he suggested that they have a memorial service at St. Gen's for the student body on Tuesday.

Gretchen then left the telephone room and checked on Mechtilde. Becky had already seen to her breakfast, so Gretchen merely picked up the tray to return it downstairs. Mechtilde smiled up at Gretchen as she bent to take the tray and patted her hand. "These will be hard days for you, dear. Take care of yourself." Gretchen, touched by her genuine concern, felt tears sting her red-rimmed eyes. She mumbled her thanks and found herself walking more slowly as she descended the stairs.

As she stepped into the kitchen, Becky rose and took the tray from her. "Can I get you some coffee?"

"Yes, thank you." Gretchen noticed the policeman with perpetual bags under his eyes seated at the table. He smiled when she came up and reached over and pulled out a chair for her. How strange to have a man sitting in Maria's chair, she thought. Suzanne was looking down into her cup. "It looks as though none of us has slept much." Gretchen was trying to break the ice of disconnectedness that had become prevalent since Suzanne burst in on the scene with the awful news.

Suzanne looked at her awkwardly then. Becky brought the cup of hot, steaming liquid to her. It smelled good. She realized for the first time that she was hungry. She noticed a slice of toast on a plate in the middle of the table. "Is this anyone's?" Everyone moved their heads from side to side and spoke at once, but Suzanne pushed the plate toward her.

"Do you have any news?" Becky asked the question and then realized that she needed to explain. "Suzie said you were using the phone when she tried to call."

That explained the click Gretchen had heard as she talked with Dr. Curran, the superintendent. "I'm waiting for a return call from Sr. Agnes. If Mr. Hogan comes before, perhaps you could take it, Rebecca. Give her as much information as you can and then see when and where the funeral will be. Tell her the body will be at Reefer's funeral home as soon as the medical examiner releases the body. We presume that it will be ready tomorrow for the wake. We need to know those times too."

It was obvious to Becky that Gretchen was back in the saddle; however, her attention, along with the others', was drawn to Suzanne who had visibly winced at the information about the funeral.

Great, thought Gretchen, she comes in and tears us all apart and then leaves all the work for us. She just sits like some helpless creature. Well, we've all been traumatized, thanks to her little nightly tete-a-tete. If Maria had come home.... Gretchen blotted out her thoughts. They served no purpose. The telephone rang then.

Gretchen went to the hallway where the telephone was mounted on the wall. "Yes?" She hoped it was Agnes. It wasn't.

"Good morning, Sister. This is Detective Hogan. I'd like to come over now if that's all right." He waited for her to agree. When she did, he said, "I'll be there in five minutes."

Apparently, he was calling from the precinct on Madison, or he may have been in the high school for all she knew. Detective Herrington had asked for a key before sending her back to the convent last night. That was when she had thought about Maria's keys for she and the detective were standing just in the hall outside Maria's classroom when he asked. She had given him a key from the rack downstairs in her office, but she made a mental note to check where Maria's keys were.

Gretchen returned to the kitchen. The policeman was having another cup of coffee. She wondered if he intended to go home or if he even wanted to. He seemed to be bending Rebecca's ear about what the life of a policeman was like. Gretchen wished Rebecca would stop being so irritatingly attentive to everyone. "Mr. Hogan will be here shortly." The telephone rang again, and Gretchen spun around to get it.

"Gretchen? This is Sr. Agnes. What's the matter?"

For once she was to the point. Vincentina must have gotten the urgency across. "Agnes." Gretchen felt tears come to her eyes and her voice trembled. "Maria has been killed. Murdered last night in our school."

"What!" There was a stunned silence. It gave Gretchen time to gnaw on her lip while she tried to regain control. The doorbell rang, and Rebecca ran past to answer it. Gretchen could see Mr. Hogan through the open door, and Rebecca showing him into the parlor. The policeman left the kitchen table with a loud scoot of his chair and walked past her down to the parlor, readjusting the wide leather belt, which contained a gun, ammunition and a baton. Suzanne must finally be moving, thought Gretchen, because she could hear the cups being stacked and placed in the sink.

Agnes was having a difficult time taking in the news. She began to ask questions for details that Gretchen hardly knew. She was struck on the forehead with a heavy object and bled profusely. Probably a skull fracture. Her clothes were torn, maybe a struggle. It happened after the parent-teacher conferences. That's when Gretchen began to focus her thinking again. She needed to check which parent saw Maria last and the time that conference was scheduled.

Agnes was getting to be a drag. Gretchen's mind still tired quickly for some reason. She interrupted one of Agnes's questions: "Agnes, a detective is here, and I need to go with him to the school. The body will be at Reefer's. When you know details about arrangements, please let us know right away. Fr. Ray will want to celebrate Mass at the funeral, and he also wants to have a memorial Mass at St. Gen's on Tuesday."

"I'm coming over this afternoon. I'll have Vincentina take care of the details here. I'll probably bring Helena too." Helena was one of the councilors and would take care of details at St. Gen's end while Agnes simply did her superior general thing, whatever that was, thought Gretchen as she hung up the telephone.

Gretchen hurried down the hall, trying to straighten her skirt. It was the brown suit and would need to go to the drycleaners after today. She turned into the parlor and just in the split second before she stepped in, she saw Suzanne moving quickly from the kitchen and down the hall as though she were timing her movements to Gretchen's.

"Mr. Hogan, I'm sorry but that was our Superior General on the phone."

"No problem, Sister." The sandy-haired gentleman stood up at her entrance. Gretchen was pleased and flattered that he practiced the social mores of a time she thought had passed. Gretchen was a little bothered by Rebecca's presence, being attentive and solicitous again!

"Rebecca, Agnes is coming and bringing Helena with her. Could you make up the rooms?"

"Yes," Rebecca said in a breathy way. It really expressed her relief. Suzie was so withdrawn, kind of dazed and not much company. Mechtilde was back to being silent even though kind and welcoming. Becky wondered if she had yet registered what had happened there last night. She waved quickly in return to Officer Quentin who had turned back to wave good-bye as he replaced his cap and left with Mr. Hogan and Gretch.

Terry led Gretchen to his car. Quentin took his own car and left for another destination. Terry drove around to the front entrance of the school on Mohammed. On the way, Gretchen mentioned about Maria's keys. She had a key ring that was plastic but had a cartoon-looking devil on it with a mustache and a yellow pitchfork. She wondered if the killer might have taken them, but perhaps they should search the music room. Hogan assured her that the room had been gone over thoroughly and no keys had been found. Gretchen inwardly fretted that the school locks would have to be changed. To Mr. Hogan, Gretchen said that she had a list of the parents who were to see Maria the night before.

Terry was interested in this list. "How long did the conferences go last night?"

"They were scheduled until nine, but most people showed up early, so I think most of the teachers left a little early."

"When did you last see Sr. Maria?" Terry felt the nun was more together than last night. She had a sharp mind.

"I didn't. Well, I came over to the school earlier than she. I did see her once when I made rounds and found Mrs. Sweeney gathering a crowd with news about Mrs. Ling." Gretchen wanted to ask him for details about Mrs. Ling but refrained. She didn't want to seem inquisitive about murders with a policeman, but she did want to check Mrs. Sweeney's information.

"What time was that, do you think?" He was parking in front of the school, again in the wrong direction.

"I'm not sure. I think it was earlier rather than later. Maybe seven, seven fifteen." They got out of the car, walked up the wide sidewalk to the front entrance while Gretchen fidgeted with her keys, and he held up the tape for her to duck under.

Once inside, she saw the tape stood between her and the path to her office. A lab man was crouched on the floor examining an area of the floor on that side. She started to reach for the tape. "Just a minute, Sister." Hogan placed a hand on her arm and realized how tense she was. "Is there another way to your office? We don't want to cut across there unless we have to."

"If we go upstairs, there's a set of stairs on that side of the main hall that leads to the office area. Students don't have access to them. Let me check if I have a key for that door." She walked her fingers through numerous keys, "Yes, this is it."

They walked up the main stairs and down the long hall. They crossed under the tape there, Terry feeling that the lab work had been completed along that section or it had already been contaminated the night before. Terry eyeballed the floor and seeing nothing, asked her to take a giant step across. They came to the door without an exit sign over it. She unlocked the door, and they walked down the stairs into a large room. "This is the faculty lounge," she announced as though she was leading a group at an open house. "My office is just down the hall, but you've been there."

Terry pulled out the gum he had been chewing; all the flavor had dissipated. As he leaned over to drop it in a receptacle, he noticed a paper towel with blood on it. Jamming the gum back in his mouth, he stooped and picked up the container. He carried it with him as he followed Gretchen into the outer office, from which they could see the main entrance door. The lab guy had apparently finished his task and left in the meantime.

"Hey, who's that? Hold on there!" Terry was taking running steps toward a small figure, who stopped in his tracks. Suddenly, Terry knew the face. The guy with the large oval eyes and larger oval mouth. Terry couldn't see the wisps of hair since the guy wore a brown cap with a visor, earflaps pulled down over his ears.

Behind Terry, Gretchen asked, "Duffy, what on earth are you doing here?"

"I come to finish my work."

"That's right! Duffy was here last night during and after the conferences to clean," she said to Terry. Then to Duffy, she said, "Duffy, you can't clean today." She walked nearer.

"Just a minute, Sister. Duffy, were you here cleaning last night?"

Duffy looked from one to the other. "Yes, I cleaned all the rooms you said. I left like you told me. Now, I come back to finish my work." Duffy felt that something was wrong; he was sure that they would yell at him. He had been so happy this morning on his way to work. He had hoped the lady in his picture would come to him again, and they would have a nice time again, but only after he finished his job!

"Can he tell time?" Terry asked Gretchen.

"I don't know." She found the question intriguing because she didn't know the answer and was surprised she didn't. "He always shows up on time," Gretchen said softly.

Terry pulled his sleeve back and extended his watch toward Duffy. "I'm not sure what time it is. My eyes are getting bad. Duffy, can you tell me what time it is?"

Duffy looked seriously at the watch. "Two o'clock. That's the bent, old man." Duffy's finger rested on the right side of the dial.

Terry's shoulders slumped. "Duffy, did you see anything unusual last night?"

"My mother let me watch the television last night. She was tired and went to bed."

Terry almost allowed his groan to be audible. The nun came to his rescue.

"Mr. Hogan means here at the school. While you were cleaning the classrooms, did you see or hear anything that was unusual?"

Duffy wasn't sure what they meant by unusual. He knew they were expecting him to answer. "No, Sister." He knew that when his mother expected an answer, to say no was the wiser course. Last night, when his mother had asked him, "Did you have sex tonight?" When he said no, she had left him alone. She only told him again that if he did, he should take his pants down so he wouldn't soil them. He didn't understand any of her admonitions, so he watched an old movie with a dog in it that saved a little boy from a waterfall. It didn't have many women in it, so he didn't have to avert his eyes frequently throughout the movie.

They were still looking at him, so Duffy asked, "May I go clean now?"

"No, Duffy. I have some terrible news. A very bad thing has happened to Sr. Maria in the music room. I have to keep the school locked for now, but on Monday, I want you to come again, and we'll see about cleaning up the music room."

Duffy looked up and began staring at Gretchen's mouth once she said the name, music room. His eyes grew into larger ovals, and he suddenly put his hand to his mouth and began wailing. Gretchen reached for him, but Duffy turned quickly, ran out of the building and down the street.

Gretchen looked questioningly at Terry Hogan. "I didn't know he cared so much about her.

Chapter 22

Becky walked up the stairs laboriously. She was very tired all of a sudden. She knew she had to prepare the guestrooms but decided she'd just lay down for a bit and rest her eyes, which were burning from the lack of sleep.

Her bed was still unmade and she kicked off her shoes and fell on the bed so that her body bounced slightly, her head lying on the pillow that had seemed so hard and uncomfortable last night. She could hear the sound of someone's voice in the telephone room. The person was crying. She remembered Maria's voice. Surely, it wasn't a deja vu experience. Could it be a ghost? Of course not! But she found herself getting up and leaning against the wall as she had done the other day, just to reassure herself it wasn't Maria.

It was difficult to understand some of the words because the crying interfered. Becky finally pieced the voice tones together; it was Suzie. She could hear her talking; her voice had the plaintiff wail of a child.

"I need you. It was awful. I can't get the sight of her blood off my mind." There was a silence. The other party was talking, but Becky could hear Suzie crying again.

"I don't care. I need you more than Ray does!" Becky began to wonder who Suzie was speaking to. Whoever it was apparently knew Fr. Ray too.

"How do you expect me to sit there at her funeral with you up there walking around on the altar? I need you, now!" Again there was silence, but Suzie was beginning to sound commanding. Becky had never known Suzie to act like that.

"Then, go to hell!" Becky realized that Suzie was angrier than she'd ever known her to be.

"O.K. I'll be there at 2:00 sharp!" That was it; Suzie had hung up.

Suzie was blowing her nose out in the hall as she walked to her room. Becky rubbed the heaviness from her eyes. She was beginning to feel stuporous. The last person she'd eavesdropped on was killed; she hoped history wouldn't repeat itself.

Becky went to the linen closet in the hall and got out the sheets, pillowcases, towel sets, and blankets she'd need to make up the rooms. The pile was too big and half her load fell to the floor, blocking her from closing the closet door. As she stooped to pick them up, she noticed Suzie looking out her door.

"I wondered what was going on. Do you need help?" Her smile was forced, her eyes bright from the tears she'd shed.

"I have to make rooms up for Agnes and Helena. They'll be coming this afternoon. I could use the company more than the help."

Suzie helped carry in the piles of bed linen, and making the beds went more easily. Becky looked over at Suzie after they'd made up one room. "I get tired so easily. I feel exhausted just making this bed. Crazy, isn't it?"

Suzie looked at her with a sympathetic smile and nod.

Becky continued, "Are you all right, Suzie? It must have been awful for you last night." Becky hoped Suzie would open up. She was never Suzie's confidante; Maria was, but maybe Suzie would turn to her if only from desperation.

"I feel like hell," Suzie said without great feeling. She bent to pick up the linen that had been placed on a chair and moved to the next room. Becky followed.

"I know Maria was a good friend to you. She was a good friend to me too." Becky felt the tears spring to her eyes and heard her words falter. Suzie reached out to her and Becky began sobbing on her shoulder. "It wasn't fair. I hope they find who did it and that creep burns in hell for it." Becky's anger flooded her insides just as her tears gushed and flooded down her face. Suzie handed her a tissue to wipe her eyes and blow her nose. They both sat down on the unmade bed.

"I thought the guy I saw might still be in the building. I don't know if he saw me. He might have heard me. I made a big noise when I was coming up the steps. I think that's why he ran away. He might try to kill me too if he saw me and thinks I can identify him."

"God, Suzie! Even if he didn't see you because it was dark, he might think someone knows him. He could think it was Gretch too."

"I didn't think of that, Beck. My God, we're all in danger. I just want to go back to my woods."

"I can't see why you can't. I think we three ought to stay at the motherhouse."

"That policeman won't let me. I'm not sure why. I told him everything. Why do you think he won't let me go? Do you think he suspects me?"

"You? You wouldn't kill your own friend. No, he said he wanted to ask some questions. I would think you could go after the funeral. He said something about tests. He should be able to ask those questions before the funeral, don't you think?"

Suzie had sat with Becky, and they lapsed into a silence that was comforting because it was shared. They occasionally broke that silence by recounting something about Maria--her music, her artistic mood swings, her emotional support. For the most part, Suzie remained dry-eyed except when they spoke of Maria's emotional support and understanding acceptance as each had experienced it. Finally, they decided to get the last room ready.

When they'd finished making up the room, Becky asked Suzie's help to make a lunch just in case Agnes and Helena arrived. "Let's try spaghetti," suggested Becky, rummaging in the cabinet for the box of angel-hair spaghetti.

"Nothing...red...please," Suzie turned her head away to gain control of her emotions.

"Sorry," said Becky. Without thinking, she said, "Let's keep it light. How about deviled eggs?"

"Sounds good. I saw some sliced ham in the fridge too."

"Want to make the brownies?" Becky offered, knowing the menu did not require two hands, but it was important to keep both of them busy, and she didn't want to be alone either.

When they'd finished and refrigerated everything, they put a kettle on for tea. "Mechtilde must be needing some company, and she hasn't asked for anything. Shall we have tea with her?" Becky had suddenly remembered the resident invalid.

"She slept through everything, didn't she?"

"Yes. I had to wake her when Officer Quentin came to the door. He wanted everyone downstairs in the parlor. She was a little disoriented at first. I think she thought she'd overslept."

"She has," Suzie said and then added the explanation, "It should have been her. She's old and ready to die, not Maria."

"Suzie!" Becky was startled.

"Don't you think Tilly is ready to die?"

"Yes, but I don't think she should just because she's old."

"It's unnatural that Maria should die now. It wouldn't be unnatural if someone Tilly's age would die."

Becky didn't like the slant in the conversation, but she chalked it up to Suzie's being so upset about finding Maria. She had Suzie carry the tray with cups and saucers while she carried the teapot, carefully adjusting the red and white checked hot pads to protect her hands.

Becky knocked loudly at Tilly's door. As no answer came, they looked at one another with some fear. What if Tilly had died? They both felt guilty and anxious at once. "Open the door a little and check," Suzie suggested. Becky opened the door and saw Tilly seated in her chair, her head bent so low that her chin rested against her chest.

"Is she dead?" Suzie's question echoed the one forming in Becky's mind.

Becky entered and set the teapot with a hot pad under it on Tilly's dresser. She walked carefully and with some dread toward Tilly. She knelt down and touched Tilly very gently. She did not move. Then she suddenly raised her head. Suzie shrieked and Becky inhaled audibly.

"What is the matter?" Tilly glanced with an alarmed look from one to the other.

"Nothing, Tilly. I didn't mean to startle you," Becky apologized.

"I believe it was you who were startled, Becky dear," Tilly smiled sweetly at Becky while she reached and patted her hand. Then she looked at Suzie, "What have you there, Suzie? I believe you've brought some tea. Can you join me?"

Becky felt suddenly better. Tilly was the only one among them who was behaving normally. Perhaps it had not yet registered about Maria, but Becky welcomed the reprieve from all the tenseness that controlled the others, herself included. She poured and passed the cup to Suzie who handed it to Tilly. They arranged themselves, Becky on the only other chair and Suzie on Tilly's bed, with Tilly as the focal point.

Becky followed Tilly's eyes as she looked at Suzie. Tired as her eyes were, Becky noticed how pretty Suzie was. She was teetering on the brink of mid-life and maturing so nicely. Becky was cute, but Suzie had always been a beauty. The kind that always made people wonder why someone so pretty would "throw her life away" and enter the convent.

Tilly asked, "How are you both doing?" Becky and Suzie darted a look to each other, wondering what the intent of the question was. Could Tilly possibly know? Tilly resolved the question by adding, "After the dreadful news."

Suzie took a sip from her cup, by which she signaled Becky that she was to answer first. Becky looked at Tilly, "Not so good, Tilly. Poor Suzie saw Maria, you know."

"I know. It must have been very upsetting for you, Suzie."

Suzie looked up from her cup. She avoided looking at Tilly. "Yes, it was very difficult."

An awkward silence followed which Becky sought to break. "Agnes and Helena are coming. They'll stay at least through the night, Tilly."

"That's good. I think it might help Gretchen let go of her sense of responsibility for a bit if Agnes comes. They'll make the decisions, and Gretchen can let go; yes, she needs that."

Becky hadn't thought of Gretchen needing to let go. Then she looked at Tilly, "How are you managing, Tilly?"

Tilly looked tenderly at Becky. "I will miss Maria so much. She was so important to us here. Maria was ardent in everything she did. Ardent about music, ardent about teaching, and she was ardent about her life, wouldn't you say, Becky?"

"That's a good word to describe her, Tilly. Maria really cared."

Suzie looked away as Tilly continued to speak. "Yes, she cared for you and for me very much. She certainly cared for Gretchen too although I doubt Gretchen ever realized that. I know that she cared for you very much, Suzie."

Suzie's head jerked toward Tilly, who was smiling at her. Suzie tried to read her eyes. Had Maria confided anything in Tilly? Did Tilly know about Gus? Suzie had no way of knowing because Tilly's eyes were kind but impenetrable. Her smile was enigmatic. All she could say was "Thank you!"

The bell rang downstairs. Suzie stood and went to the far window. She saw the motherhouse car parked out front and realized that had Tilly looked out that window last night, she would have seen Suzie parking her own car. "Agnes is here."

While Becky went to the door to admit the guests, Suzie took the tray to the kitchen. It was 12:30. They would be having lunch together, something Suzie had hoped she could have avoided.

Chapter 23

When Agnes and Helena had arrived, they both wore sympathetic expressions and gave warm hugs to each of the nuns. Gretchen, who returned from school just as they arrived, showed them to their rooms while Becky put out lunch quickly. Suzanne seemed at loose ends, still jittery and not much help.

They were long in coming down; apparently both were talking to Gretchen, getting as many details as they could, so it was 1:00 P.M. when Gretchen and Helena came downstairs for lunch. Agnes was still upstairs, visiting with Mechtilde. The four seated themselves, awkwardly, deliberately leaving Maria's chair empty and passed the time in small talk until Agnes joined them.

Helena brought them up to speed on the ailing sisters in the infirmary and the renovation of the bedrooms on the fourth floor of the motherhouse. Finally, the sisters were all having access to a bathroom between bedrooms rather than the one large bathroom situated in the middle of the hall. Everyone sitting there listening to Helena felt the banality of the conversation, but the alternative topic of conversation would have been worse so they listened as though quite interested.

Agnes finally joined them. "I'm sorry, Sisters. I wanted to stop by to see Mechtilde. She is a wonderful person, isn't she? A real blessing for you?" They began passing the eggs and ham around mechanically, nodding assent to Agnes. Then silence fell as they began picking at food they weren't very interested in. It was suddenly broken by the telephone ringing.

Becky started to rise, but Agnes told her, "No, dear. It's better if Helena answers for awhile. It might be the press." Helena rose and looked around the room for the telephone when both Gretchen and Becky motioned her toward the hallway. They all waited until they heard her answer.

Helena returned sooner than they expected and sat down quietly. Glancing up, she realized all were looking at her expectantly. "It was the priest across the street. I told him I would come over at 1:30 PM to discuss the Mass on Monday. He said that he must bury a parishioner on Monday morning at 9:30. I suppose we could have our funeral at 11:30. He wants very much to offer the Mass." Helena was addressing herself to Agnes.

"Another funeral? Poor man," Agnes was sympathizing again.

"Mrs. Ling," Gretchen spoke softly at her plate.

"Who is Mrs. Ling?" Agnes looked questioningly at Gretchen.

"A parent of one of our students. She was murdered too." Everyone heard the implied reference to Maria but chose to ignore it.

"Murdered? This neighborhood must be deteriorating faster than I thought." Agnes frowned at her conclusion. "Perhaps you should consider moving down to the motherhouse for the rest of the week."

"We--I can't, Sr. Agnes, because we have school on Tuesday with counselors coming. There will be the memorial service for uh." Gretchen hesitated and skipped over providing Maria's name. She continued, "uh, just so many details," Gretchen was trying to be polite, but she always felt that Agnes was the most impractical person she knew.

"Well, we'll discuss those details later. We only just arrived." Agnes threw her shoulders back and smiled benignly at them. Then her eyes rested on Suzanne. "I haven't seen you in so long, Suzanne. How are things out among the trees?"

Suzanne's face reddened, and she started to say that all was fine when Becky blurted, "Suzie just came from the motherhouse."

"I beg your pardon?" Agnes's look suggested that she didn't like to be contradicted. "Suzanne has not been to the motherhouse for some time, Becky. I know; I live there." She tried to sound jesting, but the sharp rebuke was there, and Becky knew enough to withdraw.

Gretchen was another case. "I beg to differ with you, Agnes. You spent the day there, didn't you, Suzanne? You only arrived at St. Gen's late last night." They all looked at Suzanne for clarification and vindication.

"Perhaps I can clear this up later." Her face was redder yet, and then she added weakly, "I did stop for my mail yesterday."

Agnes was forming another volley, not being one to lose a point, when the telephone rang again. Helena pushed her chair away from the table and went to answer it. Their eyes all followed her out the door. Then Agnes turned back to look somewhat severely at Suzanne, but Suzanne returned her look with an imploring one, saying, "Perhaps we can talk privately, Agnes. I'm not feeling very well. I still see Maria." She burst into tears. A show of emotion was what they had all been avoiding and there it was.

Gretchen looked at Becky and wondered why she hadn't reached out for Suzanne; after all, she had been Sr. Solicitous all morning. "Rebecca, perhaps you could take Suzanne upstairs."

Becky stood and helped Suzie out of the room amid her loud sobs. Becky felt that Gretchen was removing some offending presence, and Becky was correct. Emotions were an offending presence for Gretchen, who had cared for a mother who had manipulated her husband and children through emotional outbursts. It had been Gretchen's father who had told Gretchen many times to help her sobbing mother from the room.

Helena returned just then. "What's that all about?"

"They were good friends," said Gretchen, avoiding mention of the deceased in name.

Helena glanced at her watch. "That was the Telegraph wanting to know the details. I'd better go see Fr. Dunstan now."

Agnes looked at Gretchen after Helena left. "Why did you say that Suzanne was at the motherhouse?"

"That's what she told the police." Then in the pause they both looked at one another. "Agnes, if she wasn't at the motherhouse, she doesn't have an alibi. My God!" Gretchen felt a need to batten the hatches; she felt that someone needed protecting and whether that was Suzanne or the order or both, she wasn't sure. She was sure that something was beginning to form in her head, the idea beginning to emerge of two friends disagreeing about something in the dead of the night to the point of violence. The possibility that Suzanne had murdered Maria began to form in Agnes's mind too. This was not just a tragedy; it was taking on monumental proportions.

Agnes's own imagination was showing her a Telegraph headline that read: Nun kills nun in bloody brawl! When the two looked at one another again, their eyes were filled with the gleam of a wild fear, and they looked away and began to eat the food that had gone untouched on their plates.

Upstairs, Suzie continued to weep, whether in grief for a lost friend or in grief for her lost veil of secrecy in her affair with Gus, she couldn't have been able to distinguish. She knew that she now had the piper to pay; something that Maria had warned her about many times.

Becky stood nearby, waiting for her crying to subside. She hadn't leapt to the possibility that Suzanne might have killed Maria. Her mind couldn't put that image over Suzie because she thought of Suzie as a woman in serious pursuit of a spiritual life. Suzie blew her nose loudly and then blinked through her swollen eyes at Becky.

"I'm okay. You can leave me."

"I want an explanation, Suzie. You told the police that you were at the motherhouse. We were under the impression that's where you were."

Suzie looked at Becky. "I can't tell you, Becky. I would if I could."

"What are you messed up in?"

"I can't say, but it's a mess alright." She began to cry again.

"You owe us an explanation, Suzie. Where did you go all day yesterday? I mean, why did you lie about it?"

"Because I'm ashamed, maybe; I don't know." Suzie glanced at her watch. She was supposed to meet with Gus in the confessional.

"I need to go someplace, Suzie. I want to go over to the church for awhile."

"That's it? That's all you're going to say? You owe us an explanation, Suzie. Why were you so late?"

"I was with a friend, all right?" Her words were angry.

"Friend?" Becky weighed the word.

"Yes, a friend. I just got carried away because I hadn't seen this friend for awhile, and I feel guilty because if I hadn't been late, then Maria might still be alive."

Something about the explanation was still bothering Becky, but she felt sorry for Suzie as she realized that she had taken on responsibility for Maria's death.

"Maybe that's how it might have played, Suzie, and then again, we might be having a double funeral. Think about that. At least, we don't have two people dead."

Suzie shook her head. She sat, staring at the floor, noticing for the first time the weave of the threads in the throw rug by the side of her bed. "I have to go, Becky. I need to go to church for a little bit." Becky stood back then and watched Suzie walk out the door. Something was still bothering Becky, but she couldn't pin point what it was.

Suzie had left the room by a few steps when Becky followed but she turned at the bottom of the stairs toward the kitchen. She met Gretchen and Agnes who were coming down the hall from the kitchen.

"Where's she going?" asked Agnes who had seen Suzanne heading out the front door.

"To church," Becky said, glancing toward the door.

"Church? Whatever for?" Without waiting for an answer, Agnes asked, "Becky, did Suzie give any explanation as to her whereabouts yesterday?"

"She said she was with a friend she hadn't seen for a long time."

"Friend? Why couldn't she tell us all that at the table?" Gretchen's question echoed that in each of them.

"A secret friend perhaps or a friend that must be protected. Well, we shall get to the bottom of this when she returns," said

Agnes, feeling some relief that Suzanne had some sort of alibi that would not link her with Maria's death.

As they dispersed, Suzie was crossing Elias and heading for the dark interior of the church. She'd forgotten a jacket in her hurry to leave the convent, but the sun was actually beginning to warm the day, making her aware that spring was not far off. When the first warm, spring days came, Suzie noted that they always made a person more aware of the litter and of the winter's cinders that lay stretched along the street's gutters. When she entered the church, she felt the coolness of its interior, and a chill nagged at her. She folded her arms and wrapped them around her, rubbing at her elbows. She sank in a pew and leaned her face into her hands. She felt suddenly very, very tired.

Gus sat in the confessional, waiting for Suzie. He had agreed to take confessions for Ray who was busy tending to the details of Ling's funeral and the mess surrounding the murder of Maria. Helena was meeting with Ray now about Maria's Mass. Before leaving them to take Ray's confessions, Gus had said that he would certainly want to concelebrate Maria's funeral Mass.

Anyhow, Gus wouldn't be stuck in the confessional all afternoon because as soon as Ray was finished with Helena, he assured Gus that he would come and take the confessions. That might just work out so that he and Suzie could drive off somewhere and talk. She was really upset, poor kid. He wanted to stick his head out to see whether Suzie had come in yet, but he was afraid he might frighten a real penitent off.

The doorknob rattled, and Gus looked up with a welcoming smile. It was a hard-looking woman. She sat heavily in the chair opposite, smelling of stale alcohol. "Bless me, Father, for I have sinned. It's been awhile. What happened to the old curtain?"

"This is a face-to-face confessional, ma'am. If you'd like the traditional way, that's the door on the other side."

"Too late now. Well, I been hitting the bottle too much lately, Father. I also been having relations with the fella next door. He's a nigger, Father."

Gus wondered what the race of the man had to do with the sin of fornication. In her mind did that make the sin worse?

The woman's eyes didn't rest anyplace for long, but now she quickly shifted them to him briefly, saying, "That's it, Father," as she launched into her Act of Contrition.   Apparently, she doesn't want me asking any questions, thought Gus. He spoke the words of absolution, figuring her mind was pickled with alcohol anyhow. Still, for her penance, he prescribed a decade of the usual prayers to remind her of the seriousness of her sins. She fiddled with the doorknob clumsily and then exited.

Within a split second, the door opened softly and Suzie entered. He rose and closed his arms around her, wanting to kiss her, but she simply buried her head in his chest and began crying.

"I feel miserable, Gus. She's dead because of me, because of us. I never want to see you again."

Gus reeled at the leaps her mind was making. "Slow down, Suzie."

"It's punishment for our sins together, Gus. I won't do it anymore."

"You think that God is punishing you by having Maria murdered?"   Gus knew many penitents believed in a wrathful, avenging God, but Suzie was a nun, someone with an education in theology and someone who had a life contemplating God. "C'mon now."

What Gus was leaving out of the equation was the simple fact that when stressed, a person often reverts to a childhood view of God. Suzanne's mother often interpreted little mishaps as God's punishment. When Suzie was a small child, she had refused to eat the crust of her bread and later had fallen and skinned her knee. Her mother told her that God was punishing her for not obeying her mother when she had not eaten the crust from her bread. She had repeated that lesson whenever Suzie had failed to comply with her wishes.

Gus simply put his hand on her head and Suzie lay against him quietly. Ray, who had entered the church, heard the urgency in the unintelligible words that were being spoken behind the door of the confessional as Ray passed by. He decided to turn on the light of the confessional on St. Joseph's side of the aisle. Before he shut his door, he noticed Duffy leaving his mother's side and coming toward him. Duffy and his mother, when she was sober enough, were regulars for Saturday afternoon confessions.

Duffy came into the confessional and sat down. He was very agitated. "Bless me, Father. I...I hurt Sr. Maria."

Ray nearly came off his seat. Had he heard correctly? Duffy looked at Ray with an expression that reminded him of Mack's when he had soiled the rectory dining room floor by accident.

"Duffy, how did you hurt Sr. Maria?" Ray's voice came out of a very dry throat.

"I didn't mean to hurt her. I thought she wanted me to. I didn't mean to."

"O.K., Duffy. Listen, Duffy, this is a pretty bad sin." Ray didn't want to sit there and talk with Duffy anymore. He was horrified and wanted Terry Hogan to be there instead. "I think that when you take something from someone, you have to make restitution."

"Yes, Father," Duffy said, not having the slightest idea what restitution was.

"I mean you need to talk to the police, Duffy, and tell them about hurting Sr. Maria. Can you do that?" Ray knew that his face was white because all the blood was being drained from his extremities to his heart, leaving his hands and feet ice cold.

"Yes, Father."

"Alright, Duffy. I want you to go with me to the rectory, and we'll call the police. I want you to tell them that you hurt Sr. Maria."

Duffy looked at Fr. Ray, trying to understand what he was saying. It was hard to concentrate because he was still very upset. He had run around the neighborhood for a long time before he had returned home. When he did, he just went to his room and began playing with his keys but they didn't quiet him.

Finally, he burst out of his room and went into his mother's room where an old man, who lived next door, lay with his mother. His mother started to shout at him. He had been told never to enter her bedroom, but he had forgotten himself in his distress. The man jumped out of bed, staggered in his naked state over to his pants and began dressing.

His mother wrapped the sheets around her and continued to shout. Duffy's head was buzzing, and he howled, "I gotta go to confession. I sinned big!" His mother had abruptly stopped shouting, glanced over at the man stumbling in his clothes, and felt some compunction herself. After she'd dressed and tried to make herself presentable, she downed a can of beer to fortify herself, and then she and Duffy had walked to church.

"Did you understand me, Duffy? You need to talk to the police. Are you willing to do that now?" Ray was speaking slowly, hoping that by so doing it would help make a connection with Duffy, who seemed to have spaced out.

Duffy glanced at Ray's keys that glistened at his side. Ray had power. If Duffy could ever get that many keys, he too would have power. However, Duffy had to learn not to hurt Sr. Maria first. Maybe that is why Fr. Ray wanted him to talk to the police. If he told them how he hurt Sr. Maria, then the police could tell him how to get keys without hurting anyone. That was a good idea. Duffy looked at Fr. Ray with a calmer expression than he'd had for awhile. "Yes, Father. I talk to the police."

Ray sighed. Gus could continue to handle confessions. "Let's go to my house, Duffy." As they stepped out, Ray saw Duffy's mother lighting a vigil light. "Wait for me here, Duffy. I'll just tell your mother." Ray was having qualms about telling her and was only half way down the aisle in her direction when she rose and walked out the door. Ray shrugged and turned back to Duffy.

Chapter 24

Bob awoke moaning, and attempted to get out of bed, but found that he had simply rolled over on the floor. He slowly realized as he squinted around the room that he was not in familiar surroundings. He sat up and continued to look around. Some torn, yellowing lace curtain limply hung on each side of the narrow window.

Next to a tattered chair, not far from his position on the floor, were some broken crayons and a picture of what must be a bird. It had orange, blue and some black scribbles through the body, signifying feathers, he presumed. Now that he held it in front of his eyes, he sat looking at the picture, wondering why he thought it was a bird. It seemed to be making strange, unbird-like sounds.

That's when he dimly realized that a fist was banging on the door across the room behind him. Bob didn't feel ready to stand up yet and was grateful when he heard the woman calling, "Waitaminit!" He saw a tall, full-figured black woman come into the room, stop and look at him with obvious contempt, and then continue toward the door in bedroom slippers that made little flip-flaps with each step. As she walked, Bob noticed how her rear end shifted and moved under her nightgown.

She opened the door and a man's voice said something that Bob wasn't sure of. He was back to examining the bird. Maybe it was supposed to be a turkey or some multi-colored bird. He was staring at the picture stuporously when the man stepped inside. Bob glanced up and realized it was a policeman. Bob's pulse quickened and he felt a sense of impending doom although he couldn't have said why.

The woman pointed at Bob, "There he is, Officer. Walter brung him in las' night, then tell me to call the pohlice this mornin' to come get him. He's a druggie."

"Son, what are you doing here?"

He was a black man, thin and of medium height with a pencil thin mustache that ended at the corners of his mouth. He sat down in the chair to come into clearer contact with Bob's eyes. The question puzzled Bob. He tried to think. "I don't know," he said.

"Do you know where you live?"

"Yeah," Bob felt he could find his home if he could get outside and look for some landmarks.

"Maybe I can run you home, but I'll need to take a minute of Miz Atkins' time first. You wait right there, son." Bob felt the man was kind. He hoped they would be able to find his home. Still he felt that strange sense of impending doom.

The officer stood up then and spoke to the woman. "Perhaps we can talk in the kitchen?"

"Don't be expectin' no handouts, Mister," she said as she flip-flapped into another room, her rear cheeks moving sensuously under her nightgown.

Bob lay down then, still not wanting to stand up. He could hear their voices although they seemed distant. As the woman's voice grew louder, he could make out her part of the conversation.

"No, I ain't seen him since he dropped this white boy on me. So what?

"He got him a job workin' nights, I think. I don't see him when I gets home from work.

"I got five others to feed. They all younger than Walter. How I goin' to keep track of a grown boy?"

"They just pickin' on him 'cause he black; he's a good boy. I depend on him."

Bob was staring at the ceiling when Officer Jones reentered the room and was startled by his voice.

"O.K., son, we better be going now." The policeman helped Bob to an upright position, reached over to the sofa that Bob had not even noticed and picked up a peacoat. "This yours?"

Bob accepted it because he had a sense that the coat seemed familiar.

The officer looked at the woman and said, "This boy's been trippin', ma'am. I don't think you gave him any drugs, but I'm gonna need to find out who did. You understand? Now, I need you to help me find Walter. If he's innocent, then I'll do my best to see that justice is done for him."

"Big promises!" She looked mean at the policeman, and Bob decided he didn't want to stay there anymore.

The officer led the way down a hall, past three more doors, to the stairs. "You be careful on these stairs, son." Bob gripped the railing and tried to keep up with the officer who seemed to navigate the steps without trouble.

The air outside felt good against Bob's warm cheeks. He glanced up and down the street. The policeman said, "Do you know your name, son?"

Bob looked at him for a long moment and finally remembered, "Bob." He hoped it was right.

"Bob, do you have a last name?"

"Maybe," Bob answered.

"O.K., Bob. Tell me your whole name; start by saying your first name first." Jones knew that might help Bob recall his name.

"My name is Robert Francis Murphy!" It sounded as though he was reciting a lesson, but it clicked, and Bob knew that he had his name back.

"Good, Bob. My name is Officer Jones. I work over there." The policeman pointed across the street to the precinct. "This is Madison Avenue, Bob. Is it familiar to you?" Bob watched his hand move back and forth, signifying the entire street in both directions. When Officer Jones dropped his hand and looked at Bob, Bob's eyes followed the hand. The policeman took a deep breath and said, "Bob, look at any of the buildings. Does anything look familiar to you?"

Bob began to look around. He saw the little red sign of the thrift store down the block. "Yeah! That's the thrift store!" Bob turned back to the policeman. "I got my coat there." Bob felt proud of himself. He could answer the man's questions, and he felt sure of his answers.

"That's good, Bob. You must be from the neighborhood. Now, let's take a little drive and see if you can find your house." He protected Bob's head as Bob sat down inside the police car. The man had put Bob in the front seat.

The policeman made a U-turn and drove past the thrift shop. "Bob, you tell me where you think I should turn."

Bob couldn't make out where he might tell the policeman to turn, but he rubbernecked and showed his willingness to try. They crossed over Mohammed and continued down the block to Stanton. Suddenly, Bob called out excitedly, "That way!" Bob pointed to his right. The policeman made a right turn onto Stanton.

They passed a little tavern called "Bit o' the Sod" that looked familiar. Soon they came to the corner of Stanton and Grover. "There. Over there." Bob was pointing to the abandoned building that had once been a pickle factory.

In the old days, that factory, owned by an old German named Schmitt, had employed most of the Irish in the area. When the blacks started moving in, Schmitt closed his factory, retired, and that was the end of an era. Jones remembered because he was just a little kid when his parents moved into the area from Alabama. His daddy had gone looking for work at that factory but had been told that no blacks would be hired.

"That's home? Bob, are you sure?"

"Yeah. Just park here. Thanks for the ride." Bob had started to reach for the door handle.

The policeman's hand reached over to Bob's hand, "Whoa there, Bob." He pulled the patrol car to the side of the factory. "Let me go with you, Bob."

They both got out, and Bob was a little stumped. He was looking for some porch steps. He looked apologetically to the man in blue.

"That's alright, Bob. We'll find where you live. Let's get back in the car." Jones knew that he would drive further east along Stanton, toward the white section of the area. He noticed Bob looking at the tavern again as they passed and knew that Bob was familiar with this part of town.

As they passed the convent, Bob looked to his left and recognized the church down Elias. "That's St. Gen's." He gestured further to the left, "That's where I go to school."

Jones noticed how the boy seemed happy, not so much because he was remembering but because he could tell Jones about himself. He must be a lost kid inside, thought Jones. "I'll hang a left here, Bob. Maybe you can show me how you walk home from school. Just tell me where to turn."

Bob sat forward on the seat, looking intently at the school as they passed. He even turned his head back to see it. "There, that door. I go out that door, and I go down there past the church."

Officer Jones braked and backed up to prepare to make a right turn down Mohammed from Elias. As they drove down Mohammed, he saw Bob smile. "What is it, Bob?"

"I like riding in a police car. Maybe I'll be a policeman someday."

Inwardly, Jones thought, that'll be the day! His brain is fried; that's all we'd need in this city! He said in response to Bob, "That's nice. Now, Bob, keep your eye on the route. Did you walk down Mohammed?"

"Oh." Bob looked to the sidewalk. "Yeah. There it is; turn right on that street."

Jones noted Hobart. "Hey, that's great, Bob. Now, I think you'll remember the house." They had driven past two houses when Bob said, "There."

Jones pulled in against the traffic because he saw the no parking signs that lined the right side. As he got out, he glanced across the street and noticed a woman coming out of her door, curlers in her hair. She stood with her arms folded in the apron she was wearing, prepared to gawk. Bob seemed oblivious.

They walked up the sidewalk and a large man lumbered out the door. "Where in hell have you been, Robert Francis?" The man's voice caused Bob to stop in his tracks, and Officer Jones, who was walking behind him, nearly ran into him. Jones stepped around Bob then and placed himself between the towering man and the startled boy.

"What's the boy done, Officer? I'll give 'im what for and plenty!" The man brandished his fist.

"May we go inside, sir?" Jones's even tone caught the man by surprise. "It might be more private." He cut his eyes to his right and left where neighbors were looking from doors that were held slightly ajar as though the occupants didn't want the policeman to get a good look at them.

"Well." The man understood that the neighborhood was watching the spectacle, but he was looking at Jones's dark skin. He looked, to Jones, like a man on tenterhooks. Jones knew that he was taking in his color and that he'd never invite a black man into his home under normal circumstances. The man was having trouble ascertaining if this was the correct thing to do as an upstanding citizen of a predominantly white residential block, and whether being a neighborhood spectacle would be the lesser of the two evils.

Jones prodded, "It's important that we take care of some business."

"Oh. Well, come in then." He turned unsteadily and lumbered into the house.

Once they entered the house, Jones saw the plump woman shooing two gawky boys from the room. He doffed his hat when they entered and nodded to her, extending his hand, "Mrs. Murphy? I'm Officer Jones."

She glanced at his hand, overcame her repugnance and slowly extended hers to him. Jones noticed and expected her reaction. He also noticed that right after the handshake, she brushed her right hand along the side of her hip.

Jones turned back to Bob's father. I think we should all sit down for a minute. Bob's father was anguished. A nigger in his home, and he has to sit down with him, thought Jones behind his friendly smile. He's probably more worried about the neighbors' reaction than he is about what his son has done.

"It's a dark day when a son doesn't come home and has to be brought in by the police." Mr. Murphy was looking menacingly at Bob. "What's he done?"

"Mr. Murphy, are you aware that your son uses drugs?"

"He what?" Blood rushed to Murphy's face while his wife's face began to crumple like someone wadding up a sheet of paper.

"He's lucky that he didn't die from an overdose, Mr. Murphy. He is still under the influence. I found him in the home of his suspected dope peddler."

"Tell me who that creep is and I'll kill 'im."

"Leave him to the police, Mr. Murphy. I think you need to take care of your son. He'll need some treatment for his addiction. If he doesn't get help, sir, then he will kill himself some night. Bob needs your help, Mr. and Mrs. Murphy." He glanced at them and knew he had their attention for the moment. "Yelling won't work, sir."

"No, sir, I'll beat the divil out of 'im, you can count on it."

The man was actually reaching to unbuckle his belt. Jones put out a hand to caution Murphy, "No, sir. That doesn't work either. Do you remember the first time you ever took too much liquor?" Mrs. Murphy darted her eyes toward her husband. Jones continued without waiting for an answer. "I remember when I was Bob's age. My father beat me severely, but it made me more determined to do it again. So, I know from first-hand experience that a beating doesn't work. I think Bob needs some professional help." Jones extended a card toward Murphy. "This is a card with the name and telephone number where you can get some help. It won't cost an arm and a leg, sir."

Murphy looked at the card as if he was studying it, but judging by how his lips pressed together, Jones knew the man had reached the limits of his humiliation. Bob, who seemed impervious to what was taking place, would have to wing it from here on. Jones stood, saying, "Thank you for your time. If you need any further help, please let me know. My name is Jones." He replaced his cap and walked alone to the door and let himself out.

As Jones stood on the porch, glancing at doors that quickly closed in the neighboring houses, he could hear Murphy.

"No damn nigger can tell me how to raise a son. By Gawd, you sorry excuse for a son. Git up the stairs! I'll beat the hell out of you yet!"

Jones shook his head and walked to his car.

Chapter 25

John Hotchkiss awoke as he'd slept, still dressed, lying across his bed diagonally. He made several attempts before he managed to sit up. His head was pounding and his mouth full of cotton. He needed something to drink badly. He reached for the bottle on his nightstand but found it empty. He made a reach for the one on the floor but discovered that his depth perception failed him. After his third pass, he made contact, but he found only the slightest sip; however, his thirst became more acute with the slight taste of whiskey.

He pulled himself upright, using one of the pillars of his former wife's former four-poster. He walked unsteadily to the bathroom where he checked several bottles. Nothing left. He vaguely remembered going through this procedure with the same bottles the morning before. He turned to leave the room, but he banged his shoulder squarely against the doorframe, having misjudged the width.

Rubbing his shoulder, he tried to push his foot into a nearby boot. With a hand on either side, he pulled the boot on. In doing so, he staggered a few steps sideways. That brought him to his other boot, which lay on its side. He picked it up and carried it out to his living room. There in his "grading chair", he flopped down. As he held the boot, he picked up a tall, gleaming fifth of whiskey. He dropped his boot, which fell next to his foot and promptly lay up against his lower leg like an old drunken sot, and then he unscrewed the cap. He drank deeply, gurgling the whiskey down his throat.

Saturday! He had to shop for another case of his whiskey. First, he had to cash his check; then he would shop. He picked up his boot and stared at it. What was it? He felt like the boot was trying to remind him of something. He took another swig from his bottle.

He looked at the boot again. It was not polished, but he noticed that the toe was darker than the rest of the boot. He got up and walked with the boot to his kitchen. He held it in the sink and began to run water over the toe of the boot. As the water hit the boot, it was clear, but as it ran down over the side of the hard leather, the water poured off the boot, tinged red.

Stepped in something, he said to himself. He needed a cigarette. Why could he never find a bottle or a cigarette when he wanted one? They seemed to hide just to spite him. In desperation, he went to the closet and reached inside for his jacket. Unfailingly, he could find an open pack jammed in his pocket. The next problem was finding a match. He gave up the search. He was tired of looking for things. He went back into the kitchen, turned on the burner and bent down to light his cigarette, forgetting to turn off the burner.

He walked back into the living room and took another drink from the bottle. Whiskey and a good cigarette! The best way to start a day, he thought. Let other people build up all that cholesterol with fried eggs and bacon. That didn't appeal to his stomach at all. All that grease.

He was so glad it was the weekend. He could drink as much as he wanted, and when it came to classes, it would be a short week. He could look forward to Holy Week because it meant that his weekend bender would begin on Wednesday evening. That was the ticket. He liked to drink, so what of it! He wasn't hurting anybody. He just sat in his place and drank. He didn't cuss out anybody, he didn't get into bar brawls; no, he just stayed home, hurting nobody!

He took another drink and then lifted his hand to his mouth to take another drag from his cigarette, but it wasn't there. Where had his cigarette gone? He looked around on the floor. No, it wasn't there. Then he saw the smoke curling up off to the left in his peripheral vision. He grunted. He was holding the cigarette in his left hand. He'd forgotten.

Well, it was a hell of a week. That stupid kid, Murphy, siccing his mother on me like that. I told her though. I told her she didn't have a clue about anything. Her boy was no good. Stupid woman just stood there with her mouth open like an old cow. She didn't like my language, she said. I gave her some real language then. I told her she was a bitch and her son was a son of a bitch! Hotchkiss's head moved to emphasize the objectionable words, and then he smiled and reached for the bottle again. He flicked the ashes from his cigarette but missed the ashtray, and they floated down to the floor.

She was sent home acryin' that time. Serves her right! She thinks she can tell me I'm wrong! He sat there for a moment, trying to remember something. What was it? Then he remembered when Mrs. Murphy left, he had gone to his desk where he kept his emergency bottle, for times like that. He had turned while still drinking and there she was.

That stupid nun, staring at him. He hated her. He knew she was going to tell on him. He was going to lose his job because she objected to his drinking. They all did. Well, drinking was the only damn pleasure he had in life. Even his wife couldn't give him any real pleasure, not like the drinking did. His wife had told him he had to choose between her and the drinking; that's what she said and that's what he did.

Hotchkiss was seeing his wife Margie, and suddenly she looked like that nun last night who had been saying the same thing; he knew it. She had looked at him with the same disgust. No one had the right to do that. She turned and left then. He had heard her though when she came back up the stairs. Sitting in the dark of his classroom, he had drained his bottle, recounting for himself all the indignities of his life: his wife, his job, Bob Murphy and other students just like him, their stupid parents, and the nuns, those holier-than-thou Sr. Marias.

Something had snapped in him. He had walked down the back hall, still holding the bottle in his hand. It was then that he saw Bob Murphy race out of the music room and round the corner to the steps that led downstairs. Bob hadn't seen anything, but he was in a hurry to get out of the place. John Hotchkiss remembered now, going into the music room, the light from a candle dancing against the back wall. He walked down the center aisle; it being the widest and his step unsteady. That's when he saw her there. She was so still. He stepped over her and knelt down. A little moan, barely distinct, more like the breath just coming through her lips--the last breath.

He stood up then. Troubled. Should he call for help? Hell! Something inside him made him laugh. She's dead! They won't believe you! They'll say you did it! He looked down at her. She looked like someone groveling at his feet. He sneered at her. She would have brought him down if she could have. She wouldn't have had mercy. He pulled his foot back and swung it forward as hard as he could. He landed the toe of his boot against the wound at the side of her head as she lay there. He had enjoyed the feeling of power that kick had given him. He repeated it again and then again. Then he nearly lost his balance, falling backward against the wall. He took a few steps and realized that his shoe was shining with her blood.

That's when he pulled his boot off and carried it as he walked unevenly out of the room. He heard a noise coming from somewhere behind him. It unnerved him although he had turned to check behind him. He changed course then, not able to go back to his room. He turned and reached in his pocket for a key to the faculty stairs for a quick exit from the hall.

He remembered then how he had wiped his boot free of the nun's blood. He checked himself for any other signs of blood then. No, it was just a little venting of spleen. That's all. He hadn't killed anyone, but his job was safe now. No one would get him fired.

John Hotchkiss didn't like the memory, so he told himself it had been a dream and took another gulping mouthful of whiskey, held it for a moment in his mouth, and then swallowed it. He smiled and got up, glancing at the clock over the television. It was already 11:45 A.M. He had no time to shower if he wanted to get to the bank.

Mrs. Hartman was beginning to close up for the day when the disheveled man entered and made for her window. She glanced at the security guard, wondering if he had taken note. This man looked desperate. As he stood in front of her window, he reached in several pockets before he found his check. It was from St. Genevieve's High School, a paycheck. He was probably some drunken janitor the priest hired out of sympathy, she thought as she turned over the check and found it had not been endorsed. "You'll need to sign it." She slid the check back to him.

He was so drunk he couldn't locate the pen, which was in the well at his right. She pointed to it. He took the pen in hand and wrote a shaky, scrawled name across it. Mrs. Karen Hartman glanced at the teller next to her and cocked an eyebrow that said, "Oh, brother" as she bent toward her cash drawer. She counted out the money and wondered why the man did not deposit some of it. Then she reminded herself of what drunks did with paychecks-- drank 'em down!

He put the money into his jacket pocket and left the bank. She watched him get into his car and found herself praying that no innocent person would be hurt by a drunk behind the wheel. She glanced down the row of tellers and saw Edna Ferguson who had lost a teenage girl to some drunk driver. It wasn't fair that innocent people suffered because of some old drunk. Typical of that kind of incident, the driver hadn't been hurt, just Edna's daughter. Why didn't the sinner suffer, she wondered. God would have a lot of questions to answer when she got to heaven!

John Hotchkiss drove straight to the liquor store. That stupid woman at the bank had gotten on his nerves. "Sign it," she'd said in that superior way those lowly tellers had. He reached over and took a quick swig of his last bottle of whiskey. As he bounced over the curb to turn left onto the street, he saw a car driving on the wrong side of the road. He swerved back onto the "wrong" side of the road, swearing at the dumb broad. He continued driving on the "wrong" side, but a vague realization was forming that it had been he who had veered from his lane. "Well, she was a stupid old cow! She sat there with her eyes big as cow pies! She froze! Why didn't she duck me if she thought I was wrong? No, she would've let it happen! Stupid woman. She had blonde hair too." Then, Hotchkiss saw Sr. Maria on the floor as his foot slammed into her head, the toe of his boot entering the wound and blood spurting up, like a little geyser,

154

and dropping back on his boot. Another car was coming toward him, and he swerved and stayed in the appropriate lane.

As he drove another half block where a skinny tree bent bare branches toward the street, John Hotchkiss turned abruptly into the parking lot of the Sav-u-Bucks liquor store. The owner was a graduate of St. Gen's and gave him a discount on his liquor. He bought his case of scotch and then bought several bottles of vodka. He loaded them into the trunk of his car. That vodka might be a better precaution for school, he told himself. If they can't smell it, they can't trace it! Those Russkies are pretty smart, making vodka odorless, he smiled. Maybe he'd still be married if he had switched to vodka.

John scratched his crotch then, remembering that he wasn't married. A woman had walked out on him. Just like that, just like that Sr. Maria had done last night. Well, he showed her. He kicked her good. She deserved it; they all did. He slammed the trunk of his car down and walked around to get in. First, he squinted and looked at the toe of his shoe in the bright sunlight. It was dark, probably from the water he'd run over it.

John drove out of the lot, forgetting to turn left. He'd forgotten and, from habit, took a right to continue on to St. Gen's, as he did on school mornings after purchasing his emergency rations for the day. Well, he might just take a spin past the old place. He drove to Mohammed and took another right.

As he drove past the school, he saw the yellow crime tape. He slowed to a stop. He saw a cop and waved him over. The cop stepped to his window. "Hey, what's up, Officer?"

"Nothing. Just keep on moving."

"No, I work here. I'm a teacher."

"What's your name?"

"Hotchkiss. I teach English."

"Well, sir, I think you can expect to be called in for some questions. There's been a murder here last night. Now, Mr. Hotchkiss, I think you better get off the road as soon as you can. I think you've been drinking and that doesn't mix with driving. For now, though, would you please keep on moving? You're holding up traffic."

John's blood pressure rose when he heard that he might be questioned. He had to have a clear head. John glanced up into the rearview mirror and saw a car and a truck that had stopped behind him, waiting patiently. "O.K., Officer," he said as he smiled obsequiously and waved. Driving off, he muttered, "Smart mouth cop!"

Chapter 26

Ray and Duffy looked like a Mutt and Jeff couple, sitting side by side in the small row of worn, wooden chairs that lined the wall at Precinct 3. The Sergeant on desk duty, who had taken Ray's earlier call and told Ray to come into the precinct, had told them that Detective Hogan would be with them in a few minutes. Actually, Hogan was not in, but he had put out a call for him. The priest had said that it was an urgent matter, but he wanted to speak only to Hogan.

He hadn't given any reason for the request to the desk sergeant, but Ray hoped that Duffy would recognize Hogan and be able to tell him everything. Sometimes a new face could disturb Duffy's thoughts, and he was less than coherent in the best of circumstances.

In the meantime, Hogan was back at the convent. It was 2:30 PM, and he wanted to ask some questions of Sr. Suzanne. Instead, he had been met by Sr. Agnes, who had questions for him. He had fielded several. That the attacker might have been looking for money and been surprised by Sr. Maria. He had ascertained that the cask contained money. Exactly four pennies had been found at the bottom of it. Sr. Gretchen had confirmed that it contained a collection for the entire school year, just nickels and dimes, but in the past, Sr. Maria had managed to collect as much as twenty dollars for the missions. Agnes was easily satisfied with his answers. She probably didn't want to know if what she was thinking was true. She never asked why Sr. Maria's clothes were in disarray, for example.

She did add that she had learned, and at that point in their conversation, she had begun to whisper that Sr. Suzanne had been seeing an old friend yesterday and had not been to the motherhouse. Hogan thought her caution was strange, but he didn't ask why she needed to whisper. He just thanked her for her help. He was eager to find out more from Sr. Suzanne.

Apparently, Sr. Suzanne was not to be found in the house. Sr. Rebecca was sent to find her in the church. Hogan was beginning to feel he'd wasted his time coming to the convent, especially when the nun returned, explaining that Sr. Suzanne was not in the church or, if she were, she was in the confessional. Hogan tried not to show his impatience. He left his card and asked that Sr. Suzanne come down to the station as soon as she returned.

Then he declined the offers of coffee and brownies, which had just been freshly baked by Sr. Rebecca. Sr. Agnes seemed particularly distressed that she couldn't have had Sr. Suzanne there for him. She wanted to come up with alternatives, but couldn't. He simply left, repeating again that Sr. Suzanne was to come down to the station and ask for him.

Just before he left, the convent telephone had rung and the sister who answered said it was for him. He found out that the priest was waiting to see him. He put his light on the car roof and drove through the red light at Mohammed and Madison in order to hotfoot it down to the station. He zipped into the parking lot at the side of the building only to find his usual spot taken. On a Saturday afternoon too! Another of life's little frustrations. He pulled into the first empty spot he could find.

He pulled his jacket off and opened the thermos on his desk and poured a cup of coffee. He glanced down at some preliminary reports. The real hard lab data wouldn't be in until Monday. Still, he wanted Sr. Suzanne to remember times and shadows and sounds she had seen and heard. She might have better recall today because she had more than likely relived it several times since then in her mind. Funny though that the superior Sr. Agnes had wanted it clear that she was not an alibi for Suzanne. What was going on there? Hogan dropped the report he was glancing at. It contained nothing much new. The report mentioned finding a liquor bottle standing just outside the front door of the school.

Hogan pulled his tie down and loosened his collar and stepped out into the hall. He could see the legs of the two men who occupied the chairs at the waiting area. He could see the black-panted legs of the priest reaching out further than the stubbier legs of the little man sitting next to him. As he entered the alcove of the waiting area, he saw that next to Fr. Ray was the funny little guy he'd seen only that morning.

"What can I do for you, Father?" He extended his hand toward Fr. Ray, who had risen as soon as he spotted Terry Hogan.

"We need to talk with you in private, Detective." The priest nodded his head to include Duffy.

"Sure, Father. Hi ya, Duffy." He put his hand out for Duffy, who smiled as he clasped Hogan's. He made a deliberate shake that pulled Hogan's hand abruptly up and then down. Then Duffy released Hogan's hand. "Come this way." Terry led them through the door he had just walked through and into the interrogation room at the back of the large room that was filled with desks and phones. "Please, come in here. Just sit down."

Once they'd seated themselves, he asked, "Can I get you some coffee?"

Duffy glanced at him as if he was about to say yes, but Fr. Ray spoke first, "No, thank you." Duffy pulled up short just in time. Hogan sat down and glanced expectantly at the priest, realizing how tired he felt suddenly.

"Duffy has something he must tell you." Then Fr. Ray looked at Duffy, "Remember to tell the policeman what you told me, Duffy."

Duffy looked away from the priest and down at his chair. He mumbled something inaudible.

Hogan said, "Sorry, Duffy, but my old ears can't hear you. Could you speak a little louder? This room doesn't have ears, and no one else will hear you." Hogan wondered to himself if the mikes were off.

Duffy smiled at the thought of a room with ears. His favorite cartoon was about Dumbo, the elephant with big, big ears. His mother had tried to help him learn to read with that story when he was a little boy. He would always say that the picture was of Dumbo and that he had big, big ears. His mother had told Duffy that he was Dumbo with big, big ears. Duffy thought that meant his mother liked him because Duffy liked Dumbo.

Hogan watched as Duffy sat looking around with a stupid grin on his face.

Fr. Ray cleared his throat, saying, "Duffy, remember what you told me about Sr. Maria."

Hogan sat upright at the priest's words. Duffy looked shyly at him. He said very quietly, "I hurt Sr. Maria, but I didn't mean to."

Hogan instinctively reached for the recording device and started it. "Sorry, Duffy, I need you to say that again."

Duffy looked mournfully at Hogan. "I hurt Sr. Maria."

"How did you hurt her?" Hogan felt his breathing rate doubling.

"I thought she was my lady, the one in the picture. Only she wasn't. I didn't mean to hurt her."

Hogan was having difficulty following. "Duffy, how did you hurt her? I know you wouldn't hurt anyone intentionally. Just describe what you did." Was this guy tall enough to swing that cask, he was wondering?

"She was there, like the picture. I was only touching her. She's soft and I liked touching her. She didn't look at me, so I thought she wanted me to touch her."

The priest was swallowing hard, a vein in his brow pulsing. Hogan felt that Fr. Ray was fighting not to say something.

"Duffy, tell me what you mean when you say you touched her?"

Duffy dropped his eyes and moved his head from side to side. He was having difficulty in going further. Hogan glanced at the priest and nodded.

"Duffy, you must tell the policeman what he needs to know for God to forgive you." The priest didn't look at the detective, but he flushed red at his lie.

Duffy continued to look down. "I touched her here," he said, placing his hand on his chest. "I laid down with her and we had a nice time."

Hogan was beginning to understand something. "Duffy, was Sr. Maria on the floor when you saw her last night?"

"Yeah. She was in the back of the room, but I thought she was my picture."

"Her eyes were closed?"

"Yes, she kept her eyes closed like my picture."

Terry couldn't manage himself any longer. "What is your picture, Duffy?"

"The one that Sr. Gretchen gave me. I keep her in the closet, in the rag bag."

Hogan could figure it was a porno queen, but why would Gretchen ever give Duffy such a picture. He didn't need to know, he decided.

"Duffy, did you hit Sr. Maria?"

Duffy looked up horrified. "No. I wouldn't hit Sr. Maria. She was nice. She gave me a candy bar just last week. That's what she would do."

Hogan surrendered to the surreal aspect of this whole affair. "O.K., Duffy, tell me why you went to see Sr. Maria last night."

"I heard a noise. I saw the teacher walking down the hall, but I saw the dancing light in her room. I was going to turn out the light, but then I saw her on the floor, waiting for me."

"You saw a teacher in the hall?"

"Yes, Mr. Scotchkiss. I saw him coming down the hall." Fr. Ray smiled inadvertently. Duffy had only heard students identify the man.

"Did Mr. Scotchkiss see you, Duffy?"

"Hotchkiss," corrected Fr. Ray.

"Oh, no. Mr. Scotchkiss came out of the music room but I know him. He's mean to me. He isn't nice like Sr. Maria."

"Are you sure he came out of Sr. Maria's room?"

"Yes. I think he must have thought she was his picture girl too."

"I'm sorry, Duffy. Who was his picture girl?"

"Sr. Maria. I think he must have laid down with her too."

"What makes you say that, Duffy?"

"He was carrying his boot with him. He walked all crooked down the hall to the special door."

Hogan was amazed. He had more questions than Duffy would be able to answer. He wisely stuck to Duffy's course though. "What special door, Duffy?"

Duffy glanced at the keys at Fr. Ray's belt. "The one with a lock. I don't have a key to it." Duffy thought perhaps the policeman would remember this when Duffy finally finished there and earned some keys.

"Did the teacher use that door then?"

"Yes." Duffy looked innocently at Terry Hogan.

"Is that when you went inside the music room?"

"Yes." Duffy kept nodding his head. "Only Sr. Maria was already asleep. Only I thought she was my picture lady. I didn't mean to hurt her."

Hogan knew that the story would now take a circular turn. "Duffy, I want to thank you for telling me all this. I'd like you to wait for Fr. Ray. I need to talk with him for a couple of minutes, if you don't mind."

Duffy looked apprehensively at Fr. Ray. The priest placed a hand on Duffy's shoulder. "I won't be long, Duffy." Then he looked at Hogan. "Is there a place nearby where he can sit and still see me through the glass."

"Sure. Hey, Duff, you want to sit in a nice chair and watch me and Fr. Ray? I'll take you into a secret room." Duffy responded well to this offer, and Hogan took him into the room that sat between the two interrogation rooms, showing him how he could watch Fr. Ray from there.

Then he hustled back to Fr. Ray.

"O.K., Father. Who is this Hotchkiss?"

"He teaches English at St. Gen's. If we could afford better, he wouldn't be teaching there, I can assure you. Do you think he killed Sr. Maria?" The priest was agitated.

"Don't jump to conclusions, Father. We've got a lot of investigation to do yet. But Duffy has been helpful. What is it you don't like about this guy Hotchkiss?"

"Oh, he's belligerent and belittles the students. I think he has a drinking problem too."

"O.K. I'll have him in for questioning. I have a list of teachers from Sr. Gretchen, so I must have his phone number and address. Now, I guess Duffy won't disappear on us, will he, Father?"

"I doubt that very much. Oh, yes. On the way over, he kept asking if you were going to give him a key. I'm not sure, but I think it must be a reward or something." Ray looked down at his collection and fingered through them. "Here." Ray detached one from his ring. "Would you give him this one? It used to fit the garage door at the rectory, but I had that changed to an electronic opener." Ray placed the key in the palm that Hogan held open.

They walked out and Hogan went into the viewing room. Duffy was standing, nose pressed against the mirror, trying to figure out where they had gone. Hogan smiled and stood watching him for a moment. "Hi, Duffy."

Duffy spun around, completely surprised to see Hogan.

"Hey, Duffy, I want to express my appreciation to you. I have this key for you. You like keys, don't you?"

"Yes." His eyes opened wide with excitement as he reached for the key. "Fr. Ray has a lot of keys. He's important. I will put this key with my others." Duffy dug deeply and awkwardly into his pants pocket and pulled out a key chain. At the end of the ring, a little devil dangled. Hogan's eyes opened wide.

"Are those your keys, Duffy?"

Duffy looked at him and then looked down. "Sr. Maria gave them to me." His cheeks colored.

"I thought she was asleep when you saw her, Duffy."

Duffy hung his head. "She was. I took them. I'm sorry. Are you going to put me in jail?"

"When did you take them?"

"Afterward. After I laid on her."

"Oh, boy." Hogan let out a long sigh. "Duffy, I think we have to sit down again. Fr. Ray?" Hogan led them back into the interrogation room and gestured toward the chairs at the table.

Fr. Ray was puzzled, but simply took Duffy's hand and led him to the nearest chair. Ray looked at him questioningly, but Hogan simply pushed a button to record. "O.K., Duffy. Tell me how you laid on Sr. Maria."

Duffy looked up at Fr. Ray beseechingly, and Fr. Ray, who frowned when he heard the question, tried to clear his face and nod encouragingly.

Hogan was growing irritable. "C'mon, Duffy, I need to know this, or I may have to take the key back. You have to earn it."

"I have to finish the work." Duffy had managed to correct Hogan without realizing it. Hogan and Ray smiled at each other. They stood silently though. "O.K." Duffy looked from Hogan to Fr. Ray. He said plaintively, "I just laid down with her. I touched her too. It felt good." Both men looked at one another over Duffy's head. Ray felt alarm rising in him.

"Did you open her blouse and touch her breasts?"

"Yes." Duffy's head lowered further.

"Did you pull your pants down?"

"Yes. My mother told me to." At the end of that statement, Duffy looked up at Terry Hogan as if that made it all right.

"Did you insert your penis into Sr. Maria?"

Duffy looked confused. Fr. Ray was the first to realize that Duffy didn't know what Hogan was talking about. "Duffy, do you know what a wee-wee is?"

Duffy nodded. "Mr. Hogan wants to know if you used your wee-wee when you were," Fr. Ray swallowed hard, "on top of Sr. Maria."

"Yes. It felt good and she didn't open her eyes, so it was O.K."

Hogan pushed the button. He looked at Fr. Ray whose eyes mirrored the sadness in his own. "I guess you get to keep the key, Duffy."

Duffy smiled brightly and Hogan wanted to punch him hard.

Chapter 27

Hogan was sitting at his desk, writing up the report. Well, he might have the rapist and the killer as two separate individual actors in this unfolding crime. It would explain the several footprints, but not completely. Duffy's could have been the set down the main stairs, but what about the side stairs. Hotchkiss had gone down the other stairs. Hogan wondered what forensics would say about the bloody paper he'd pulled out of the wastebasket. But there were more culprits here, and he hoped this Sr. Suzanne might lead him to some elucidating information.

Just as he took the last drink of coffee, the telephone rang on his desk. "Hogan here."

"Are you going to make it home tonight?" It was Millie.

"God, darlin', I don't know. What's up? Any trouble?"

"Goodness, Terry! I think your job is making you paranoid. The kids are fine and I'm fine. It's just that Liz called and wanted to go out to dinner. If you won't be home, I might take her up on it. I could use some girl talk."

"Go ahead, Millie. Have some fun. I'll catch up with you later." The desk sergeant had stepped in with Sr. Suzanne, who was looking paler than Terry remembered. Terry rose and walked over to meet her and then saw that Sr. Agnes was standing behind her. He also noticed Joe Curtins, who was at his desk, glance up and check the younger nun out. She was a good looker. "Thanks for coming over, Sister." Terry stressed the title for Joe's benefit. "I'd like some privacy, so would you follow me to the room at the back there."

She nodded and glanced quickly at Joe in passing. As Suzie continued past him, she felt instinctively that he had turned to scan her from behind. Sometimes when that would happen, she would turn back and catch them at it, but this time she would be doing good to walk a straight line to the distant room. Besides, Agnes was right behind her. Suzie hadn't seen it, but Curtins turned from looking Suzie up and down to get sizzled by Agnes's acidic stare.

Suzie was still thinking of Gus. They had to end their meeting abruptly because a penitent knocked on the door. Usually, not many confessions were heard on a Saturday, but Holy Week was coming up and people got concerned about their Easter duty.

She'd returned reluctantly to the convent and was accosted by Agnes as soon as it was known she'd walked through the door. Agnes wanted to know about her long-running excuse about visiting the motherhouse once a month before dropping by St. Gen's. Agnes was relentless in her questioning, and Suzanne, emotionally played out, had told her everything. It wasn't that Agnes was a harsh woman, but she had exhibited very little compassion with Suzanne. She'd said they would talk further, but that Suzanne was to go with her to the precinct and ask for Detective Hogan. He had questions for her about "the incident." None of them could yet refer to what had happened as Maria's murder.

After entering the room, they were offered a seat at a table. Suzanne realized that the darkened wall at the end of the room was probably one of those mirrors that served to conceal an observation post. She vaguely wondered if someone was eavesdropping on her.

The detective asked if she and Agnes wanted something to drink. Agnes had declined, but Suzie had asked for a coke, and he'd looked surprised and left to find one. While he was gone, she laid her head on her hands that rested on top of the table. She felt very, very tired and wished she could just go to her cabin in the woods. The detective seemed to be taking a long time.

Hogan had been stopped by Herrington on his way back with the coke for Suzanne. The damn machine had eaten his money the first time. "Remember that kid you had in for questioning?"

"Which kid?" Hogan asked with an irritable edge to his voice.

"LeRoy something-or-other. They found him in a dumpster next to the thrift store. Had a bullet through his skull and one through the heart. The perp wanted to make sure."

Hogan sighed. "Have we got any leads?"

"Not yet. I wonder if it has anything to do with his fingering Atkins."

"We'll bring Jo-Jo in. I figure he knows what's going down in his territory." Hogan was standing, shoulder pointed toward the interrogation room, and holding the coke away from him, trying to give little signals to Herrington that he didn't have all day to listen.

"You got somethin' goin' on?"

"Yeah. The nun's murder. I'm talking to a witness."

"O.K. Pecker wants to see us Monday at ten. Hope we get the lab stuff by then."

"Me too. See you." Terry hurried back to the room. Pecker was Captain Charles W. Peck. Everyone who worked under him referred to him as Pecker. Some said the name reflected his infernal hammering when an investigation did not go speedily forward. Others said it referred to the pecking order he had established. Still others said it referred to his, hmm, what did Father Ray call it? When Terry entered the room, he was grinning.

Suzanne looked up immediately. She took the coke and smiled her thanks. She fished in her purse and pulled out a bottle of Advil. She shook two of them into her hand and popped them in her mouth, washing them down with the coke.

"I know this has been a very difficult day for you, Sister." Suzanne knew he couldn't know the full truth of his words. "I'll try to keep this brief."

"I don't remember anything more."

"That's probably true, but it might be helpful if you'd begin with your visit to your friend."

Suzanne was startled. He noticed her look. "Sr. Agnes mentioned that you'd been to see a friend and that explained the confusion regarding your whereabouts."

"Oh." She took another drink from the coke.

Terry wished he'd taken time for a cigarette. "Is your friend in the city?"

"Yes."

"I need you to fill in the details, Sister. Like where, when, why. That sort of thing."

I drove into the motherhouse around 3:30 as I recall. After that, I visited with my friend until around 9:30. I was supposed to meet with Maria in the music room around that time, but I got a late start."

"Yes. Where does your friend live? I'd like to know how long it took you to get to the school."

"I." She stopped, looked down, and frowned. "I was visiting Fr. Gus Spellinger at St. Hildegarde's. I left there sometime after 9:30 and drove to the school."

Terry was quick to realize that hanky-panky was involved between this priest and the nun sitting in front of him. It saddened him, but he had long since been robbed of a naïve attitude about people of the cloth. As a young cop, he'd been assigned to arrest a priest/pedophile. A chaplain had told him that a cop's life was a little like the priest's life in a confessional. There was no place for foolish idealism for either one.

"And when did you arrive?"

"At ten o'clock." Suzie saw his frown and knew he didn't believe her. "I got there earlier, but I couldn't go in. Fr. Ray was walking his dog, and I didn't want him to stop me. He wasn't aware that Maria and I met in the music room of the school. I just drove down Mohammed to Madison and turned around and came back."

"O.K., did you notice anything unusual outside the school." Terry was thinking of the whiskey bottle that had been found at the main entrance. Maybe the drunken teacher was in evidence.

Suzanne took another swig from her coke, closing her eyes. She sat there with her eyes still closed for what seemed like a full minute. "Yes, I remember this kid running down the street. It was different running. Not just running like a person does to catch a bus, but wild, desperate running."

"Where was he headed?"

"Down toward Madison. He was a white kid. There were some black guys on the corner, selling dope." She looked pointedly at him, and Terry understood in her look the accusation that this was taking place under the noses of the police and why weren't they doing something about it. "I figured he was running down there to get a fix."

"Did you notice anything about him? Any description?"

"I remember my lights picking him up. I noticed his tennis shoes. And he had a dark coat. There was something about it." She was looking intently at the wall just beyond him. Terry wondered if our memories worked like movie projectors when she continued, "Yes. It was a navy jacket."

"Navy. You got the color?"

"No. Well, I guess it was blue, but I mean, it was…what do they call it?"

"You mean a pea coat?" Terry felt a surge of adrenaline.

"Yes. The collar was turned up, and I remember thinking that if he'd had the little white hat, he would have looked like a sailor—except for the shoes. He had on high top tennis shoes."

"Anything else you noticed?" Terry was still hoping she would have seen the teacher.

She thought for a moment. "Yes, down on Madison, I turned around in the parking lot next to the thrift store, and there were these two black guys. The place is crawling at night. I was frightened and thought maybe a hold up was taking place. One guy had his hands up, but I thought he was pleading with the other guy."

Terry leaned forward. "Tell me what they looked like."

Suzanne thought they were far afield, but she didn't care to talk about Maria's death and continued. "The short guy, the one with the stocking cap, was holding a big boom box that was blasting away. The other guy just looked scared. I can't remember much about him. The other guy looked mean. I didn't waste any time in turning around."

"If I showed you a picture, do you think you'd recognize the two of them."

"Yeah, maybe, probably." Suzanne had always been observant and a stickler for detail. She had a hobby with photography, and people commented about her good eye for details that no one else would notice.

Hogan got up and left her. He went out and looked for Herrington. He found him in the men's room, washing his hands. "Herrington, I may have a witness for you. Get the mugs on Jo-Jo and LeRoy."

When they entered the interrogation room, Herrington was with Hogan. After introductions, Herrington placed before her the front and side views of several young males. She picked out Jo-Jo immediately and then, after a moment of hesitation between two others, fingered LeRoy. Herrington smiled broadly and thanked her.

"What did I just do?" Suzanne asked when Herrington left the room.

"Seems like murder was happening everywhere last night, Sister. You just identified the suspect and the victim. You placed them together at the murder scene. Nice going."

"It's not much of a consolation."

"I know. Life doesn't offer a whole lot of that, does it, Sister?"

Their eyes met and locked. "No, I guess it doesn't, Detective."

"Shall we continue?"

Suzanne knew that Hogan meant her arrival at the school. "I came into the school, using the side door that Maria had fixed for me. I removed the tape so that it would lock again. When I started up the steps though, I hit something hard and metallic. It rolled around and made a loud noise. It scared me. I went upstairs slowly because it was dark and my eyes hadn't adjusted yet. When I got upstairs, I saw a movement down at the end of the hall. Someone was moving down there."

"Was the person tall or short, man or woman?"

"I guessed it was a man, and if I had to say, I think he was short. But it was very dark. He was headed for the main staircase."

"Did you go that way?"

"No, I went in to find Maria. It was dark, and she usually would have been at the piano, waiting. She wasn't, so I went back to the alcove to turn on a light. When I turned around, I saw her there." Suzanne began to cry.

Hogan waited patiently. "Was there anyone else around?"

"No. I began to worry that the shadow I'd seen was the killer and that he might be waiting to kill me. I had a hard time leaving. I went a little crazy."

"That was your car with the parking violation?"

She almost smiled. "Yes. I drove like a maniac down the alley and ran into the convent. I didn't even shut the door, come to think of it. If a murderer was on the loose, that wasn't too smart."

Terry smiled. She looked like the inner pressure had been released. He knew it was always better to talk and get it all out, every sordid detail. "You have been a big help, Sister. I want to thank you for coming down today. I or Detective Hennessey will probably need to speak with you again, so I need to repeat my request that you not leave town."

Chapter 28

Ray drove Duffy home and went inside with him to speak with his mother. At first, it seemed she wasn't at home. The place had a dank smell to it. Duffy said that "Mommy" might be back in her bedroom, but he didn't seem willing to check. So Ray told Duffy that he would come back that evening to check on him and to see if his mother was home. As he pulled the door shut, he heard her yell out a warning to Duffy to stay the hell out of her bedroom, and Ray decided to continue his exit from the house with more haste, closing the door quietly behind him.

When he returned to St. Gen's, confessions were over, and Gus was sitting in the rectory kitchen, drinking a beer. He looked bad. "Gus, I'm sorry about the confessions. I came over to relieve you but got called away."

"No problem." Gus looked at Ray for a moment and then looked back down at his hand for no reason that was apparent to Ray.

"Mind if I join you? This has been a helluva day." Ray reached into the refrigerator for a Budweiser.

"You said it!"

"You seem down, Gus. Can I help?" Ray sat down opposite Gus, who was running his hand through his hair.

"I got a problem." He momentarily drummed his fingers on the table.

"Only one, not bad, I'd say!" Ray was trying to be upbeat because most of Gus's problems lately had to do with fixing his busted boiler.

"It's bad." He took a drink, looking over the can at Ray. "I've been having an affair, Ray."

The news didn't surprise Ray, but he felt his heart sink a little more under the news of a brother priest's infidelity. "Yeah?" He was encouraging Gus to go on since he figured there was definitely more to the story.

"It's out."

"What do you mean?"

"I mean that it's known."

"By what means?" Ray expected to hear that Gus had a woman pregnant.

"What the hell is that question?" Gus was not at all in a happy mood. He had never barked at Ray before.

"You're talking in generalities, Gus. Care to be specific?"

Gus sighed and squeezed the can. It made a little click as he did so and then fell on its curved side. Gus leaned back and his eyes took in the ceiling, then he looked down at his hands again. "It's Suzanne. She was with me last night. I'm her alibi, I guess. She'll have to tell the police. She says Agnes is on her trail too. She's been telling the other nuns over there that she's been going to the motherhouse as a cover to her coming to my rectory. Anyhow, that blew up in her face today when Agnes arrived and commented that she hadn't seen Suzie in a long time. On top of that, she blames herself, and me too, for the fact that she was not with Maria on time. She thinks she could have prevented the murder."

"Maybe she could have."

Gus looked sharply at Ray. "Maybe not; maybe she saved her own life by being with me!"

"That's possible too. Either way, it's all academic, as they say. So what's going on inside you?"

"Hell!" Gus looked briefly at Ray and then looked away again. "She's gone funny on me. We had a good thing going, dammit!"

"Are you worried about the bishop? If Agnes knows, she'll probably tell him."

"He'll give me a slap on the hands. Some counseling, I guess. But, hey, I'll probably get transferred out of the city, probably some rural parish. No, I guess I'm not worried."

"Are you worried about Suzie?"

"Yeah, a little. Agnes is not a sweet, understanding lady. She'll probably rake Susie over the coals, and she's a little vulnerable right now. She was pretty hysterical with me earlier. But, damn, it's over, you know."

Ray was aware that his brother priest had no compunction for his actions. In his own weariness, Ray imagined that rather than a priest sitting across from him, an overgrown baby was sitting there, crying for the nipple that had been suddenly removed.

"I'm sure you'll both land on your feet and be better for it, Gus." Ray heard the hollow ring his words had, but he found he didn't care.

Gus looked at him coldly. "Yeah, well, I guess I'll see you at the motherhouse on Monday. I gotta get going."

Ray nodded and noticed he hadn't drunk any of his Budweiser. When Gus left, he walked to the sink and slowly poured it out. He felt like he wanted to hit something hard, so he did what he always did when he felt like that. He called Mack who had been sleeping under his desk upstairs. On all fours, Ray roughhoused with Mack and mused at how gently Mack grasped Ray's wrist between his teeth.

Ray fed Mack then and drove back to Duffy's house down Stanton. As he passed the convent, he wondered how Gretchen was doing. He suspected that she would be busy keeping a stiff upper lip, but Ray felt she was probably quivering inside.

He pulled up into Fenton Place and walked to the door, hoping that Mrs. Duffy was sober and in a good mood. He figured he was asking for too much, but he was running on fumes at the moment.

Mrs. Duffy opened the door. Her eyes were squinted suspiciously, but when she recognized him, they opened wide, and a saccharine smile spread itself over the lower part of her face while a hand clasped the lapels of her bathrobe tighter. He felt revolted.

"Father! Do come in." She turned immediately to straighten up the place. He saw her try to hide a bottle in the pocket of her bathrobe. "Please sit down, Father. I'll just be a moment."

She fled to the back, presumably to put on a dress. He wondered where Duffy was and then heard him clear his throat behind a curtain. Duffy glanced around the curtain cautiously and smiled at him when he saw that his mother was not in the room with Ray.

"Hello, Duffy. Are you all right?"

"Yes, Father. Are you here to talk to Mommy?"

"Yes, Duffy. I think we have to tell her about last night."

Duffy rocked slightly from side to side. "She'll be mad at me."

Ray felt genuine compassion for Duffy. Ray wouldn't want the woman mad at him either. A regular banshee! "Well, she might be, Duffy, but the news about Sr. Maria is pretty upsetting for everyone. You too?"

"Yeah." Duffy looked past Ray at his mother who was coming down the short hall, smoothing her hair down. She was wearing her best dress, the one she bought when she buried Thomas, her late husband and Duffy's father, at least that's what she thought, but she was never really sure. In fact, she wondered if having sex with two or three men on any given day might have caused her son's retardation. She wasn't exactly sure if the variety of sperm might not have all entered the same egg and duked it out and poor Duffy was the result.

She looked at Duffy and motioned him toward his room. Duffy looked doubtfully at Ray, which caused a stronger resentment to rise in her. "Duffy, you are not needed here."

"It might be good for Duffy to stay. You see, my visit concerns him, Mrs. Duffy."

It was not easy to wear a stern look in her eyes for Duffy and a smile for the priest, but that is exactly what Eleanor Duffy managed. "Very well, Father." She sat down on a dilapidated sofa and waited for Ray to speak. Duffy continued standing, but Ray had the strange sense that although his feet were firmly on the floor, Duffy was dangling there between them.

"Maybe you could just sit there, Duffy." Ray motioned for Duffy to take a seat next to his mother. Ray, of course, had no idea that he was sitting on Mrs. Duffy's chair. Duffy shuffled toward the sofa, and his mother gathered the skirt of her dress away, fearful that her clumsy boy would wrinkle it.

"Mrs. Duffy," Ray used her name in the tone in which he began his homily each Sunday and for the same purpose--to get her attention away from her dress and her son. She looked at him then. "Today, your son came to me with some information that was difficult for him to share."

The mother glanced quickly at her son, a glimmer of concern in her eyes, but she looked back at the priest, eager to hurry him to the worst that she feared; namely, that he had impregnated some girl at school. She knew that she would insist that the little hussy had seduced her son who was not mentally competent enough to seduce anyone.

"Duffy has been experiencing, uh, a sexual awakening lately. Perhaps you're aware of that?" Ray was finding words difficult. He didn't want her to start shouting but he didn't know how to prevent that either.

She moved in the sofa seat, restlessly. He was going to have to hit her with it now. She pushed her tongue around her dry mouth, preparing her defense.

"By now you've heard that Sr. Maria was found dead in the high school last night."

"Well, yes. My Gawd! You don't think my Duffy did it?" Her eyes were bulging.

"No, no, Mrs. Duffy. It's just that your son found Sr. Maria afterwards, shortly afterwards."

"Oh, well." Mrs. Duffy settled down. Perhaps her son had reported the matter to Fr. Ray, and the dear priest thought of her son as a hero, simpleton though he was.

"Duffy thought Sr. Maria..." Ray glanced at Duffy and rephrased, "Duffy mistook Sr. Maria for a sexual fantasy he's been having." Ray saw she was about to question that her son could have a fantasy life and hurried to the point. "He might have tried to have sex with her." Ray glanced down at the floor quickly and steeled himself.

"He what! He had sex with a nun? A dead nun? My God!" Before either he or Duffy knew what was going to happen, she stood and backhanded her son soundly. His right jaw was red. "You Satan! A nun!" She was standing over her son.

Duffy began to cry, and Ray sprung to his feet and caught her hand just as it was about to slap her son again. "Mrs. Duffy." Ray heard his own voice commanding the woman. He had never heard that tone and quality in his voice before.

Apparently, she hadn't either. She stopped and realized that a priest was there and she'd taken the Lord's name in vain several times. Tears started to her eyes. Duffy just sat, doubled in on himself, sobbing.

"Duffy didn't mean to hurt her! He feels very badly, Mrs. Duffy. I think we have to keep level heads here!" She seemed to have herself in check. "Now, let's sit down." Mrs. Duffy sat down next to her son, less conscious this time of her dress. Ray found his own seat and noticed that his leg muscles were spasming.

"I was afraid of this day," Mrs. Duffy said, shaking her head from side to side.

"I think we have to work closely with the authorities, Mrs. Duffy."

"They'll be taking him away, won't they?"

"I think so." Ray looked quickly to Duffy. However, Duffy seemed to be somewhere else, oblivious of their conversation.

"I just want you to be prepared for that. But I wanted you to know that Duffy meant no harm to Sr. Maria, and that he has been helpful to the police."

They sat then and looked at one another. Somehow Ray felt the silence was important and so the three of them sat in the cramped living room for several minutes. Finally, Eleanor Duffy sighed and Ray smiled wanly at her. Then he told her that he would be available to walk through the hearings with her and that she could call him at any time.

When he drove back to the rectory, he found himself repeating the words, "Feed my sheep" over and over. Ray was eager to be greeted by Mack and as the big dog danced toward him, he knelt down and buried his head in his fur. Ray began to cry then and Mack licked his tears.

Chapter 29

Saturday evening, her husband had made an excuse about going to a Holy Name meeting at the Church. Indeed, there was such a meeting, but he wasn't headed there. She knew that and knew as well that he would be home very late, stumbling up the steps and fumbling with his key, cursing.

Tonight, she was glad to see him gone. He'd beaten Bob mercilessly and forbidden her to go into his room to see to his wounds. He didn't even allow her to take her boy some supper. By then, she was too tired to argue with him about it. She'd had enough with her other boys. They were always so frightened when Bob got his beatings. You'd a thought it was they who were being beaten rather than their brother. They'd pleaded with her to stop their dad. She told them she couldn't. She knew that if she interfered, he'd wind up beating her and that would be worse on her boys. Instead, she huddled them to her there in her kitchen and began to pray the rosary aloud with them.

Downstairs, their sweet prayers were asking for mercy while upstairs the thwack, thwack of Murphy's belt went on incessantly. She'd stopped in mid-prayer when she heard a body fall on the floor above them. She half hoped it was her Jim who'd dropped from a heart attack. Maybe she'd be better off, raising her three boys unaided like Mrs. Sweeney. Then, she heard Jim yell at Bob to stand up like a man and the thwack, thwack continued. She had remembered her prayer again then and noticed that the boys' faces were turned upward. They might have been mistaken for angels except for the fear in their eyes.

179

Well, she was carrying bandages and medicine up the stairs now, sure that Murphy wouldn't be back. The room was quite dark. She knocked. Sure and there wouldn't be a sound. The boy was probably unconscious the whole rest of the day. She opened the door and called softly for Bob. She could see the filtered light from the low sun, just beginning to nibble at the horizon to make its way down, creeping around the narrow window blind. Just enough light to enable Betty Murphy to see that the bed covers were in a heap. She walked over to the bed and gently reached out. She felt her inner alarm jangle her nerves again when her hand touched only soft covers and no son's body.

She called aloud then, "Bob?" No answer. She crossed over to the door and found the light switch. She looked on either side of the bed and found no son. She looked under the bed and in the small closet. Still, no Bob. She crossed to the window and raised the blind. Sure enough, the window stood open behind it. A slight breeze entered, lacking the bite that it had just the evening before.

"My Bob's run away," she said to the room, and tears started in her eyes. By the time she had run down the stairs, the tears were running down her face. The Murphys had no telephone. She knew the Thompsons two doors down had one, but she couldn't bring herself to reveal anything of her problem to them. She had to get hold of herself.

"Jeremy!" She called loudly, and the boy appeared from down in the basement where he was making a scooter for himself and his brother from scraps of wood and a broken pair of skates he'd found in an alley. "I want you to lock the door after me and don't you answer it unless it's your father or me, you hear me?"

Jeremy was mildly troubled. He knew that his mother was quite upset and serious about her orders, but he rarely opened the door and certainly never at night. He was more interested in his project downstairs. He liked the downstairs because he had already become convinced that the world above it was not a safe one.

Betty Murphy pulled on an old gray sweater that had been her husband's and walked with determination down the steps. She reached the sidewalk and then wondered which direction to take. She could turn right and walk to the precinct and get help to search for her runaway son, or she could turn left and go to the tavern to fetch her husband. Normally, in emergencies, she would go to the tavern. Once when Sean had fallen from a tree and split his chin open, she'd had to go get Jim. She had looked through the windows of the tavern to see if her husband was there. One of the men noticed her and called to her husband. She'd never had to set foot in the divil's den yet!

She turned left toward her husband's hangout as if tranced by the memory but quickly reversed herself. No, this time if he found Bob, he'd finish the job and kill the boy sure. Maybe her son was taking himself to St. E's emergency room, knowing how badly he was hurting. Maybe that nice Mr. Jones would take her there. Well, he was black as the ace of spades, but she couldn't help believing he'd meant to help Bob. There was something gentle about him as he'd tried to reason with Jim, she'd noticed that right from the start.

Betty Murphy headed down Mohammed. As she did, she passed the church and signed herself. She had been keeping an eye out for Bob all along and hadn't seen anyone at all. Old Mr. Haggarty, yes, but he might as well be a ghost. She then remembered she'd yet to make her Easter duty, and time was running out. She'd have to harangue the whole of them to get them all to church. The boys didn't have a fit example in their father, she knew, but still she'd insist he'd do this much for them. Besides, he had plenty to confess what with his drunkenness.

At the school, she noticed an older man standing with his missus, pointing along the sidewalk and down Mohammed. As she neared them, she smiled. She wondered why older men always wore hats. His was straw and had a pretty blue and green band. Thankfully, the weather had warmed now, and a person could walk about without even a sweater if they'd a mind to.

The old man turned his head toward her and said, "Evenin'. Ain't it awful what happened last night?"

"What is that now?" She didn't want to dally with them and continued to walk past but had turned around to face them and slowed her pace just a bit to appear sociable.

"Nun was murdered!" The straw hat shook back and forth.

"A what? A nun? Jesus and Mary! Are you sure of it?" She stopped dead in her tracks.

"It's come to that now. This neighborhood used to be a proud one. The drug people stand openly on that corner down there, and they don't do anything about it." He was frowning, and Betty knew that he meant the police. "It gets dark and I and Janie here are inside with our doors locked, let me tell you."

"Me too! My goodness. Murdered?" Betty Murphy's head shook its disapproval and she picked up her pace. She surely wanted to get back home before dark what with a murderer on the loose! When she finally reached the corner, she saw no gang hanging around. Perhaps the man was wrong or perhaps it was still too early. Betty noted to herself that people always did their sinning under the cover of darkness because they were ashamed of themselves. The precinct was in sight now, and her pace slackened once again. She was breathing hard from the exertion of her hurried pace.

She passed a dark young man with a swaggering walk just a few yards from the precinct entrance. He was quite tall and she was careful not to turn her head as they passed, but her eyes strained the muscles that held them in their sockets so that she could see him peripherally if he made any move at her as she passed. She fought looking over her shoulder but at last gave in. Surprisingly, he was no where in sight.

Betty Murphy nearly passed the entrance to the police station in her distraction and checked herself awkwardly, opening the heavy door to enter. A bare floor, dirty too, greeted her. She walked forward and emerged into a little waiting area. No one was around. That struck her as strange. Why someone could walk right in and steal something! Where were the police? She walked to the desk, which being quite high came to her shoulder, preventing her from looking over to scan the area behind it. Then a door beyond the desk opened and a uniformed man came forward, wiping his hands on a paper napkin.

"What can I do for you, ma'am?" He didn't smile since he was still swallowing a chunk of his roast beef sandwich. She didn't notice because her eyes were looking at his badge, which caught and reflected the light.

"I need to see someone about my son. He's missing."

Just then Jones came through the door to her right. She heard the swoosh of the door and looked in his direction, recognizing him. "Oh, Mr. Jones! I'm so glad to see you."

Jones looked up at her quickly and after a moment, his face indicated that he remembered her. "Hello, ma'am. What brings you down here?"

"My boy, the one you brought home." Tears welled in her eyes and her face began to crumple.

"Here, ma'am, why don't you sit down here?" Jones guided her to a bench along the wall. He glanced at the desk sergeant, who shrugged back at him. They both knew that Jones had worked a double shift and was on his way home, bone-tired. "Now, what about the boy? Bob, wasn't it?"

"Yes, my Bob. Well, my husband really lit into him this time. I feared for him, really." Betty wiped her tears with the cuff of the tattered sweater. "He wouldn't let me even check on him, so I waited only until just now but he's gone."

"Where's your husband?"

"Gone drinking." Betty Murphy didn't care if she was being disloyal. She needed to find Bob and was willing to spell it all out to anyone who might be of help.

"Did Bob leave a note or anything?"

"Goodness, I don't know. I didn't see one right off. The window to his bedroom was open. He just jumped down from there, I think. I'm afraid he ran away because he felt I didn't care." She began to cry harder at the thought.

"Ma'am, I think the boy knows you care about him. It's evident to a stranger like me, you walkin' all the way down here like that for the boy, so I'm sure the boy, who sees your love all the time, surely knows. Bob isn't dumb, now, is he?" Mr. Jones was smiling and his teeth shown a pretty white against his dark skin. She didn't notice the bags under his eyes.

"No, no. Bob's not dumb. He's just having a hard time right now."

"Well, now, ma'am, do you remember me saying that Bob was addicted to drugs?"

Betty hadn't given that much thought. "I believe you did."

"I have a suspicion that Bob is out prowling for a fix." He could see she didn't know what he meant, so he explained, "Bob's looking for drugs. The drugs he took last night have probably worn off. When that happens, the drug addict has to find more."

"Bob is a sick boy." She was making a statement but seeking confirmation from the policeman.

"Yes, he is, ma'am. He needs help. Do you still have that card with the numbers on it? You need to make the telephone call, ma'am, and get Bob some help." Just in case her old man had destroyed the information, he reached in his pocket and held out another card to her. Jones found himself passing out more and more of these cards with each passing week.

"Now, ma'am, let me drive you home." She started to object, but he read her correctly. "No, I'll take you home first, and then I'll look around to see if I can find Bob."

"Oh, officer, you are so kind. I can't tell you how much I worried myself all the way here. I'm sure glad you were coming out that door." She glanced toward the desk, certain that the man behind it would not have been any help at all.

Jones stood up, and she followed him out the door she had entered. He led her to the parking lot just next to the building. He unlocked the door to a rusted Pinto. She got in and he walked around to the driver's side. She was a little surprised that police cars looked so ordinary. He smiled as he got in and said, "This is my own car, ma'am. I was just about to go off duty, but don't you worry now. I know this neighborhood pretty well. I'll find him."

They drove quietly the short journey to her home on Hobson. When Jones pulled up, he looked quite seriously at her. "Ma'am, if I find your son, and he's high on drugs, I'll call you. But I don't want to speak to your husband. I don't think he can handle it very well." She nodded her agreement. "So if he answers the phone, I will hang up and wait. If you can't answer, then I'll call back and let it ring only 2 times. I'll repeat that again just a little bit later. That way, you'll know that I've found Bob and he's all right." Betty Murphy was impressed with his intelligence. She had always thought his race was capable of producing only dull-witted people.

Jones continued, "But, regardless, I want to keep Bob in the hold. That's a room down at the precinct. I don't want to bring Bob back home in that condition."

Although her heart pained at the thought of her Bob being locked up, she understood. She wanted no more beatings. "I understand. Thank you, officer."

"Now, you can come down tomorrow and get him, but maybe you ought to wait until the afternoon."

"Thank you, sir."

"That's alright; now you don't worry, ma'am."

"I'll never forget your kindness to me, Mr. Jones." She was so overwhelmed by his kindness that she forgot that she had no telephone for Mr. Jones to enact his plan.

As she hurried into her house, he felt sympathy for her, a feeling he didn't often allow himself to feel in his job. Jones drove down Hobson to Stanton. He decided to check out the pickle factory. He'd heard a rumor that a gang was doing business out of the vacant building. In fact, he had intended to check it out first thing on Monday, so he might as well do that now while he was at it. As he approached the corner of Stanton and Madison, he saw a tough-looking kid with a blue cap.

The kid had seen Jones too, and he put his fingers to his mouth and uttered a loud whistle. Jones knew it was a signal. Jones turned left onto Madison, and as he approached the empty building, he saw four or five boys running in front of him, away from the building.

He drove past and at the end of the block, turned around and came back. He wanted to give the gang time to disperse. He didn't want to alert them to the fact that he knew about the use of the building. Not yet anyway. He looked around and felt that the boys were long gone.

He got out, gripping his flashlight. He could see a beaten path along the side of the building where the ground sloped along the basement windows, one of which had been broken out and cleared of glass. He knelt and stuck his head through, flashing his light around.

As he swept the floor, he didn't see anything. Then he swept the beam along the far corner and something much larger than a rat moved. Jones made the effort to squeeze himself through the window frame. He was glad he was in fighting trim, as his father had called it. Jones walked to the corner and flashed his light on a pea coat that began to unfold to reveal a boy beneath it. Bob was gone on a trip somewhere. His pupils dilated.

"O.K., Bob. Wake up, boy." He slapped his face just hard enough to get the boy's attention. He was greeted with a ridiculous smile. "I'm getting tired of finding you like this, Bob."

Jones pulled the boy up and pushed him up through the window. Jones felt sweaty and dirty by the time he crawled through. This was more work than he wanted. He wondered if Cora Lee would forgive him for not going to church with her tomorrow morning. He felt that he was pretty much carrying Bob back to his car. The boy's legs were totally uncoordinated.

Jim Murphy was just beginning to stagger homeward when Officer Jones was thumbing through the telephone book. There was no Murphy listed on Hobson. Then he cursed himself. "Damn! She was too proud to admit they don't have a telephone." He sighed. He'd have to drive by their house and hope that the father wasn't in.

Jones was leaving the Murphy residence, having received Mrs. Murphy's assurances of undying gratitude for the third or fourth time, just as Jim Murphy was vomiting into the gutter at Stanton and Hobson.

Chapter 30

Sunday afternoon, Agnes and Helena returned to the motherhouse. They brought Mechtilde with them, but only after she had been reassured that she was not being permanently reassigned to the motherhouse. She insisted that she return to St. Gen's after the funeral on Monday.

After the wake, held with vespers, Helena walked down the administrative wing of the motherhouse to her office. She flicked on the light and sat down in the comfortable, black leather swivel chair, after carefully closing the door to her office. She pulled her glasses off and rubbed her eyes, thinking that of all the women who had served on the governing council and whose pictures she had passed coming down the hall, none had faced a situation like this.

Yes, Gertrude, back some thirty years ago, had that car accident in which four sisters, all young and healthy, had been killed. That had been it though, the sum total of problems that shocked or shook the community to its foundations. The community had been scandal free all of its existence.

What a horrible weekend, Helena summarized. The telephone at St. Gen's had been warm to her touch each time she had used it because she seldom had not used it. She had to call the bishop who was sending his auxiliary bishop in his place since he would still be at a meeting in New York. Ray and Gus would also concelebrate as would Fr. Schmalzer, the motherhouse chaplain. There would be others, but Sr. Aidan, her secretary at the motherhouse, had taken care of that list.

Thank God for a community, she thought. Sr. Beatrice, just completing her Master's in liturgical music, had begun gathering the choir and preparing the liturgy, including the vesper service for the wake that evening, for which she and Agnes had returned in time.

She'd also had to call the funeral home, and although she was reassured that their best make-up person could make Sr. Maria presentable for the wake, she had decided single-handedly not to have an open casket. Maria's body had been released by the medical examiner late Saturday, and the business all seemed too rushed. They needed to have her body for the wake by Sunday's vespers.

Maria's family was upset and wanted to see her as soon as possible. They had made quite a fuss about the closed casket. Fortunately, Aidan had a good head on her shoulders and a tactful, compassionate way with people. In the end, the family members were satisfied to grieve over the framed picture of Maria that was placed next to the casket.

Helena had suffered qualms about making the decision and clearly the director at the funeral home had been eager to prove that he had the best make-up artist around. Still, she wanted things to be simple, and she didn't want people coming up to view Maria and looking to see where she'd been hit.

It was not generally known that she had also been raped. Most of the sisters still didn't know either. Detective Hogan had told them about Duffy's confession. What could be done for such a man? It was just as well that he would be housed away from regular people lest someone else get hurt. Thank heavens, he wasn't roaming around their school any longer. Imagine the law suits!

That was part of the reason Agnes and she hadn't announced that Maria had been raped. No use starting an uproar at this point with parents browbeating their girls and being suspicious that every unwanted pregnancy had been Duffy's doing.

Helena put her glasses back on and picked up a paper from her desk. It was a copy of Beatrice's liturgy plan and the music. Helena appreciated her efficiency. She wondered how she'd take the news that she was to finish out Maria's year at St. Gen's. She could teach just the music classes, which would leave her enough time to complete her thesis. Helena knew that Beatrice had high hopes that she would be allowed to remain at the motherhouse and compose her own music as well as run the liturgies there. Ah, well, she was young enough to wait for her dreams to come true.

Beneath that sheet was another list. Aidan too was efficient and got the job done. It was a relief to Helena. Basically, all she would have to do was be at Agnes's side and tell her what to do next. Agnes! Helena had been nominated for superior general along with Agnes. However, Helena was not a crowd pleaser like Agnes. Agnes had an air about her when she walked into a room. If Helena behaved like Agnes, she would have described herself as political. She didn't think of Agnes as political though. She was just a gloss-over type of person. She was not good with details. So, when Agnes was elected, it was no surprise to Helena. And when Helena was elected to Agnes's council, she wasn't surprised by that either.

From Helena's observation point, the Superior General was the glitter person. She was the community's liaison with the public and with church officials. Those on the council were chosen because they could get a job done and keep a Superior General on course. This weekend was sufficient proof of that for Helena. Her experience of serving with Agnes in this crisis had convinced her that her theory was true.

The last sheet of paper was the press announcement. In one of several conversations, Aidan had told her that the press and TV journalists were calling the motherhouse, frustrated because they couldn't get anything but a busy signal at St. Gen's. The reporters were each, in turn, frightened that a busy telephone meant one of their colleagues was making contact and walking away with the scoop. They hadn't any better luck with Fr. Ray. He never seemed to be at home.

Aidan had said that the news programs were showing footage of the exterior of the school and reporting that a murder had purportedly taken place there Friday evening. Helena had seen the van from Channel 4 driving by when she'd gone to see Fr. Ray Saturday about the funeral arrangements.

In fact, some reporters had begun storming the convent. That's when she stepped out and referred them to the motherhouse and Sr. Aidan. Then she and Aidan had conferred about what would

HELLBENT

be said. She had decided already not to mention the rape or the fact that the police felt that there was more than one person involved.

Then that morning, Sunday, at Mass, Fr. Ray had spoken quite compassionately to the people. She had not been particularly impressed with Fr. Ray Dunstan until then. He seemed so ordinary. She was now a bit embarrassed that she had liked Fr. Gus Spellinger. He's always had some sparkle to his personality, she'd thought. She felt he was a person with some get up and go. Unfortunately, he was!

That stupid Suzanne! She'd fallen for him and now what a mess that was. So, by Tuesday, she would be placed in an in-patient treatment facility with more nuns and priests like herself. Helena wondered if such a treatment facility was a wise choice because being thrown together, they might just re-partner with new people and live out the same mess they had been in prior to entering the program. But Agnes seemed desperate, so she'd jumped at the facility since they had an immediate opening.

As for the sisters there at St. Gen's, they seemed to have borne up surprisingly well. Rebecca and Gretchen both had insisted on returning to the parish after the Vespers at the wake. No amount of talking could sway them. She could see Gretchen's point though. Someone had to be there for the school to function with some normalcy on Tuesday. Fortunately, they would be in session only two days, since Easter vacation began with Holy Thursday.

But Gretchen had also refused their offer to spend the holidays at the motherhouse. People would be troubled by their absence, she'd said, and that would foster rumors that the school was closing. So she and Rebecca would stay at St. Gen's convent and participate in the Holy Week services at the parish. Gretchen was dutiful, if nothing else.

Helena pushed her chair back. Maybe she'd take a walk on the grounds before she turned in. She looked back at her desk, her hand on the light switch, and fantasized Gertrude in her chair. "A sex scandal and a murder/rape! They'da blown you away, honey!" She flicked off the light and walked down the hall with an air of authority. Tomorrow, the devil would have his due, she said to herself as she stepped out to enjoy the starlit, spring night.

Chapter 31

Ray was driving Gretchen and Becky back to St. Gen's. The three of them had attended the wake service Sunday evening. Each one had a personal heaviness that seemed to merge into a collective sadness that enabled them to take comfort both in the physical proximity to one another and in the silence as they rode together.

As they neared the west central part of town where the residences gave way to tall buildings and shrubs to fire hydrants, all three became aware that they were reentering their real world, the world of St. Gen's. Even if they had been unconscious of the casket in the center of the chapel at the motherhouse, the music would have forced them to consider matters beyond this life. But being out of the city, surrounded by trees that were just beginning to suggest a hint of fuzziness as their leaf buds grew to bursting, made them feel they had escaped the gray, smelly, and now vicious world of St. Gen's.

Gretchen broke the silence with a little sigh and then said, "There's no escape. We have to face it."

"The people? I think they'll be hurting more than ever. Violence so close to home, I think it's got people panicky," Ray said quietly.

Gretchen wasn't thinking along those lines but more about dealing with the students and the faculty and organizing the counseling sessions. She'd pretty much given up the idea that they could have a normal hectic week prior to the Easter holidays.

Becky's thoughts went in neither direction. She had lost her two mainstays: Maria and Mechtilde. Life was going to be without

191

a buffer for her with Gretchen from now on. Not only had she lost her friend and her mentor of a sort but also her innocence about humanity with the knowledge that Suzanne had turned out to be such a hypocrite. She wanted to collapse into tears and yell and scream obscenities all at the same time. Nothing that had happened was fair.

"We never know how good we have it until it gets really bad, do we?" The question had slipped idly from Becky.

Ray glanced up at her in his rearview mirror. "You're sounding a little like Mechtilde."

"I miss her. Do you think they'll let her come back with us tomorrow?"

Until she mentioned the return, Gretchen thought Becky was speaking about Maria. "I hope so. I can't see how they can deny an old woman her wishes, especially since it's not asking anything of them to let her return." She caught herself too late and feared that they might misinterpret her as complaining that Mechtilde's return was asking something of the two of them.

"Are you two going to be all right being alone tonight?"

Gretchen looked at Ray and wondered what on earth he thought he could do about it anyhow. "We'll be fine." She sounded tired and picked at a loose thread in her skirt.

He let them out and waited until they waved and had shut the door of the convent behind them. Becky didn't feel like going upstairs immediately and asked, "Gretch...en, do you want some tea? I think I'll just go and see what's in the fridge. I want something, but I don't know what."

"Yes, Becky. I'll take some tea."

They had just managed making some sandwiches and brewing the tea when the doorbell rang. They both looked at each other and decided to go to the door together.

"Hi!" It was Ray. "I decided to walk Mack down this way, and I noticed the downstairs lights were still on." Mack was dog-smiling up at Becky and wagging his tail. Becky figured that Ray didn't want to be alone just yet either.

"Are you hungry, Father?" Gretchen seemed to have surmised the same thing.

"Uh. Well, if you have something prepared."

"C'mon back to the kitchen, Fr. Ray. We have lots of left-over chicken salad." Becky bent down and stroked Mack's side. "Mack might be hungry too." Becky glanced quickly at Gretchen to see if she objected to the dog entering the house, but Gretchen was already heading back to the kitchen as though she hadn't noticed.

Mack sat contentedly on the kitchen floor next to Fr. Ray as the three of them sat around the table. They felt the comfort in one another's physical presence that they'd felt in the car, driving back from the motherhouse.

Ray brought the subject up first. "You know, I feel like I missed so many opportunities to know Maria. I was just so damned caught up in my own life."

"I was thinking the same thing," said Gretchen, but her eyes grew watery as she said it. "She was sunshine here, and I think I was the gloomy cloud that stood in the way."

"Gretch! I don't think that's wholly fair." Becky was trying to rescue Gretchen although that is precisely how she herself felt about Gretchen.

Gretchen winced at the nickname. "No, I think it is. It's too late. She's gone, but I hope they catch her killer soon. I hate to say it, but I want him to pay for her life in some way. Not death, just the loss of his freedom and that everyone knows what he did. I think I don't want him protected by the secrecy that cloaks him until he's arrested."

They listened to her carefully and measured her feelings against their own.

"I want him caught and I want to see him," said Becky. "I've even fantasized staring hatefully at him and cursing him too. I think I want him to hurt."

"What about you, Fr. Ray?" Gretchen wondered what the mild Fr. Ray might have to say. His homily that morning had actually been moving, pitched toward trying to ameliorate the suffering of his people. He'd described the Pieta to the people and then spoken of them as a parish being called to be the Madonna, holding the dead limp body, not just of Sr. Maria and Mrs. Ling, but of the people who kill, maim, and hate others. We have to hold the spiritually dead among us and mourn for them. We must pray that God gives them life anew just as God will give Sr. Maria and Mrs. Ling new life, he'd said.

Ray shifted in his chair and looked thoughtfully. "I have always hated violence. I have always questioned the authenticity of the Christianity of people who have lost a loved one in some violent act and demanded an eye for an eye. I think that this is the first time that I have wanted to strike back at someone, you know. I look at the fear in people and at their shock that someone so innocent has been killed."

Ray sighed and continued, "And tomorrow, I will have a funeral Mass for the mother of two children. She came to this country, looking for a better life for her children. She and Maria are both just good people, looking to make life better for others. Sometimes, I feel my faith in God being shaken.

"I ask God, 'Why these people? Why not the drunks, the bitter people who abuse their children? Why not wipe them off the face of the earth?' Then I listen to what I'm thinking and wonder where my Christianity is."

"I know the place, Father." Gretchen was surprised that the two of them could think so similarly yet be so different as they conducted themselves in their ministry.

They all fell into being quiet with one another after that. None had a solution for the other, and if they had, they would have found only platitudes to utter. It was wiser to remain silent.

Ray stirred after awhile. "It's been good just sitting here with you. Maybe I ought to do this more often."

"We'd welcome that, or I would." Gretchen looked at Becky to speak for herself.

"Ray, I would too."

They nodded to one another, and Ray stood and walked toward the door, Mack immediately following. They were standing in the hallway as he placed a hand on the doorknob. "Uh, does that go for Mack as well?"

They all smiled and nodded affirmation. Mack seemed to understand that something about him had been said and romped to each nun before being recalled by Fr. Ray.

Gretchen went to the door and locked it after Fr. Ray had stepped out. Then she turned to Becky. "Tomorrow is going to be long. I want to attend the funeral for Mrs. Ling too."

"I'll go with you," said Becky, who was about to return to clean up the kitchen.

"Becky." Gretchen called, and Becky stopped and turned around.

"Leave them, why don't you? We'll do them tomorrow."

Becky was surprised. "O.K. I am kind of tired."

They started up the stairs. When they reached the top, Gretchen said, "Becky, I don't know how to thank you. For coming back with me. I know they wouldn't have allowed me to come back alone."

"I know. I wanted to come back, Gretchen. Maria's body may be at the motherhouse, but her spirit is here."

Gretchen went into her room and stood against the door. What was it that had picked at her attention as though she hadn't quite been getting it? "Yes, it was something subtle about Becky. Ray had said she sounded like Mechtilde. There was a new depth to Becky that Gretchen had either not detected before or that had not been there before.

Chapter 32

Betty Murphy fixed a cup of tea and, for the first time that she could remember, didn't care whether the mister wanted a cup or not. She'd waited on that man hand and foot and cleaned up after him. Last night, he'd come home as drunk as ever. She despised him in that condition, but last night she was grateful because he was too in his cups to notice that Bob was not in his bed. Well, truth to tell, he'd never looked in on the boys, not even when they were babies. Raising them was her task, he'd said from the start.

She'd had a hard time rousing him for Sunday Mass. Such a time that proved to be! Doris Sweeney sat two pews ahead, sniffling into her handkerchief all during Mass, making a show of her rosary. It was all for the poor, dead nun. Well, there'd been another murder. That poor Chink woman! Yes, and what would Jim Murphy do if Betty had been murdered! Then he'd have to be busy about raising his sons!

Well, Jim nearly had made them all miss Mass what with raving about Bob not being there. She told him he had stayed the night with friends. Yes, she lied to him. Never mind, she'd confess it when she made her Easter duty. But if she'd told him the truth, they'd all have missed Mass. As it was, Betty had a hard time keeping her head up, knowing that Bob was in a jail. It would get out eventually, and there'd be the divil to pay. Bob bringing such disgrace on them.

Well, it was probably that Chink girl friend of his that brought him down that way. Those people dealt in opium and lotus blossoms. Now they were coming to this country and bringing their trashy ways with them.

However, the truth had come out when she laid the table for Sunday dinner. Jim had a couple of beers by that time. As it turned out, they had a terrible fight. She'd told him that Officer Jones had found Bob and that he was down and out with the poison in him and that Officer Jones had kept him down at the police station to protect him from the savage beating her fine husband would give Bob. Yes, a nigger policeman said that to her. Jim was outraged. In the heat of the argument, Betty had told him that policeman was acting more like a father to Bob than Jim was.

With the heated yelling, she'd been fearful that he would strike her, but he hadn't. She'd simply looked boldly into his eyes, daring him with her steady gaze to do it. In the end, he'd simply dropped his hand to his side and walked away. Even his dinner was untouched. The boys seemed so relieved when he'd left the table that they both ate double portions.

She'd heard Jim go to the kitchen, looking for some dinner an hour later. She found herself smiling over the mending she was doing, hearing him mumble about nothing left of his dinner. After he'd made himself a sandwich, he came to her as she sat by the dining room window for the light. She stopped her mending and looked at him expectantly. He didn't complain about the food to her as she had expected. Instead, he asked what the policeman had said about Bob. That's when he told her that she had better be the one to fetch her son lest he light into him.

There was a glistening about his eyes as he said it, and she wondered if it were really possible for Jim Murphy to cry. Well, she was so angry with him that she didn't care. If Jim felt like a failure as a father, he certainly had earned the right.

After that, she'd gone to the station, and the policeman seemed to know what to do. She signed some forms and promised that she would be getting her boy some help and that she would not allow him to leave town. Her son might be wanted for some questioning. She swore quite seriously upon her own mother's soul that she would find a telephone to call that number Officer Jones had given her.

She had every intention of doing so too, especially after the fine policeman, O'Reilly he was and a fine Irishman too, assured her that the treatment wouldn't be expensive at all. Some sort of sliding scale he said that slid to near zero if you hadn't any money for such things.

So Betty Murphy, coming home with Bob, had thought to herself that whether she had a husband or not, she was just as alone in the raising of her sons as Doris Sweeney ever was. She would take charge of Bob now. Indeed, all the way home, she'd informed Bob that he was a grief to her and to his brothers, setting such a poor example and being no different than his own father. She told him how he had to be strong now and take a pledge to never touch the poison again. Bob had said nothing, not a word, the whole way home, so ashamed he must have been!

Now as she sat drinking her tea, she was trying to figure how she would make the call. She knew of a public telephone way down at the laundry. She'd overheard Mrs. Thompson say that she'd used it before they got their own. Betty didn't like the idea of going down to that part of the neighborhood, but she had to summon the courage if she was going to rescue Bob from the clutches of Satan. And just to be on the safe side, Betty Murphy intended to say a rosary to God's holy mother every night until that task was completed.

In the meantime, she would be on her son every minute. With no school tomorrow, he would be cleaning up his filthy room and scrubbing all the upstairs rooms. Indeed, the house would be shining and glistening in greeting this Easter to come. She smiled at the thought of it. Cleanliness is next to godliness, her own mother used to say. Bob had said he just wanted to go to bed when he got home. She told him he was to sleep down in the basement. Jeremy had complained fierce and she'd boxed his ears just a little. Then, she'd locked Bob into the basement, feeling he fared better in her basement than in Officer Jones's holding room.

Jim had spent the afternoon and evening outside, throwing a ball to Sean and Jeremy. Yes, both Jim and Bob were sheepish around her, and she was surely going to take a lesson from Doris Sweeney, she was. They'd know there'd be hell to pay if they tried to object to her placing some order on this house. Indeed!

Chapter 33

Terry Hogan rose early Monday morning. He looked in at his son and then his daughter. They were soundly sleeping, safe from a world gone awry. For how long though? That was the question that had bothered Terry ever since he'd set his family up in this suburban neighborhood. Terry knew that drugs were spreading. The affluence made it clear that they were easily obtainable. Kids seemed to be losing their motivation and didn't have serious goals anymore. He shook his head and walked downstairs. Whenever he looked at his children, inevitably he became pessimistic about the culture as a whole, which he felt was going to hell in a hand basket.

Terry filled his thermos with the coffee that Millie had set up last night with the automatic timer on it. That way, Millie could make his coffee and not have to get up at the ungodly hour that he did. She'd been faithful to him, through thick and thin, and Terry felt she deserved her rest. She was raising the kids practically single-handedly as he saw it anyway. Terry twirled the red plastic cup onto the thermos and then headed for the precinct.

At his desk, he found the note about warrants that Herrington had requested for the arrest of Walter Atkins and Jo-Jo Crowe. Herrington and Big Mike Rafferty would be taking care of the grilling. Terry was supposed to continue with the nun's story, as they'd named it. Ghoulish humor was a necessary coping mechanism among the homicide guys. Besides Sr. Suzanne's ability to finger Jo-Jo and place him at the scene of the crime, Herrington would attempt to get Walter to plea bargain and see if he would finger Jo-Jo.

Jones had turned up a Mrs. Duffy who had seen Walter strike the Ling woman in the alley. Seems that Mrs. Duffy had just come from the bathroom at the back of her house and was sitting on the edge of her bed when she saw what took place. She could readily identify Walter since he was, to use her words, "that tall nigger who stands around on the corner." So Walter would be told he was charged with murder, but with a little cooperation with regard to Jo-Jo's murder of LeRoy, they would bring the charge down to armed robbery and murder would be changed to manslaughter. That should put two punks out of action for awhile.

Now, Terry had to work on identifying the numerous people who tracked Sr. Maria's blood throughout the school that night. Duffy was one such suspect. Duffy had fingered the teacher. So Terry would be grilling the guy Duffy called Scotchkiss. Good enough; however, there was a missing piece. Two tracks used the side stairs. One of those was Sr. Suzanne's. So Terry Hogan had to find out who the missing person was. He was anxious for the lab results. He drummed his fingers on the table nervously; then he unbuttoned and rolled his shirt cuffs back while noting the time. It was 8:00 o'clock. It was a good time to rouse the teacher, a time when he couldn't get his excuses together. Terry dialed John Hotchkiss. If a policeman dropped by, that would arouse the man's suspicions. Calling him and asking for a voluntary interview would keep the man calmer and less prepared to defend himself.

Jones came into the office just then, dragging a recalcitrant Jo-Jo. Terry smiled and gave a smart-ass wave. Jo-Jo sneered at him. Hotchkiss was taking his time answering. Finally ring number eight was interrupted as the man fumbled with the receiver.

"Harrow." The garbled greeting was followed by heavy breathing.

"John Hotchkiss?"

There was a pause, and Terry imagined the fellow was staring at the receiver. "Who's this?"

Hmmm, paranoid, huh? Terry liked to psych people out. "Mr. Hotchkiss?"

"Yeah." The voice was diffident.

"Sir, this is Detective Terence Hogan. I'm in charge of the murder investigation. You have heard that a murder occurred Friday night at St. Gen's High School?"

"Yeah. Sr. Gretchen called off school. She told me about it then."

Terry noted on the pad in front of him: Not broken up about the death. "Sir, I am attempting to set up a schedule of interviews with the faculty. I understand that everyone was at the school that evening."

"No, I left early. She wasn't dead. I saw her in my classroom before I left."

Terry wrote: Defensive as hell! "Yes, sir. I am interested in any lead and the fact that you spoke with her before her death may provide some assistance to me in my investigation. Now, are you able to come in, say," Terry paused and then continued, "How about nine o'clock?"

"Well, uh. Nine o'clock? How long will the interview take? I'm kinda busy."

Terry smiled. "Well, that's a little dependent on what you can remember. Based on what you've said, it probably won't be more than a half hour." After making sure the man knew where to come and who to ask for, Terry gave him a sunny, dapper good-bye.

Terry got up and paced then. He needed the lab results. Herrington had been bugging the technician all Friday night. Grant money had enabled them to hire someone to keep the lab going 24 hours. It was a significant breakthrough for the homicide division. They'd closed more cases in the last year than they ever had in one year according to Terry's recollection.

That was also why the meeting with Pecker was predictable. He was used to seeing developments and things happening. Well, Herrington would have something to report on the Ling murder and that might shut Pecker up, but Terry needed some lab reports in order to have something to say.

Just then Herrington came up. "Peck wants us now. He moved the meeting up. Seems he's got another meeting for later."

"Hell! I don't have a whole lot more," Terry snapped the pencil he held.

"We'll just have to listen to him rant and rave. What can he do? He knows he's jumping the gun by having a meeting on Monday anyhow." Herrington's experience and the fact that he was about to retire kept him from developing acid indigestion, a diagnosis that anyone suffered who had a scheduled meeting with Peck.

Terry Hogan followed Herrington out of the room and down a side hall to the Captain's office. It was a well-appointed office, considering the poverty just outside the window, which was barred. Terry always found that incongruous.

"Sit down, sit down." Captain Peck closed a folder and looked at them. His thick, curling eyebrows hung over his dark eyes, which were, in turn, enveloped in dark circles. Add his beakish nose and Peck looked something like a large bird of prey, not an owl, but more like a vulture. Terry wondered if having that image in his mind was what made him so uncomfortable at these meetings. As he sat down, the thought flashed in his mind that he should think of something more positive, but as he looked across the desk at Peck, the idea shriveled and died.

"You two are my best, you know that." Peck's attempt at a smile that revealed a gold-capped tooth, resulted in a smirk. Both men nodded appreciatively, but they didn't believe a word they heard. They knew this was merely a standard prelude to something less flattering. Peck cleared his throat and then looking from one to the other, stated fiercely, "We've had a rash of crime lately. This may be a poor neighborhood, but we've been relatively peaceful in the past. Not like this anyway." He realized that he had exaggerated the safety of the neighborhood. "I mean it's getting to be a murder a night. Punks happen all the time, but women! Mothers of children, for godsake! And worse, a nun! Nowhere, nowhere in this city has this happened before!" He was working up his oratory, and some of it was straight from The Morning Sun's editorial.

Peck suddenly leaned back in the plush suede chair. "Now, tell me what you've got." Then Peck looked deliberately at both of them, adding, "And you better got something, gentlemen!"

As if they had discussed a strategy beforehand, Herrington leaned forward just as Terry Hogan leaned backward in their respective padded chairs. "Well, Captain, we're moving forward on the Ling murder. Very handily, very handily. In fact, Terry here, has been of immense help with my investigation."

"How's that? Hogan's on the nun's story." Peck had leaned forward with a frown. Terry knew that he owed one to Herrington for trying to soften things up for him.

"One of his witnesses had information that tied our suspect to the scene of the crime and to the victim. So, we now have our suspect in custody. That shouldn't take a whole lot of time to wrap up."

"You're speaking of the Ling case?"

"Not exactly, sir. I'm speaking of a witness in the nun's case. Hogan was able to get some helpful eyewitness stuff for us to crack a punk's murder that ought to provide leverage for me to use to get a confession in the Ling case. So this breakthrough was essential." Terry was amazed at Herrington's quick maneuvers through the landmines. He'd managed to get the fact that LeRoy's murder would be solved first, much to the Captain's chagrin without his being able to berate his detectives for not having their priorities straight.

"Is that right? Well, that's good. I want that creep who killed that poor woman in record time. It's difficult for women not to be afraid to walk outdoors when they know someone is out there. Helen," Peck looked at them and added unnecessarily, "my wife, is really upset. She does some volunteer work over at St. Hildegarde's. They have soup and sandwiches for people once a week over there. She's afraid to help now."

Hogan wondered if the Captain was so simplistic as to think that the culprit behind these crimes was someone like Walter Atkins rather than the drugs themselves. This was not the time to challenge his thinking, not when he was dealing with his hysterical wife.

"O.K., so we'll have some arrests within a day or so. Good work, Herrington. We'll miss you when you retire." Herrington leaned back as Peck looked sharply at Terry Hogan. "Now, Hogan, don't tell me you spent all your investigative time on the nun's story, digging up witnesses for Herrington. What do you have?"

"Captain, you know the nun's story occurred twenty four hours later, so I'm not as far along as Herrington." Terry knew he had erred by beginning with an excuse.

"Hard work, Hogan. That's what solves cases, not excuses!"

"Yes, sir. The nun's murder is a little more complicated than the usual armed robbery that turned violent. We have four sets of tracks that lead from the crime scene. However, it's coming clearer that each of these tracks belongs to persons who worked independently and quite possibly were not aware of the others."

"I beg your pardon? What do we have here? Four different people all trying to kill the same person? Murder on the Orient Express was a movie, Hogan!"

"No, sir." Terry glanced at his watch conspicuously. "You see, I have identified two of the sets of tracks. As a result of interviews so far, I think I have another set identified. After an interview scheduled this morning, I may have a clearer idea of who killed Sr. Maria." Terry knew that the final statement was the one that Peck was looking for.

Peck sat back and picked up a pencil, which he used to beat a steady rhythm on the edge of his desk. "Good. Good. I want that killer. We need that killer. I know you're a Catholic, Hogan." Peck glanced quickly at Herrington. "You too, of course." He narrowed his eyes as he looked back at Terry and said meaningfully, "And so is Mayor Haggerty. This is the number one priority here. Understood?" His eyes burned. Peck was a Methodist, but Haggarty was a lameduck mayor, and Peck needed his support when he would make his much-rumored bid in next year's mayoral election.

"Yes, sir. And to that end, I would like to get on with the investigation. I have a suspect to question, sir." Terry leaned forward as though he was about to rise from the chair.

"Go to it, men!" Peck stood and leaned over to shake each one's hand firmly. This was always the moment in such meetings that Terry imagined Peck as General Patton, sending his officers out to do battle. Pecker was surely a character! Terry hoped the rumor that Peck was going to run for mayor wasn't true. He imagined their fair city would fast resemble a military compound if that happened.

When they were safely beyond earshot, Terry clapped Herrington on his shoulder. "You did good in there. Thanks for softening him up for me."

"No problem. I thought you were going to get yourself in some stink for a minute. But you pulled it out. You think you'll get this wrapped up?"

"God, I hope so. What worries me is the second set of footprints that lead down the side steps."

"Well, good luck, Terry." Herrington stopped at the coffee machine. "Want one?"

"Never touch the stuff. I bring Millie's brew with me instead." As Terry walked to his desk, he heard Big Mike Rafferty singing softly as he held Jo-Jo's rap sheet in his hands, "I only have eyes for you!" Terry stopped and asked Big Mike what was up. Big Mike was wearing his devilish grin. "I'm psyching myself up for this little fart, brother."

Chapter 34

On Monday, Becky and Gretchen rode with Fr. Gus Spellinger to the funeral at the motherhouse. Fr. Ray had to accompany the body of Mrs. Ling to the cemetery for graveside services after the funeral. He expected to leave the cemetery and just make it to the motherhouse in time for the eleven o'clock funeral for Sr. Maria. Gus was none too talkative, so they were silent for most of the trip out.

They arrived at ten and dropped Gus off at the visitors' dining room where a breakfast buffet awaited the gathering priests. Then they headed into the motherhouse to meet with old friends who were gathering from the various convents all over the city and beyond. Becky ran first off into Linda, her classmate. "Hey, Beck, how's it going? I'm so sorry about Maria."

Becky had gone this round the evening before, but it was more limited. She wondered if she could keep repeating the same old assurances over and over for an hour. She tried to get Linda talking about herself, but she wouldn't bite. Finally, she remembered that Linda was always into gossip. "Have you heard if Mechtilde will return with us today? I know she wants to come back." Becky thought Mechtilde wouldn't mind being offered on the sacrificial altar of gossip if it meant turning attention away from the reliving of Maria's death.

"You don't know? I'd think they'd tell you. Yeah, they will but not just yet. You heard that Beatrice is going to be picking up Maria's music classes?" Satisfied that Becky had not heard this tidbit, Linda looked conspiratorially around her. "She's not a happy camper either." Linda looked around once again and then leaned closer to Becky. "I'm surprised that they told her before the funeral. I hope she can get through the liturgy today." Linda straightened up and continued. "Anyhow, she and Mechtilde will go to St. Gen's together on Easter. Mechtilde's supposed to get a thorough sales talk on the joys of retiring to Gaynes Hall, but I don't think Agnes expects Tillie to bite, do you?"

Becky hadn't known this and wondered if Gretchen already knew and why she hadn't told her. The news of Beatrice coming posed a relief to Becky because Beatrice was about her age and might be something of a companion. "Well, the place tends to grow on a person. She'll be fine." Becky saw Suzanne at the coffee machine and excused herself.

She waded through the crowd of nuns, stopping to hug this one and comment with another until she reached Suzie, who by now had taken her coffee mug and moved to the trays of donuts.

"Hi! You're looking better than you did last night." Becky slid between Marie Kevin and Suzie at the donuts.

"Oh. Yeah. Well, I took some melatonin and slept better. Thanks. How are you?" Suzie's complexion was not as pale, but her voice lacked enthusiasm.

"Let's get out of here, O.K?"

Suzie looked relieved. "Good idea. Let's check out the study room down the hall." Unfortunately, there was a small gathering of nuns in their fifties who hadn't seen one another in several months. They were laughing uproariously. Suzie backed up and led the way to a small supply room. They leaned against the shelves.

"Have you been clued in about me?" Suzie set her mug on the shelf that came to her shoulder as she bit into a bowtie glazed donut.

"No. How'd the questioning go down at the station?"

"Oh that. I don't know. The policeman was more interested in the two guys I saw next to the thrift shop that night. One of them was killed."

"No kidding. God, what a night for you."

"Oh, I didn't see the killing." Suddenly, she was seeing Maria on the floor again. She had suffered several flashbacks to Friday night.

She also found herself jumpy around stairs and used the elevator at the motherhouse, which was generally reserved for the elderly. They had looked questioningly at her last night when she'd crowded on among all their walkers and wheelchairs. But she'd tried the stairs. There'd been a loud noise from above, probably someone just let a door bang against the banister on the landing above, but it was enough to send her trembling to the elevator. She saw Becky looking at her, concerned.

"I'm fine. I just wander off. I can't get the image of Maria on that floor out of my mind."

"Maybe a doctor can help."

"I guess I'll have plenty of help by tomorrow." Becky looked at her blankly. "You haven't heard. I'm being packed off to a program for sickos."

"Why?" Becky had the feeling that her universe was starting to spin at warp speed again.

"Because Agnes thinks I am." Becky tilted her head with a questioning look, and Suzie decided she should tell Becky the truth. "My friend, the one I told you I was visiting with? Well, it was Gus Spellinger. We've been kind of hitting it off." Suzie paused and forced herself to say it. "We've been having an affair. Agnes wants me to get some psychological treatment."

"Suzie. Oh, Suzie. I thought you...never mind." Becky didn't have words because her mind was trying to sort through what Suzie had just told her.

"You never thought I was that sort of girl?" Suzie expected that holier-than-thou attitude from the older nuns but not from the younger ones.

"No. No, I meant that I thought you kind of had it together. I mean you're a hermit and out there with God."

"Sometimes, God just isn't enough. I gave him most of me," Suzie thought she sounded perfectly together. Why should one small affair raise the eyebrows? Agnes had gone ballistic over it, and now Becky was standing there like she'd just been slapped.

Becky wanted to remind Suzie that God was enough for tons of people and that her vows had proclaimed as much, but she said, "Suzie, I'm sure this will be difficult for you. How long will you be gone?"

"Maybe a month, probably more. The average stay is six months."

"Wow. What's to become of your hermitage?"

"Agnes won't let me go anywhere. I wanted to ask if you would go out and pack up my things. Would you have some time? I have a list upstairs of things I need sent to me. The rest can be boxed and left here at the motherhouse."

"Sure, Suzie. I'd be happy to do that. Let's get the list." Becky wanted to do anything but continue the conversation.

They stepped out into the hall where Becky saw Mechtilde being rolled past in a wheelchair. She called out and the little parade stopped. As Becky leaned over to give Mechtilde a hug, Suzie said, "I'll get the list and give it to you in chapel. It's almost time for Mass."

"Oh, Tillie! I've missed you so much." Becky heard the heartfelt quality in her own voice.

"My sweet Becky! They won't let me come home with you tonight, but I'll be there when Beatrice comes."

"When's that?"

"I doubt it'll be until Easter Sunday sometime. She'll dawdle as long as she can, poor dear." Mechtilde looked as far over her shoulder as she was able. "Gloria dear, why don't you go on? Becky can scoot me around for awhile. That's all right with you, isn't it, Becky?"

"Sure, Tillie. I'd love to chat with you."

"Then let's go outside. The sun is shining. Isn't that wonderful for Maria?" The sun and clouds were taking intermittent turns at predominating over the day's proceedings.

The mention of Maria's name, a reminder of their purpose for being there, sent a depth charge into Becky's abdomen. She wheeled Mechtilde out into the courtyard and pulled up to a stone bench. She seated herself so that she was facing Mechtilde.

"Are they treating you right?"

"Most efficiently, shall we say?" Mechtilde smiled. "I'd rather have you and your tea though." Then Mechtilde looked seriously and asked, "What's the matter, Becky?"

Becky studied her for a moment. "Am I such an open book?"

"You choose to be so with me, yes."

"Do you know about Suzie?"

"Yes. It's the buzz around here. I feel for poor Suzie. She's got herself into a scrape and doesn't even realize what she's done, but who can throw the first stone?"

"A lot of people feel they can."

"Yes, they do. But you know, Becky, they are as oblivious to themselves as Suzie is to herself. Birds of feather flock to throw stones, hmm?"

"Tillie, that's a mixed metaphor of the worst dimension!" Becky wrinkled her nose.

"I know. Shocking, really! What time is it, Becky dear?"

Becky started to look at her watch and then heard the ten-minute warning bell sounding inside.

She bent forward to hug Mechtilde once again. "Thanks, Tillie. May I drive you to your destination?"

"Yes, dear. Get me to the chapel on time. In my younger years, they used to tell me that I'd be late for my own funeral. Well, I don't want to be late for dear Maria's."

As Becky wheeled Mechtilde, falling into a line that was moving in the direction of the chapel, she wondered why the words of a song about marriage had been used by Mechtilde to refer to a funeral.

Chapter 35

Gus heard the warning bell with relief. The bishop had been cool when Gus had greeted him. Obviously, Agnes had already bent his ear. When they'd had a brief moment, the bishop had leaned toward his ear and indicated that Archbishop Madison wanted to see him after the Chrism Mass on Holy Thursday.

All Gus could see was the grim irony of being called on the carpet on the day that celebrated the institution of the priesthood. The fingers that had once been anointed with chrism and wrapped as a sign of his ordination would now be rapped soundly because he'd been a naughty boy.

As Gus vested, he saw Ray. Ray didn't return the look of recognition, and Gus wondered if Ray was studiously avoiding looking at him. As it turned out, they were paired for the procession, in a place of honor, preceding the bishop. As they came toward one another to get in line, Ray smiled easily at Gus; Gus immediately felt better.

Once on the altar, facing the congregation, Gus scanned the faces of the nuns and lay people in the pews. His brother priests were in chairs on either side of the altar of sacrifice. Out in the first row of pews, Agnes was quite prominent and had a somber expression. Helena stood next to her, singing with fervor. About ten pews back, hidden for the most part by a tall nun in front of her, he finally saw Suzie. She had dark circles around her eyes. Not once did she look at him. They'd done a number on her, he was sure, making her feel unworthy and guilty. He felt himself aroused and looked away quickly.

The funeral was filled with pomp and circumstance. The bishop delivered a long and arduous homily, thrown together in less than a day and drafted by some aide. Probably Bananas; that is, Fr. Joseph Bononos. In the seminary, they'd begun teasing him by calling him "Good Nose", but since he did have a rather bulbous nose, they found the teasing had hurt his feelings. In good humor, they changed the word play into Bananas even though he remained suspicious that they had merely softened the reference to his nose while snickering quietly behind his back.

Whatever, Bananas had redrafted the homily too many times, and the bishop couldn't keep the previous drafts from invading the last one. He strayed several times from the text and awkwardly transitioned to the present text each time. Even Ray yawned audibly at least once. Then Gus saw Suzie look at him, but aside from the recognition in her eyes, she let nothing show on her face. He knew she would be on his side of the aisle at communion time. He wondered if she would look at him then.

Finally, the bishop stopped and returned to the president's chair. One of the nuns came into the sanctuary then to offer the Prayer of the Faithful. She had a slight limp and legs that reminded Gus of a baby grand piano. She prayed for victims of violence and for those who committed acts of violence. Gus wondered if the guy who murdered Maria felt the prayers of this chapelful of nuns.

Gus let his eyes glide over the nuns and then he glanced left. He saw the hard face of a man whose eyes and mouth were a male version of Maria's. He must be her older brother, Gus decided. The family resemblance was strong. The woman next to him kept dabbing at her eyes with a Kleenex that had been wadded up in her palm. Maria, like all nuns, had two families, one the members of her religious community and the other, her blood relatives, who knew little about her community. Yet here they were, joined for better or worse. They had all been assembled for the better, which had been Maria's profession of vows, and now the worse, her death, was being shared.

Finally, at Communion, as Gus and Ray stood side by side distributing the consecrated hosts, he found himself focussing on Suzie again. She should be reaching him shortly. He glanced beyond the communicant in front of him but didn't see her. He glanced toward the pew where she had been sitting but she wasn't there. Then he saw her. She had switched sides and was coming toward Ray. Damn! She probably blames me! Hell! Gus said to himself as he repeated the words: "The Body of Christ."

Chapter 36

Hogan went to his desk. No report yet! He sighed, loosened his tie and reached for his thermos. Big Mike stood up and walked back to Terry's desk. "Looks like you're turning into a twenty-four-hour man, Terry."

"It feels like it. One of these days," then Terry Hogan looked at the tall man standing there before him, "Do you think there will ever be one of these days where we put in regular hours?"

"Have you found one yet?"

"Nope. We're just a coupla masochists, huh? Hey, Mike, my teacher didn't show up yet, did he?"

"No one's been around here. Oh, yeah. Jones was here a minute ago. He collared Jo-Jo, but you were here then." Big Mike fluttered the pages on Jo-Jo that he held in his hand. "That is one mean dude."

"Yeah. I think he took care of LeRoy. That nun said when she saw them that LeRoy looked like he was pleading. I just bet he was too."

"My momma always told me that when you plays with fire. Hey, how was Pecker today?"

"Well, now that's one constant we can count on around here."

"Figures. You know he wants to run for mayor?"

"I heard. God, I hope it's not true."

"Ah, Terry, wouldn't you vote for him?"

"You would?" Terry gave Mike a look of incredulity.

"Sure. I figure that way he would owe me for a change. I'd say, 'Mr. Mayor, sir, I worked my buns off for you, and then I voted you in office. Hey, I figure you're in for giving me and my fellow police officers a break. I'd like a twelve-week vacation every year!'"

Terry looked up at Mike, "So, you don't have anything to do, huh?"

"I'm waiting on Herrington. He's with Jo-Jo. They haven't brought Walter over yet. Besides, I was wondering what's happening with the nun's story. Did you see the paper this morning?"

"Is it worse than yesterday's?"

"Oh, they just rewrite the story. This one's got a picture of her. She looks like an angel. Wait a minute, I'll get it for you."

Hogan looked up the list of teacher's telephone numbers that Sr. Gretchen had given him. Mike returned with the front page of the newspaper. "Murdered Nun Buried Today!" was in large, bold lettering splayed across the top of the page. Beneath was a picture of a smiling woman, her blonde hair flowing softly to her shoulders. Her eyes were bright and clear. "She looks like a nice person, doesn't she?"

"Yeah. Who would want to kill her for a few dollars? That's what my wife said this morning when she saw it. She said that if a nun like her gets killed for that, who stands a chance anymore."

Hogan groaned. Everybody's wife was at it. Thank heavens, Millie stayed out of his business. She never commented about any high profile case. "We'll nail the son of a bitch, Mike."

"Yeah, I hope so. Oh, here comes Walter. I'll see you later, Terry."

Big Mike was taller even that Walter Atkins who was a bit subdued by that fact. Mike had walked up close to him to impress him and then motioned to the room he was to enter without saying a word. The officer who had brought him from a holding cell, then uncuffed him and told him he was waiting just outside the door. As he said it, he'd rested his hand on the butt of his gun.

Mike paced slowly along the table and walked up behind Walter and paused, causing Walter to turn his head to check what he might be doing. Walter's neck muscles were paining him. When he'd tried to run, a couple of the cops who chased him had pushed him down, and one of them had hit his shoulder with a baton. Down deep, Walter knew it had been a warning blow, but he was secretly nursing a grudge.

Maybe a lawyer would help him sue for abuse. Still, he knew he'd need more bruising. He'd tried to be smart with the guard, but he wouldn't bite. Looking at Mike, Walter didn't cherish the idea of smarting off to this guy. He was big enough to do serious damage. No lawsuit was worth that.

Mike let Walter strain to look long enough to satisfy himself that Walter was not physically comfortable, then he walked on, taking another pass around the table, saying nothing. Walter shifted uneasily. Suddenly Mike turned and leaned across the table, towering over Walter. "So what the hell did you get from that poor woman?"

Walter had a startled response, pulling his head back quickly. He said nothing.

"You're up for murder one, you know."

Walter looked surprised. "I didn't kill nobody."

"Yes, you did. We got the goods on you. Witnesses. Your gun is being checked for the woman's blood right now." Walter swallowed hard at that news. "We'll find her blood along the little creases where the handle is affixed to the butt of your gun, Walter. I can see your sorry excuse for a lawyer now when our prosecutor asks Dr. Derringer (Mike made up the name and was amused by it, but didn't show it) to tell the jury about the blood. Then we'll have Jo-Jo under oath, telling about your drug dealing and drug use. No jury I ever knew feels kindly toward a drug dealer."

Walter shifted and wet his cracked lips with his tongue. "Jo-Jo is my frien' and he'd never say that."

"Yeah, he would. In fact, he's telling Detective Herrington that right now. You see, Jo-Jo is in a lot of trouble too. It seems he offed LeRoy, and if he can get a lighter sentence for that, he'll sell you down the river. Some friend, huh?"

Walter looked disturbed and glanced around the room. Mike continued to press. "So, it's good-bye to freedom, Walter. Your mama can make trips to the pen up there in Beaverville now rather than those short hops over to Juvey. Yeah. It's always hard on the mamas." Mike paused and took out a piece of gum and slowly and studiously unwrapped it and then fed it into his mouth.

"You got Jo-Jo sure like you sayin' you got me?"

"Well, his case is a little weaker. He ditched his gun, but we'll find it."

"No, you won't."

Mike looked slyly at Walter. "Why, Walter? You know where it is?"

"Maybe."

"Hmm. Look, Walter, I like you. I mean, Jo-Jo is a runt. He thinks he's big, but big guys like us should run the world, don't you think? Anyhow, if I had to choose between you two, I'd want to put that sucker away before I put you. If you can help me out, then I'd cut a deal with you probably. Although we have an ironclad case with you." Mike paused as if he were about to rethink himself and rescind the deal.

"I can help you, but you gotta cut a deal first."

"Yeah, well, I gotta know what kind of help first." Mike imitated Walter's pitch and tone exactly, but Walter was too agitated to notice. He needed a fix and his body was growing desperate in its demands.

"O.K., O.K. I know where the gun is because Jo-Jo told me to get rid of it. He say he killed LeRoy because LeRoy told the cops that I killed that Chinese lady. He took care of LeRoy for me, so I had to hide the gun. That's what he say."

Mike was amazed. He had a confession but he also realized that Walter's prints were on the gun. Jo-Jo was not stupid by any means. "All right, Walter. I'll have to go out and talk to the prosecutor's office about a deal. You wait here."

Terry had just hung up the telephone. Hotchkiss had not answered, and he was now a half-hour late. Mike walked up to him and shook his head. "Have you seen Herrington?"

"Yep," Terry leaned back in his chair. "He's in the john. A new development?"

"Yeah. I've got an admission of guilt, but I think the gun that Jo-Jo used may be contaminated with Walter's prints. He's ripe for two murders, and Jo-Jo may be back on the streets."

"Man!" Terry stood up and hitched his pants. The desk sergeant had just come in and signaled to him. "You and Herrington get that mean little bastard, one way or the other." Terry walked out and saw a man who looked ready for skid row leaning against the counter. "Mr. Hotchkiss?"

The man looked at him. "Yes." His mouth curved downward by force of habit.

"Come this way, if you don't mind." Terry caught the smell of liquor from several feet away. He glanced over the man's shoulder to Dick, the desk sergeant. Dick had been wounded, chasing a bank robber and now had a serious limp. He had adjusted to the dull routine behind the desk rather well. Terry often wondered if he'd become gun shy and welcomed the quiet life. Dick pinched his nose between his thumb and index finger, noting that he too had smelled the stale alcohol on the man.

Hotchkiss, who seemed distantly familiar, didn't stagger as he walked through the door toward him, so Terry had concluded that he was sober. The two interrogation rooms were busy with Walter and Jo-Jo, so Terry led Hotchkiss down the hall to a small room near the Captain's office. Some officers used it for a gathering place when they came in off the beat. The coke, coffee and snack machines lined the wall. Since it was Monday morning, the room was empty.

"Would you like something? Coffee?"

Hotchkiss nodded. "Yes, thanks. This is different. On TV, the rooms appear a bit more sterile."

Terry looked around, thinking to himself that it did look sterile. "Yeah, well, you know TV. They never get it right."

"I know just how you feel. I'm an English teacher. Ever notice how teachers are presented?"

Terry looked at him and decided to use the opportunity. "Yeah, they're always every kid's pal."

"Yeah. And the kids are basically no problem. I mean they're mildly bored. Not reality, at all."

"What is it really like?" Terry handed Hotchkiss the coffee and sat down across from him. He'd decided to give himself a coke. He couldn't bring himself to drink the coffee and Millie's was out of reach at present. Hotchkiss looked at him skeptically. "No, I mean it. I was just thinking that I might try teaching. This stuff is getting too old, you know." Terry's voice sounded as naïve as he was capable of making it.

"No way, pal. You don't want teaching. There's no reward in it at all. I know they show these teachers who turn around a kid's life, but it doesn't work that way. Kids don't trust adults. They take pleasure out of making you feel crappy and worthless. They rebel at every assignment."

"Hmm. Sounds awful." Terry was reminded of Pecker's ability to make his detectives feel worthless and crappy. "Why do you stay in it?"

"Nothing else to do. I mean, once you're trained for something, you gotta stick with it. I mean, an English teacher. What else could I do?"

Trained, thought Terry. I guess he thinks he's a seal or a dog act. Yeah, he's a dog all right. Terry tried to inhale by looking down, breathing close to his chest. The guy really reeked.

"Yeah. I think if I didn't stop off for a coupla beers every night, I wouldn't be able to do this job." Terry had spoken more softly and tried to look as if he were confiding a dark secret.

"Yeah, I know what you mean. They don't know how to write, but I have to read the crap they hand in. If I didn't have something to swallow, I'd go crazy." He looked at Terry with watering eyes. Terry knew Hotchkiss wished he would produce a couple of beers then and there.

"Yeah, well, that's life, I guess." Terry felt that he'd better switch the course of the conversation or Hotchkiss would start fixating on liquor. "Mr. Hotchkiss, I remember you saying something about Sr. Maria. Oh, I'll need to record our conversation now." Terry produced a small tape recorder and clicked it on. Hotchkiss stared blankly at it.

"Mr. Hotchkiss?" He seemed to have tranced out.

He looked up suddenly at his name. "Uh, call me John."

"Sure. John, you mentioned seeing Sr. Maria the night she was killed."

"Yes. Uh. Yes, she came into my classroom." Hotchkiss was sitting upright but rigid. He was putting on a good front, Terry thought.

"That was during the teacher conferences, was it?"

"Say, do you mind if I get a coke. I'm awfully thirsty."

"Sure. Hey, stay there. I'll get it for you." Terry wanted to be the friendly cop still, and this gave him a chance to reassure Hotchkiss that he was not being adversarial. Still, he couldn't help wondering if Hotchkiss rated the coffee as bad as Terry did.

Terry sat down again after handing the Pepsi to Hotchkiss who drank deeply, making a gurgling sound in his throat.

"Yes. Well, it was just at the end of the conferences as I recall." Hotchkiss set the can down, but held it with both hands as if it were physically comforting to him to do so.

"May I ask what the exchange was? It helps me to understand her frame of mind."

"Uh. I think she wanted to discuss some student. I'm not sure. It was a very brief exchange." Hotchkiss seemed to breathe a sigh of relief. His shoulders relaxed. Apparently, he'd gotten beyond what he considered the dangerous part of the questioning.

"And then she left?"

"Why, yes. She went down to the music room."

"And where did you go?"

Hotchkiss was startled by the question. "Me? I, I, I left then."

"I've been up to the school, and I've seen several sets of stairs that could have been used. Did you use the main steps?"

"Uh. No. I needed to go into the faculty lounge downstairs, so I took a shortcut. There is a set of stairs that leads into the faculty room."

"I think I've seen those. You have a key to open the locked door?"

"Yes. Well, we all have a key."

"I see. And in terms of time. Did you go down those stairs immediately after Sr. Maria left your room?"

He stirred uneasily and took another long drink from his Pepsi. "Well, I did. Yes."

Terry wiped his hand across his face and held it longer over his mouth while he looked long and hard at Hotchkiss. Then he shifted in his chair and leaned his elbows on the table between them. "John, I need you to remember this part very carefully. There's always the chance we have witnesses. Would you care to try to answer that question more precisely?"

Hotchkiss was alarmed. His eyes darted quickly from Terry Hogan to the wall behind him. He decided to try to bluff. "I doubt there were any witnesses. Everyone was out of that school quickly after the last parents went through."

"John, you are trying my patience. Take my word for it. We have witnesses." Hogan bluffed back, knowing that Duffy's testimony wouldn't hold up in court.

"All right. I didn't want to implicate him, but I did see someone leaving the music room. He was running like a bat out of Hades, so I went down to check on Sr. Maria."

"Uh, huh."

"Well, she was," he hesitated, not knowing if saying more would do him damage.

"Uh, huh," Terry prodded.

"She was on the floor at the back of the room. She was dead."

"Why didn't you call the police?"

"I don't know. It was unnerving. I guess I wasn't thinking straight."

"What did you do when you saw her body? I mean did you examine it or touch it in anyway?"

"No. I just saw it and took off. That Bob Murphy might have doubled back."

"Bob Murphy? Is he the one you saw?"

"Yes. I presume he killed Sr. Maria. It certainly explains why he was running out of the room."

"And which exit did he use?"

"The side stairs. He was in a hurry to get out of there. He and I had an altercation earlier that day which ended in his being suspended from school. I guess I thought he had been looking for me, for revenge, I thought. I don't know why he would have smashed her head in."

"So you saw that she had sustained a head wound?"

"Yes. I mean it was apparent. I knew Bob Murphy was headed for trouble, but I didn't think he'd do something like that."

"How did you know it was Bob Murphy? I mean if you got a good look at his face, perhaps he saw you."

"No. I saw the back of him. It was him. That long hair and that ridiculous peacoat that he never takes off. He wears it in class even."

"I see. Well, Mr. Hotchkiss, you've been of immense help to me."

The man looked relieved but too tired to smile. "That's all, then?"

"Well, you have helped us complete our identification of the footprints we found. Now, I know that one set belongs to you and one to Bob Murphy." Hotchkiss smiled slightly, his confidence growing. Hogan continued, "Now, the prosecutor won't just take your word for that. He'll want some tests run. So, I'll have to collect the shoes you wore that night and, of course, I'll have to get young Mr. Murphy's too. If everything matches up, then we'll be able to nail our suspect and clear up the investigation of those who remain innocent."

"Oh." Hotchkiss saw no problem. He knew his boot matched the prints that went down the stairs to the faculty room. "I was wearing these. I have a pair of sandals in the trunk of my car. If you want these, I'll get them."

"Well, let me walk out with you and save you the trip."

Hotchkiss felt alarm. He remembered that he hadn't removed a case of vodka from his trunk. "No, no problem. I'll be right back." He was backing out of the door.

Hogan watched him walk hurriedly through the room and out the swinging door. Man, he thought, and it's only Monday morning but it feels like Friday night. He'd have to talk to Sr. Gretchen about Bob Murphy. Then he remembered the funeral for Sr. Maria. He would be late, but he decided to attend. Terry smiled as Hotchkiss came back in, ironically holding the boots high as though carrying some sort of banner.

Chapter 37

Hogan stood at the back of the crowded chapel, having arrived just as the Offertory procession began. There was an impressive array of the diocesan clergy, headed by the auxiliary bishop with a young attendant, more than likely not long ordained, who took pride in handling the miter and crosier for the bishop. Hogan did not take communion, preferring to watch the crowd, scanning for a murderer among them.

After Mass, he joined the crowd that made its way toward the cemetery on the motherhouse grounds. People dispersed into groups, talking softly to one another. He smiled as a few women in front of him had difficulty with their heels sinking into the ground that was now in full thaw.

Fr. Ray had seen Terry when he stood among a crowd at the gravesite, and his eyes had indicated his recognition. Terry thought Fr. Ray was a gentle sort, probably never raised his voice. He was a good Joe, ordinary, who could be counted on. Terry watched as Ray quietly stood back while the bishop's man moved in front of him to place the miter on the bishop.

There it was. A huge open hole in the ground. It comes to that. Terry heard Peggy Lee singing in his head, "Is that all there is?" It was a question weighing on Terry's mind. He worked so much with the hopeless and endless succession of murders that had only increased with the drug trade.

He let his eyes take in the faces of the crowd across from him. They were the faces of good, law-abiding people, to be expected since most were nuns or priests. There weren't many tears among them.

Yet such a profound and silent sadness that Terry felt it weigh on his own heart.

Then he saw Sr. Gretchen with Sr. Rebecca standing next to her. Somehow, they seemed smaller than he remembered them. Maybe vulnerable was a better word. Terry was beginning to wish he hadn't followed the crowd to the cemetery, but he wasn't in a position to push his way through to leave now. The familiar prayers and responses came easily to Terry although he didn't attend that many funerals. His altar boy days were indelible, he supposed.

Yet everyone responded quickly and unerringly—"and let perpetual light shine upon her". He wondered why these prayers could be so easily remembered. He'd noticed that at Officer Kilpatrick's funeral a year ago. Maybe we're so preoccupied with death that everything about the experience imprints itself irrevocably, he thought as he let out an audible sigh that caused the person in front of him to turn and check to see that he wasn't fainting or worse, adding to the number dead.

He watched as the nuns filed past the coffin, sprinkling the coffin with holy water and then leaving. Terry moved then. He wasn't completely sure why, but he wanted to catch up with Sr. Gretchen.

"Hello, Sister," Terry said as he drew alongside her.

She turned to look at him and recognized him immediately, "Hello, Officer Hogan."

She still didn't have his rank down and Terry smiled a little. She struck him as such a precise person. "I just wanted to offer my condolences, Sister."

She stopped walking then, and as others made their way around them, a few casting curious glances his way, she smiled slowly. "Thank you. It was good of you to take the time to come. Would you like some refreshment? There's some available in the dining room."

"Oh, no. I just wanted to come. I guess it being a sister and all." Terry was surprised at himself. He was finding it difficult to speak, and he felt his throat constricting.

Gretchen patted his arm. "It's been hard on all of us. You shared our shock and our sorrow the other night. It was good of you to complete the journey of it all with us."

"Will you be staying at the motherhouse for a few days?" Terry shook off her sympathy and resurrected his professional self.

"No. Sr. Rebecca and I will be returning to St. Gen's this afternoon."

"Could I call on you later today, or tomorrow, Sister?"

"Why, yes. Is there something more you know?" Gretchen felt her pulse quicken.

"I just need a little more help from you. We're making progress, Sister." Terry turned to leave; the crowd that had been moving past them had begun to thin out.

"Officer," Gretchen called. "You could come by the convent this evening if you want."

Terry found his car in the motherhouse parking lot. He had blocked another car when he came late and found no other alternative parking space. Fortunately, the other driver had not yet come for his car. Terry wanted to hurry back to the precinct, sure that by now he would have the reports, but the sun warmed his car and invited him to take his time. He rolled down the window and a pleasant breeze flowed in.

As Terry entered the city, he noticed the litter along the streets. It depressed him. He always wondered what sort of people they were who didn't pick up after themselves. Millie had always bragged about Terry to her women friends. Terry always picked up after himself, she'd say. Well, it wasn't that hard to do, and, besides, a person should take responsibility for himself. By the time Terry Hogan pulled into his spot at the precinct, he wasn't in a good mood.

As he stepped inside, he noticed Joe Coolidge wad a sheet of paper and toss it at the trash basket. It hit the lip and dropped to the floor. "Hey, Joe Cool. You missed!" Terry called to him from two desks back.

Joe twisted his body to look who had called to him and then turned his head to survey the wadded paper, which lay near the leg of his chair. He looked back at Terry and shrugged his shoulders as if to say that it didn't bother him.

"Damn it, Joe. Pick the trash up!"

Joe looked at Terry and shook his head in disbelief. He did pick up the offending paper and pop it in the can though. "What's your deal, man?"

Terry leaned his butt on the desk across from Joe. He knew he wanted a cigarette, but he was trying to stop again. "I don't know. It's spring outside, I guess."

"Spring makes you unhappy?" Joe spoke sarcastically. He leaned back and pulled out a pack of cigarettes from his shirt pocket. "Want one?"

"No, I'm quitting again." Terry waved his hand as if pushing them away.

"Maybe that's your matter, man." Joe proceeded to light up his cigarette and blew the smoke down to his side, away from Terry.

"Maybe. I'm sorry, Joe. I was driving back from the nun's funeral, and I saw all this litter that careless people leave behind. It gets to me, you know."

"The funeral, huh? How's the investigation going? I hear Pecker is avidly interested in wrapping it up."

"Yeah." Terry wandered back to his desk. Some malaise was working on him. He sat down and loosened his tie. The large brown envelope lay on his desk. He opened it and began to read the reports.

Four separate tracks were identifiable. Of the two on the side stairs, one was a woman's tennis shoe and the other was a man's, probably a high top tennis shoe. The third set of prints that ended at the doorway of the music room was also found on the faculty lounge stairs and were made by a man's boot, and the last set, down the main stairwell, was from a small man's shoe. Terry saw his witnesses falling into place: Duffy, Hotchkiss, Sr. Suzanne, and the new player—Bob Murphy.

He turned more pages to look for the cause of death. His eyes lit on a semen report. Apparently, Sr. Maria had not been raped. Semen was found outside her body however. Terry laughed.

The poor schmuck! He couldn't even aim his wee wee right. Terry glanced up and saw Joe turned around, looking at him. Reports were never funny. Joe probably figured he was cracking up. Well, maybe he was.

Finally, he found the part of the report he was looking for. A heavy object, metallic, had caused severe abrasions and a hairline fracture. She had lost consciousness from the blow. However, death had been caused by repeated blows from a pointed leather object, possibly a shoe or boot. "Jesus!" Terry stared at the words and reread them. He read further details. The leather was suede and left several particles impaled on the fractured bone of her temple. "My God!" Terry spoke aloud and realized that Joe was again looking back at him, his ear attached to the phone by his right hand.

Terry stuffed the material back into the envelope. He looked at the outsized envelope, which lay on top of the stack of papers and memos on his desk. He had failed to get it to the lab before he left for the funeral. He scooped it up. He would personally drive the boots to the lab right away. Then he remembered that the wad of bloody paper he'd found in the faculty lounge would be analyzed that day. Man, if it connects the boots to Sr. Maria, we've got our killer! Terry Hogan was whistling as he passed Joe at his desk. He didn't see Joe's expression, but Joe sat shaking his head, mumbling to himself about what a strange guy Hogan was.

On his way back from the lab, Terry fully intended to stop by St. Gen's, but he found himself so weary that he headed for home. He was grateful to see that Millie was home. She looked surprised to see him so early. She had just asked him that morning if his shift had been changed since she had expected him to go back on nights again.

As he came into the kitchen, she surmised even more about him because she came toward him and put both hands to his cheeks and kissed him gently. They stood hugging for quite some time, saying nothing.

Chapter 38

Tuesday had come with a rush. Students entered the school with stricken faces. The counselors had arrived half an hour earlier and had immediately set up shop. First, students were sent to homerooms where teachers briefed them on the day's agenda. Then, everyone filed to St. Gen's for a memorial Mass.

Fr. Ray tried to tailor the past Sunday's homily to the adolescents, but they seemed too upset for any words to register. Gretchen decided that hormones simply didn't mix with life in general or life specific, for that matter. As she listened to what seemed to be constant body motion around her in the church, she wondered if the Lord hadn't overdone it. Someday, she sighed to herself, they'll calm down. Then she thought of Suzanne and wondered if for some people hormones never simmered down. She heard her own audible sigh then.

Afterward, she felt that much of the morning had a dream-like quality to it. Classes went on as they would have on any other school day, except that when students reached the point in their schedule where they would have been with Sr. Maria, they found themselves with a counselor in the classroom instead.

Gretchen found little knots of students, usually girls, feeding on one another's hysteria, but she had been cautioned by a counselor not to intervene or shoo them along. It went against the grain, but Gretchen complied. These people were the experts, supposedly.

At ten thirty, Terry Hogan stood waiting in her office for her return from touring the hallways. Fortunately, the secretary had forewarned her that "that policeman" was waiting for her, or she might have been startled to find the man there. She had forgotten that he had told her at the funeral that he wanted to see her. As they stepped into her office, Gretchen knew that her nerves must be frayed because the very sight of this man had caused every muscle she was aware of to become taut.

"Sister. I'm sorry that I didn't make it over yesterday."

"That's quite all right, Officer. We got back a little later than I expected. You said you needed my help?"

"Yes, Sister. I need to have an address of one of your students. Bob Murphy."

"Bob? Did he do something? I suspended him on Monday, but since school was cancelled, his suspension is in place for today." Her questions all had an edge to them and the tension in her was obvious to Terry as well.

"I'm sorry, Sister. I've been abrupt. I just need to ask him some questions. We're working with witnesses, Sister. Sr. Suzanne might have seen him out on the street that night."

"Oh." She was sitting on herself as a result of her spate of anxiety.

Terry felt she'd bought his line about witnesses. He saw her walk to the file cabinet and remove a folder. The action was so reminiscent of their first encounter that they both thought of Mrs. Ling.

She looked at him, hesitated for a moment and then asked, putting aside her private advice to herself, "Have you heard anything more about Mrs. Ling?"

"We have suspects in that case, ma'am...Sister." Terry corrected himself. The slip indicated how tired he was.

"Officer Hogan." She hesitated again and glanced away for a moment. "I heard a rumor that poor Mrs. Ling had been raped."

The thought troubled her, he could see. "No, Sister. She was brutally beaten to death though." He wondered if she had a priority about the crimes. Maybe women did that. He'd have to ask Millie about that, he decided.

Her face relaxed, but it was barely discernible. Hogan's practiced eye alone could detect it. He decided to risk something he never would have usually. "Sister, I trust you can keep a confidence?"

She looked puzzled. "Yes, of course."

"I wouldn't want you to tell even the other nuns yet."

She answered a little more slowly. "All right."

"Sr. Maria was not raped either."

The relief across her face was more than apparent. He heard her whisper, "Thank heavens."

"Do you think she suffered or do you think she died quickly?"

"She was unconscious when she died." He saw that she was so tired, she couldn't quite understand his words. "No, she didn't suffer."

"Thank you, Officer." Gretchen sat down then, looking down at her hands.

"Sister?" When she looked up, he saw the tears in her eyes and was surprised. He heard himself urge her gently. "Could I have Bob Murphy's address?"

"Oh, yes, of course. I'm sorry." She reached for a message pad and scribbled the name and address. "Here. They don't have a telephone." Her voice indicated that she was somewhere else.

He nodded and left. When he saw the secretary gather up some papers, he felt compelled to tell her, "I think Sr. Gretchen needs a few minutes alone. Can you give them to her?"

The secretary backed up. "Yes, sir," she said with wide eyes and a kind of awe. She too was running on automatic, Hogan noted.

As Hogan left the building, he felt a little better though for having done that.

Chapter 39

When Terry Hogan had shut the door, Gretchen grabbed a Kleenex and wiped her eyes, then blew her nose, and started talking to herself. The words were along these lines: "Get hold of yourself", "Buck up, this isn't the time," "You can do this later, in the privacy of your room, but you have to take care of others now." None of them had the desired result.

Tears streamed down her face, slowly at first and then a regular torrent. Images overpowered words. Maria lying there in a pool of blood, gone, never to return. Why hadn't she looked to make sure everyone was out of the building? She'd just done her usual thing and hurried home to her own bed.

Maria sitting at the dining room table, trying to avoid a confrontation about the music budget. Gretchen always chiding Maria about something or other—her hair, her demeanor with students, her carelessness with regard to dismissal so that desks and chairs were out of alignment—an endless assortment of ways to communicate that Maria was not up to her standards. Now, there was no way to make it right.

Gretchen felt such a spasm of regret. Maria had always been so loving to her students. Gretchen began to feed self-recriminating words to herself. She reached again for her fourth Kleenex and blew loudly. Then she took a deep breath and heard her grandmother proclaiming loudly within her, "No use crying over spilt milk!"

Gretchen's tired mind reasserted itself then, and she began to wonder when the word changed from spilt to spilled. She took another Kleenex and wiped her eyes again. She resisted going into the little bathroom behind her to check her eyes. She knew they were red. "What of it?" She said as if challenging herself.

She stood to straighten her skirt and looked down her front. She brushed some lint from the Kleenexes away. Then she noticed the file on Bob Murphy. It had remained open. She glanced at the gridlines where his grades had been posted since his freshman year. Basically, he was an average student. Then her eyes fell on the last quarter. His grades had taken an abrupt fall. Strange, she thought. Something stirred in her.

Gretchen went to the file cabinet again. She retrieved the file she was looking for. She opened Liu Ling's file. Although she was a "B" student, Liu's grades had taken a precipitous fall in the last quarter as well.

Gretchen stepped out of her office where the secretary looked at her with such an understanding look that Gretchen was taken aback. It was a look that clearly invited Gretchen to confide. It was the look of a woman who was not just her own children's mother but the world's mother. However, Gretchen was in her professional mode again. "Holly," Gretchen always thought the woman's name was childish, but she had no control over it, since Holly was offended when Gretchen referred to her as Mrs. Thompson. "Would you see that the first available counselor comes to my office as soon as possible?"

Holly looked surprised. She immediately assumed that Gretchen was in crisis. Her eyes were red. Her demeanor brave. Gretchen was surely a holy woman although Holly found her somewhat unfeeling at times in her dealings with truant students. Holly knew how difficult it was to get children on time for anything. But Sr. Gretchen needed her now, so Holly went into crisis mode, jumping up and moving quickly down the hall. Her skirt swayed in quick jerks, her heels clicking heavily against the terrazzo floor as she walked importantly down the hall. She was a woman with a mission. Gretchen needed a counselor.

In Room 224, she knew the class would soon be over. She would stand at the door and wait for the students to come pellmelling out. As she stood there, she could hear the counselor's voice muffled by the closed door. It sounded soothing, and Holly felt that she had successfully found the right counselor. Poor Sr. Gretchen would, no doubt, find solace and comfort from this person.

A student must have been talking next because Holly couldn't hear any sound. That's when she noticed the garish voice of Mr. Hotchkiss in the room just across the hall. She instinctively disliked the man. Well, she hated him. He treated the students like scum.

They might be poor, but that was no reason to put them down the way he did. Her own Penny came home in tears the first day of school. He had belittled an answer she'd dared to give on the first class of the year. As a result, she never dared speak aloud in his classroom after that. It was as plain as the nose on a person's face. Penny's grades were wonderful, all A's in every class but Hotchkiss's, where she was struggling to pull a C.

The bell rang then and students poured into the hall like rushing, spring creeks, emptying into a river of humanity. Holly watched them with the same compassionate look she had given Sr. Gretchen. "Give me your tired, your poor," she quoted to herself as she watched. Holly had once fancied herself a poet. She liked words. Perhaps that is partly why she resented Hotchkiss and her Penny's poor grades in English. She was sure Penny had the same penchant for words that she had.

Abruptly, Holly realized that the room had emptied and she stepped inside. "Excuse me."

A very young man glanced up. He had a jacket on but no tie; in fact, he was wearing a polo shirt. He had been sitting on the desk with one leg slung over the edge, supporting himself with the other. "Yes?" His voice was mild.

"Sr. Gretchen would like to see you in her office. Immediately," she added. He seemed so mild and calm that she thought he might need a little goading.

He gathered a paper up and glanced at it. "I don't have another group until 2:00."

Holly was incensed as he followed her down the hall. She couldn't believe that it would have entered his mind not to go immediately. What did it matter at all, his schedule, when the principal had requested his presence? When they arrived at the outer office, she asked him to take a seat. Then she knocked at the door and tried to put on her most professional behavior.

"Sister, the gentleman you requested is present."

The young man heard Gretchen reply, "Well, show him in."

When Holly turned and walked up to him abruptly, saying, "Sister will see you now," the young man showed his amusement. Holly did not share the amusement and took her bruised ego to her own narrow desk where she was compiling the day's absence list.

John Harrow walked into the principal's office. He had already observed Gretchen at Mass and had concluded that she was a conscientious woman who repressed her emotions. Perhaps she was ready to talk. He had understood that she had been the first on the scene when the police arrived to check out the murder.

"May I be of help, Sister?" Harrow still carried his childhood experience of nuns with him, so his question was a studied response that he had prepared on the way down to the office, following the officious little secretary whose skirt whipped from side to side in her self-importance.

"Yes, please, sit down." Gretchen remained behind her desk.

Harrow noted mentally that she needed to be in control. He sat down and crossed his leg, trying to assume an open posture that would help her to feel no threat from him. He would need to let her feel in control.

"I'm sure this has been very upsetting for you." His voice sounded thin from overuse. He was used to listening, but the students had wanted to hear from him before they were willing to reveal their feelings. For the most part, the adolescents were typically self-involved, fearing for their own safety in a school where a murder had taken place. They were frightened too by the neighborhood, but that seemed more racially based. John had concluded that a great deal of work needed to be done in that area, and he planned to suggest further work with St. Gen when he got back to the diocesan School Office.

But the woman who sat in front of him had emotional ties to the deceased. Here was real emotional catharsis that needed to be done. Harrow felt just a little privileged, if he were truthful with himself.

"Yes, of course." Gretchen had eyed him at first, but then decided his comment had been appropriate.

"Would you like to talk about it?"

"It?" Gretchen suddenly realized the impression the counselor was under. "Uh. I'm not sure what my secretary told you." Gretchen became self-conscious about her red and puffy eyes. She had stopped to put eye drops in them, but they probably had not removed all the red quite yet. "I wanted you to give me some information."

"Oh." Harrow's train of thought hung in the air like the trailing wisp of smoke when one blows out a match. The stench of it was in his nostrils.

"Yes. A month ago, I attended a workshop at the school office about drug use. I vaguely remember the profile. Would you be willing to run it by me again?"

Harrow shuffled his feet. This was not the stuff for which he had been trained. He wanted to make a difference in people's lives. Empower them, not just recite some laundry list of characteristics. His voice assumed a slight monotone as he ticked off the signals. When he spoke of absenteeism and isolation and falling grades, he noticed her eyes grow attentive.

"Would you look at this student's record?" Gretchen handed him Liu Ling's record.

"Yes, the dramatic shift indicates that something is troubling the student. However, you can't conclude from this alone that drugs are involved." Human behavior was a complicated matter, and Harrow was always slightly impatient with administrators who all seemed to have a penchant for simplifying everything. Harrow remembered now a nun he'd had in high school who had admonished him to study harder for better grades. Some years later, Harrow discovered his dyslexia.

"Look at this student's record, would you?"

"Yes, his grades have tumbled."

"It's the same quarter for both, don't you see?"

He didn't see, but she expected him to conclude that drugs were involved in something that could easily be a coincidence. He looked from the record to her and said nothing.

"They are friends," she urged. "As a matter of fact, I see them gathered with other freshmen of a morning. Not every morning, mind you. I'll try to remember which students, but I suspect that if I check the records, I'll see the same trend."

"It's possible, Sister. Don't get me wrong. You may be on to something." He decided to give her one last opportunity. "I know that there are many problems for an administrator and certainly drugs wreaking havoc among teens is one of them. However, you have a murder to deal with. I'm sure it would benefit you to have an opportunity to focus on that too. You have provided so well for your students, perhaps…."

"Thank you, Mr. Harrow. You've been of some help. As you said, my students are probably in need of you right now. I wouldn't want to take up any more of your time."

John Harrow found himself, proverbially, picked up and dusted off. As he exited the office, he noticed the secretary give him a hurt look. As he walked back to the classroom, he glanced at his watch, stopped by a water fountain, wiped his mouth afterward and decided that teenagers were a lot less complicated than their adult forms.

Chapter 40

Betty Murphy had grown tired of keeping up with Bob. He awoke that Tuesday morning sopping wet. She knew it was a fever and hoped to God that the welts, some of which had scabs, had not become infected.

She'd had him strip and changed his bed linen. She'd placed him in her bed. Jim had promised to remain sober for the rest of his life and had gone out to seek a job. He'd promised to return with new and gainful employment by that night. She'd kept him on the sofa downstairs for two nights running, which generally had the desired effect of motivating him in whatever direction she needed him to go at the time.

She was also relieved in a way by Bob's fever and skin rash. It gave her an excuse to keep him home from school. He had been suspended for Monday, but the classes had been cancelled for that day. Without a telephone at hand, she couldn't call to see if Bob's suspension carried over to Tuesday or not. Maybe if her dear Jim came home with a real job for a change, they too could afford a telephone like the Thompsons. It might uncomplicate her life. Still, she had to find a way to call that number Officer Jones had given her.

She was sitting at her kitchen table, sipping a cup of tea, looking at the card that the kind Mr. Jones had given her. Drug Rehabilitation...Councilors available 24 hours a day...call.... The doorbell rang and Betty Murphy put the card back into her apron pocket.

A tall, sandy-haired man stood at the door. Probably one of those salesmen, the kind with encyclopedias one couldn't afford, thought Betty as she opened the door.

"Good morning, ma'am." He reached inside his jacket and pulled out his billfold. He was saying his name, but Betty Murphy heard nothing. She only saw the badge and sucked in her breath. Her hand went to her mouth as though making an independent effort to snatch the breath back.

"Ma'am, is this the Murphy residence?"

She came to herself as he started to repeat the question again. "Yes, yes 'tis." Her heart was beating wildly now.

"Ma'am, may I come in?"

"Saints alive. Is it my Jim or Jeremy? Sean, is it?"

Terry seldom forced himself through a door, but she was going wild on the other side of the screen door. He initiated opening it. "Ma'am, no one in your family has been harmed. I just need to speak with you for a moment."

"You're sure now?"

"Yes, ma'am. You have my word on it."

"Well, then, please come in, Mr...uh." She looked at him helplessly.

"Mr. Hogan. Shall we just sit there, Mrs. Murphy?" Terry gestured toward the worn chairs in the immaculate living room.

"Of course. No," she said. Terry hesitated halfway to the chair. "I'm sorry. I've forgotten my manners, sir. Would you be for a cup of tea, Mr. Hogan?"

"No, thank you. My visit will be brief."

"Yes. Well, then." She walked slowly toward the other chair and sat down, resigned to begin talking with a policeman, a prospect that could not bode well.

"Ma'am, I'm investigating a crime that occurred at the school on Friday night and so...."

"Oh, Jaysus. Wasn't that awful, now? That poor nun! You don't think...."

"No, I just have to do these many interviews of possible witnesses, you see."

"Oh, I surely didn't see no murder. Indeed, I'd have gone and told you all about it, wouldn't I though."

"Oh, I'm sure you would, ma'am." Terry Hogan heard his words come with a bit of her lilt. It was obvious to him just then of the effect of generations in America on most of the Irish. Indeed, his Irish blood had been tempered, melted in a pot somewhere that left a world of difference between himself and this woman; yet he felt a kind of kinship anyhow. "However, I was wondering if your son Bob might be available for me to ask a few questions. I was just over to the school where I learned that he was absent today."

"Bob? Oh, he's upstairs, he is, suffering from some kind of outbreak. I think he must be having the measles or chickenpox or some such."

"Is that right now?" Terry's eyes were twinkling; he was having a good time talking with this woman. "Well, that explains his absence. Do you think he's feeling up to my asking a few questions?"

"Oh, I doubt it." Mrs. Murphy was aware that this man's conversation was pleasing to her. He seemed to be enjoying her, and she felt herself flirting just a little, but then she warned herself that the man was a policeman who wanted to be talking to her dear Bob. She chided herself that she must be a mother first and foremost.

"Is that right, Mrs. Murphy?"

"Oh, yes. He's upstairs just moaning in his bed. He wouldn't eat a thing. It's my hope that he's finally sleeping, so restless he was."

"My. Will you be taking him to the doctor then?"

"Well, not just yet, I won't. I'll just see how it goes with him."

"My. It's difficult. You see, Mrs. Murphy, my boss will be none too pleased with me today. He sent me to talk to all these students who might have seen something, but I'm having such a hard time locating them." Terry could see that the woman was enjoying him, so he decided to try for her sympathy. However, they were interrupted by a blood-curdling scream. It came from upstairs.

"My God." Mrs. Murphy looked up and then back at him. "Could that be Bob?" She rushed quickly up the stairs. Terry went swiftly behind her. As she flung open the door, they saw Bob standing on his bed, looking earnestly at his arm, scraping his fingernails against it.

"Bob dear, what is it?" Mrs. Murphy crossed quickly to Bob, who blinked at her, trying to piece her face to a memory. Then he began to whimper, and she folded him in her arms. "Oh, dear." She looked back at Terry Hogan, who saw in her eyes an appeal for help.

Terry wasn't certain he should approach the bed, since he suspected that what he'd witnessed was a case of the D.T.'s.

Betty Murphy sat on the bed and held her son, rocking him like a small child while he cried. "What is it, lamb? Mummy's here, now. Do you hurt?"

Terry thought he heard something about spiders. From behind her, he spoke softly, "Mrs. Murphy, he may need some water. I'll just go down and get some, if I may?"

"Oh, please. You'll find a glass on the lower shelf, first cabinet to the right of the kitchen sink."

Terry took the steps quickly and strode into the kitchen. He saw that the cleanliness of the living room extended to the kitchen. He noted also that her precise directions led him unerringly to a shelf of odd-sized glasses. He returned to the bedroom, extending the full glass toward Mrs. Murphy. She smiled up to him as she took it.

"Here, now, son. Take a sip and you'll feel better, I'm sure." Bob drank thirstily and Mrs. Murphy looked a little relieved, taking the glass from her son. Bob edged away from her and seemed to drowse immediately.

Terry leaned forward and whispered, "Maybe you and I can just go out in the hall for a minute, Mrs. Murphy."

She glanced fretfully at her son but got up and walked out of the room. "Can we just leave the door open? Thank you. Well, that was awful, wasn't it, but you see how it is. Bob can't be answering questions, sir." The spell of their easy conversation had been broken. She was a protective mother again, and Terry Hogan was a policeman again.

"Mrs. Murphy, I think your boy needs to go to the hospital. His fever has him delirious, wouldn't you say?" Terry tried to resurrect the trust he had been building between them.

"You think so?" Her eyes were pained and worried at the mention of the hospital. She looked down, then leaned forward to look in on Bob again. She looked back at Terry and studied his eyes intently for a moment. She was trying to decide something.

"Mrs. Murphy, I have a son Bob's age. I worry about him too. May I take you to the hospital with him?" He knew the wiser course would be to call an ambulance, but Terry sensed that she couldn't endure the neighbors coming to stare as her son was removed on a stretcher.

"Could it be the sickness that Officer Jones told me about?"

"Jones? Did he say something about Bob?"

"Well, he found Bob when he went missing Friday night. I was so frightened. He'd brought him home on Saturday morning but Bob was not at all well. He disappeared again on Saturday. It's just not like Bob to be doing that." Tears welled in her eyes and she had no more words.

"Mrs. Murphy, is Bob doing drugs?"

She was looking down, trying to hold the tears back, her lower lip trembling, but she managed to nod her head. He instinctively put his hand on her shoulder, and she began to weep. He knew it was stupid and against his better judgment, but he put his arms around her as she stepped toward him and let her tears gush. Her sobs wracked her body. He simply patted her as though he were burping a baby. What if this was Millie, he kept saying and he felt Betty Murphy's pain.

When her sobs began to subside, and he'd given her his handkerchief to blow into, he stepped back just a little. "Bob needs to get the poisons out of his system, but he needs the help of doctors. Let me take Bob to the hospital. I think the sooner, the better. He's still responding to you, but it might get worse."

She looked up at him with alarm. "Worse?"

Terry didn't realize how naïve she was about drugs. "His body is craving the drugs. The longer he goes, the more he'll crave them. Bob's in pretty bad shape, but it'll get worse before it gets better. It's better he have a doctor to help him through this."

She studied him carefully and then made a decision inside herself. "What should I pack?"

"Nothing. We'll just take Bob for now. Let's just bundle him up so he doesn't get chilled. Can you put a pair of pants on him and shoes?"

Betty Murphy walked quickly to a smaller room and rummaged quickly through a closet. She came forward with the required clothing. She looked at Terry and directed him to the downstairs closet to get a coat.

As he bounced down the stairs again, Terry was thinking about what a brave woman Betty Murphy was. Something about mothers enabled them to handle emergencies with their children regardless of how they were feeling themselves. He jerked open an ill-set door and saw a large, gray sweater and--a navy blue pea coat.

Chapter 41

Ray was getting into his car on Holy Thursday after lunch, having just left Gus's rectory. Gus was being transferred immediately to St. Suzanna's parish in the small town of Quackenville near the diocesan boundary. The parish name's irony was not lost on either of them and Ray kept to himself his thoughts about the name of the town.

Gus was moping around though because he felt he was being banished to a remote area, far from the action. Ray had told him to be thankful that he didn't have to worry about the boiler anymore. St. Susanna's might be a rural parish, but it probably didn't have the money problems he'd had at Hildegarde's.

As Ray turned the ignition key, he realized how suddenly bright the sun was. It had been a mainly cloudy day, but every now and then, the sun had come out bright and warm. He wished he'd remembered his sunglasses, but he hadn't. He'd just have to squint with the best of them. The Hildegarde parishioners were to be directed to St. Gen's for the Holy Week services. Ray wondered if the combined parishioners would fill at least half the vast nave of his church.

He admitted the prospect was motivating him to prepare the Holy Week liturgies more carefully, but these services were favorites of his anyway. They told a story, he thought, that was coherent and simple: passion, death, and resurrection. Pain, sorrow, and then joy. Ray sighed. He felt mired in the passion and death part, and wondered if there was any redemption.

Duffy had voluntarily been placed in the state hospital for evaluation, and Ray had to console Mrs. Duffy who had been more than a little soused for the occasion, carrying on about how she'd tried to be a good mother and where had she gone wrong. Bob Murphy was in the hospital being treated for drug addiction, and the foster parent of Liu Ling and her brother had notified the authorities of their drug withdrawal problems too.

Ray had been busy all morning with his parishioners. He'd visited Bob at the hospital and that's where he'd encountered the Murphys. They had been denied access to their son, but as the pastor, Ray had been able to see him briefly. He tried to impress on Bob's parents how much better Bob looked, but the reality was that the boy still had a rather sallow appearance.

Jim Murphy himself did not look much better; he struck Ray as unsteady and uneasy. In contrast to her husband, Betty Murphy seemed a pillar of strength; yet, she seemed to be vulnerable, standing there in a world of bustling professionals, not fully comprehending what they were telling her. She was glad to see Ray and drank in every word, looking for good news in everything he said. He probably invented the rosy report for that reason. She needed something to hold onto.

As he pulled out of St. Hildegarde's parking lot and headed home, he decided to drop by the convent to check how things were going there. He had meant to get by the school, but time seemed to slip through his fingers. People can sure eat up time, he concluded, as his mind went over his day.

Becky answered the door and smiled at him. She still looked tired to him, but she was quick to reassure him that his visit came at a fine time. They'd just finished their lunch. She beckoned him back to the kitchen, then called up the stairs for Gretchen.

The three of them were seated at the table once again, Ray taking a drink of the apple juice Becky had offered him. Although Becky looked tired, Gretchen looked exhausted. Still, she had smiled at him as she took her seat and declined Becky's offer of a similar glass of juice.

"Gretch, I'm sorry I didn't get over to the school these days. I really intended to."

"I understand. It's all right. I'm just glad it's over."

"Did things go O.K., nothing earth shaking, I hope?"

"It seems to have gone well, but I think this is one break we all need. I'm sorry that you can't get one. This is a priest's busiest time of the year."

"That it is. We'll be having the parishioners from Hildegarde too."

"Really?" Gretchen's eyebrows lifted with the question.

"Oh. Well, it's not out yet, but Gus has been reassigned, effective immediately. His successor hasn't been named."

"Reassigned?"

Ray heard the sharpness in the word and lowered his eyes. He waited for the tirade but it didn't come. He glanced up and saw the two women exchange a knowing look that held scorn in it. "The bishop probably thinks the country will give him a change of pace, less stress." Ray realized his words were not making any impact, but he continued, "He'll have the time to think about his life and make some decisions."

Becky surprised him by being the first to speak, "How sweet! Suzie gets counseling and Gus gets a cushy job in the country. Maybe the bishop thinks country girls know better."

Ray felt himself squirm. She was right; it was the merest rap on the knuckles. Ray glanced at Gretchen, who was looking at Becky. They fell silent again.

Ray needed to break the silence. "I'm not trying to defend him. I can't defend what he did. They both screwed up."

Becky laughed. "You said it!" Ray laughed too at his unintended double entendre and even Gretchen smiled. The tension melted.

"Ray, on Saturday morning, Gretchen and I are going to Suzie's hermitage. We just want to get away for awhile, but we also have to pack up her things there. Would you like to go along?" Becky was giving him a peace offering.

Ray hesitated. The vigil services were the most complex in preparation. He liked to have his church immaculate. In fact, he'd asked Betty Murphy to collect some women and give the church a real cleaning.

"It's just an hour away." Gretchen had spoken.

"Mack can come too. The fresh air will do that poor city dog some good."

"You guys need transportation?" Ray grinned at them.

Becky smiled back sheepishly. "We were going to ask to borrow your car."

"I may not fit into your time frame. When are you leaving?"

"We'll fit into yours, just so's we can have a picnic out there." Becky was definitely urging him. He decided to take the invitation more seriously.

After taking another round of apple juice, he asked, "I need to get Betty Murphy and her crew set up at eight o'clock Saturday morning. I could be ready to leave by nine. I guess I can work on my homily out there while you two pack up things." Then he realized what he'd just said. "Are you moving her furniture out?"

Gretchen replied, "No, just her personal things. We'll box them up and put them in your trunk. We've plenty of storage here, don't you think?"

"It's a deal then! Only when we get back, you two have to help me get set up in church."

"Ah, what's a bit of charcoal, a few candles!"

"After this week, you're probably right, Becky," Ray said and then he drained his glass. "Say, do you have another refill?"

"Sure, Ray." Becky jumped up and got the pitcher from the refrigerator. "Gretchen, are you sure?"

"Well, I think I will have one." She suddenly felt as though she had something to look forward to.

Chapter 42

Terry felt a stir around him as he read the report before him. He had an appointment with the D.A. in about an hour. He looked up to see Peck standing in front of him. He had that contorted smile of his, revealing the edges of gold that lined the front two teeth. Terry found himself standing up abruptly. Peck never mingled with the men. If he wanted to see one of them, he arranged for that person to come to his office.

"Congratulations!" Terry was stunned and looked around. Peck was looking around too. "We need men like you, Hogan! You get the job done! Yes, and in record time. In one week, you've cracked this case. We're proud of you!"

Hogan hated how Peck was making an example of him. He wasn't congratulating Terry but rather castigating the others for shoddy work. Hogan mumbled his thanks and wanted Peck to go away.

Peck continued in his loud voice: "In fact, I want to call a news conference and announce that we have a suspect and will make an arrest before day's end. That'll wrap things up for the weekend. It'll be in Saturday morning's paper, Hogan, and the people of this fair city can have a peaceful Easter Sunday!"

Terry recognized the politician's language. Hennessy caught his eye. Hennessy was standing well behind Peck, and with his hands held up in a vee, he was nodding at the others with a goofy grin, mocking a politician at a victory celebration. Hogan did not suppress his own grin.

"Yes, Terence, my boy, and I want you right there beside me. You deserve the credit. You've been very dedicated." He glanced at the other men and nearly caught Hennessy in his act. "So, Terry, meet me at 2:00 this afternoon. I'd like to hold the conference just outside the precinct door." Peck turned on his heels and walked with great dignity back to his office.

They all held themselves in silence. Terry thought the men in view resembled boys who were holding their breath as they descended in water and would soon be laughing and hooting as they broke back through to the surface. That is what happened. Terry got the ribbing he expected. Herrington began by lifting his thermos and sniffing deeply. "Yes, sir, boys, it's the coffee. Terence, my boy," he mocked Peck's tone of voice, "please do ask Millie to make provisions for all of us. We so want to be just like you."

Big Mike leaned over Terry's desk, "Ask him to make you captain when he leaves for the mayor's office."

Finally, the nonsense stopped and Terry was able to return to arranging the paperwork for the D.A. He was standing again, taking one last drink of Millie's coffee. He first raised his cup in the direction of the men and then drank. A few groaned, some chuckled. He was feeling pretty good, come to think of it. As he passed Herrington, he heard the man get up and follow him. As they stepped out into the sunlight, Herrington took out a pack of cigarettes and offered him one.

"No, I'm off them again."

"Yeah? For how long, you think?"

"For good, I hope. What's up?"

"You did good, Terry. In spite of the ribbing, I want you to know that you're a good cop, real good."

Terry felt his throat grow tight. Herrington was a hero of sorts to him.

Herrington glanced down the street and then down at the sidewalk in front of them. "Terry, I just heard some more on the punk killing."

"LeRoy?"

"Yeah. Walter has to take the fall for his murder."

"Man! I wanted to nail that Jo Jo."

"Stupid kid! Still his prints are all over the gun. But don't worry, Terry. That's what I wanted to tell you; Jo Jo did get nailed."

"How's that?"

"Just this morning, somebody did him in. Jones found his body down by the pickle factory. He says that he heard rumors of another gang trying to take over the Mandrakes' territory."

"Hmm. The beat goes on."

"I like to think of it as one more down."

"Only it means one more up. You ever get tired of it, Herringbone?"

"Used to be, I'd get tired of it once a week or so. It's gotten better though. Now, it's two, three times a day."

"I envy you retirement."

"Yeah. I hope I can. I mean, I'll miss you guys, but I don't want to be coming around, visiting, and going home to mope because I'm not part of it anymore. Know what I mean?"

Terry wasn't used to these confidences and changed the tack, "Herrington, do you think Pecker will run for mayor?"

"Naw, Terry. He's too little a fish. He's trying to impress Dan Laughlin, hoping to get out of this precinct. Gee, he'll probably be captain in your neighborhood, out in the lovely suburban Willow Wood."

Terry lightly tapped Herrington's shoulder with his fist. "Just my luck, he'd move in next door."

They turned away from one another then, but Herrington called to him as he opened his car door. "Terry, were you asking because you want his job? Serious?"

Terry waved a disgusted hand at him as he went back inside to get his report for the D.A.

The D.A. had been impressed with the evidence presented in the reports. The wadded paper had fragments of the suede boot as well as Sr. Maria's blood. The boot matched those fragments and definitely contained hair, blood and skin from Sr. Maria's body. It wouldn't take very much to get John Hotchkiss to crack. Hell, they'd only have to keep him dry for a day and set a cold beer at the end of the table.

Those were Terry Hogan's thoughts as he stood well behind Captain Peck who wore his uniform as he stood before a couple of TV cameras and proudly announced that a suspect was about to be arrested. He tried to make it quite sensational although the media had been disappointed that the arrest had not already occurred and that the name was not yet to be released. Peck was a little distressed that they were so testy. He had expected them to fawn over him.

When it was over, Terry smiled as Peck left him to stalk off in ill humor, grumbling about how ungrateful they'd been. Then Terry went directly to his car. He was headed home to Millie. What the guys didn't know was that it was Millie, not her coffee, that kept Terence Hogan motivated and dedicated. He found himself eager to get home although he knew it was Friday night and he would be on call.

Chapter 43

On Saturday, Ray had been able to pick up Gretchen and Becky earlier than promised. They were eager to get away from the city. They jammed empty boxes into his trunk and a huge cooler into the back seat. Gretchen urged Becky up front with Ray while she sat beside the cooler. Becky retorted that Gretch was just afraid that Becky would have the picnic goodies all eaten before they got there. Ray had decided to leave Mack behind in the rectory and once in the car he concluded it had been a wise decision because Mack would have pestered Gretchen about the picnic lunch the entire trip.

Ray felt them all relax as he drove onto the interstate. Gretchen held the paper with the directions on her lap. In another half hour, he noticed she laid her head back against the seat. It was the first time he'd ever seen her in a relaxed state. It made him smile. Becky, on the other hand, chatted more and more animatedly.

Ray had brought the morning paper, and it lay between them. He hadn't a chance to read it yet. Betty Murphy had come early. She'd pleaded with him that she hadn't yet had a chance for her Easter duty and would he hear her confession.

"Just ahead, Father. Take that exit." Gretchen was all attention and pointing with her finger to the right. He wondered why she needed to give him the direction of the exit since it was quite obvious. "Little Valley Road," he said to indicate that he was there. He smiled because he was simply reading the sign they all could read.

"Look at all those glorious trees!" Becky spread her hands wide, nearly clipping Ray's shoulder with one.

"They are beautiful. They've leafed out already. I wonder when that happened." Gretchen seemed to genuinely question whether they'd been in a time warp.

They finally came to the gravel road turn off that led them through the wooded area to the long driveway that wound them through a mix of pine and oak and maples to the little cottage that served as Suzie's hermitage.

As they stood looking around them, Becky began to swirl around, "It's so quiet! Just listen!"

Gretchen laughed and said, "Quiet? All I hear is you!"

"No, the birds! The sound of spring!"

Gretchen looked at Ray and shook her head. "An English teacher!"

"Let's have a look inside," said Ray who found his curiosity piqued.

They entered a small house, consisting of two rooms. The larger served as kitchen mainly, but one side had a sofa with a large picture window that looked out at a small clearing in the woods. The second and much smaller room was a bedroom with a bath. The place was neat enough. There was a coffee mug and cereal bowl left in the kitchen sink, and a bathrobe had fallen from its hook to the bathroom floor.

As they looked, no one said anything. They opened no drawers or doors, feeling a little like intruders. Ray broke the silence: "I feel like we're the three bears."

Gretchen moved to a window and began unlocking it. "It's stuffy in here, don't you think?" A pleasant breeze entered the room as Ray opened a window on the opposite wall. Becky opened the refrigerator. She took out the milk and smelled it. Her offended look announced that it had gone bad.

"Well, let's get organized, shall we?" Gretchen decided that the bad milk, which Becky was now pouring down the kitchen sink was her cue to rally the troops and get a job done. Becky and Ray looked at her, each experiencing disappointment. Gretchen read their expressions as simply the reticence of people who would rather play than work. "Becky, you take care of the refrigerator. Leave anything that's still usable in the refrigerator for the time being, and when we go, we'll just put it into our cooler to take back with us. Fr. Ray, would you bring in the boxes? Let's see, where did I put the markers and tape."

"You didn't," said Becky. "I have them in my bag. It's on the floor of the back seat."

Gretchen was taken aback that she might have forgotten something so essential to the packing and chagrined that it was Becky who had remembered the essential items. She walked with determination to the bedroom, having left the more difficult job of going through Suzie's personal things for herself. She opened the dresser drawers and placed their contents on the bed.

Nothing too disturbing there, she thought. Perhaps she feared she'd run into a stack of love letters, but there was nothing, not even a clandestine photo of Fr. Gus. She was in the closet, gathering the clothing that hung there when she heard Ray dropping boxes on the floor behind her.

As she removed the hangers from the clothing, she presumed Ray had gone back for more boxes. She returned to the closet shelf after finishing with the hangers. Ray had actually taken a box into the bathroom, where he'd begun to pack up the shampoo, soap, and Lady Schick. He was amused that there was such a thing as a Schick razor for women. He stuffed the Kleenex into the box and opened the medicine cabinet. He saw the toothpaste, the floss, and the pill bottles. Having just become aware that drugs had infiltrated the school, he felt compelled to examine the bottles. One was for the relief of cramps. One was Caladryl, which Ray recognized handily along with the aspirin bottle. The next though was a bottle of birth control pills. That upset Ray, bringing a mixture of feelings—anger, revulsion, sadness. He decided to spare Gretchen and Becky the experience and shoved the pills in his pants pocket. He would flush them down his toilet when he got home.

He closed the medicine cabinet door and saw Gretchen's face just then reflected in its mirror. "Ray! I didn't realize you were in here."

"Oh, I thought I'd help pack. The rooms are too small to have two people moving around, so I came in here."

"Oh, that's fine."

253

"I'm finished now. Can I be of any help?"

"Becky is gathering up the personal belongings in the other room. We'll be able to pack up in a hurry. Why don't you take a look around outside?"

Ray and Becky met at the doorway and each stepped back and then forward simultaneously in the little dance that people do when they meet at a doorway. Finally, Becky came through at Ray's insistence. She was carrying a sweater, a nail file, and a pair of sandals. "There's a lovely afghan out there too, but I left it." Becky stole a swift glance at the array of clothing on the bed. She looked back and her eyes rested on a box, which Gretchen had managed to pull down from the closet shelf. Gretchen followed her eyes.

"It's stationery and her address book. I think we should just forward it to her as is. I didn't want to just go through it bit by bit."

"Yeah, I feel like I did when we went through Maria's things, except that Suzie's not dead."

Gretchen's eyes filled with tears. "In a way, I think she is." Becky looked at Gretchen then, but Gretchen stooped to pick up a box. "Becky, would you begin to pack all the clothes just in front of you there. I'll pack the things she specifically asked for in this larger box."

They worked diligently and, within an hour and a half, had everything boxed. Becky looked at Gretchen then and said, "I'm starved!"

Gretchen had to admit that she felt hungry too, but she glanced at her watch to note the time as though she expected her body to adhere to the clock. It was 11:30. "It's early! I guess the country air…." She had looked up from her watch to see Becky, who had been watching her, smiling amusedly.

"Gretch, you're such a stickler for a schedule!"

"Well." Gretchen felt she needed to defend herself. "I've spent a lifetime following one."

"And chasing kids so they follow one."

"Yes, that too." Gretchen smiled a little. "Let's get Ray. I wonder where he went?"

The fact that Gretchen had skipped Ray's title did not escape Becky. "You sent him outside. I bet he got sidetracked. It's beautiful out there. Let's eat out! A real picnic."

"The ground will still be damp." Gretchen remembered her grandmother warning her as a child that if she sat on damp ground, she'd get hemorrhoids. She didn't know what that was then, but she had ever since studiously avoided sitting on the ground, damp or not.

Becky had gone into the living room and returned with the afghan. "We can spread this on the ground." Gretchen conceded defeat because she didn't want to bring up her grandmother's malediction. Obviously, Becky had never heard it before and chances were that Ray hadn't either.

As they stepped out in the bright, warm sunshine, they saw Ray sitting on an old stump about fifty feet from the cottage, his bright red shirt in stark contrast to the dark bark of the surrounding maples. Becky called out, "Hey, Santa Claus, you want some lunch?"

Ray turned and waved. He came toward them. "I was watching a doe with her fawn. It was great."

"Wow! Where are they?" Becky was moving to the spot where Ray had been.

"Beck, you startled her when you yelled. The animal world demands silence. They don't like a noisy world." Ray took the cooler from them. "And I found a perfect spot to have our picnic." They fell in line as Ray led the way through the trees.

After five minutes of ducking branches of maple saplings, Gretchen called from behind, "How much farther? It looked better back at the cottage." She was eyeing the damp clumps of dead leaves that lay all around the forest floor.

"Just up ahead. Wait 'til you see this." Ray was enthusiastic if a little winded himself.

True to his word, suddenly they came into a large clearing. There was a spring-fed pond with the clearest water any of them had remembered seeing. They stood in awe. The sunlight warmed the area and seeped into their bodies as far down as their spirits. Becky walked forward, mesmerized by the water.

"Look, there's a bug crawling on top of the water!" Then she shrieked and jumped back, laughing. "Fish!"

They both joined her at the water. "Those are tadpoles, Beck."

"Oh. Baby frogs! Aren't they cute?"

They stood for a while longer, and then Gretchen spread the afghan out near a log. She thought she might be able to sit on the log at least. Ray came up and pulled up the afghan. "I don't think I'd sit on the log. Too many ticks might be waking up. Besides, snakes hibernate under logs too." Gretchen moved quickly to follow him.

"Over here, Ray. Then we can see the water too." Becky staked out a place that would give her a chance to watch for more tadpoles. The grass was sparse there, having given way to a swath of violets.

They ate hungrily, feasting on fried chicken, chips, and Oreo cookies. Gretchen had poured iced tea for them into the plastic cups she'd found on a forgotten shelf back at the convent. After they'd finished, Ray laid back, letting the warm sun relax his muscles. The ground was still cool, so he told himself that when one side was done, he'd turn over and let the other side cook for awhile.

Becky stretched her arms out behind her, supporting herself on them as she looked out at the water. Her eyes couldn't get enough of it. Gretchen gathered their paper plates and was about to ask if anyone wanted more tea, but stopped when she saw how relaxed and contented they were. She pulled her legs from underneath herself. She'd hoped to avoid contact with the earth by using her legs as a buttress, but they'd become quite cramped. It felt good letting them stretch out in front of her.

"Why do you think this wasn't enough for Suzie?" Becky addressed the question to no one in particular. There was a long silence that followed.

Gretchen finally ventured a response. "I think for part of her, it was." Becky turned toward Gretchen, and Ray opened his eyes and looked at her. "She was here for a year; it must have satisfied some part of her." She sounded a little defensive.

"But you speak of her like she had different parts, Gretch." Ray's voice was mild and not accusatory.

"I think she did. Maybe we all do to some degree. I think we're not altogether whole." Gretchen had the same feeling she'd had at supper the night that Maria had been killed. Mechtilde had been talking from the depth of her wisdom, and now Gretchen felt she was tapping some hidden root of wisdom in herself.

Ray sat up, knees bent, fingers playing with the laces of his sneakers. "We talk about our fragmented society all the time. You're saying that fragmentation is true of each person as well?"

"Yes, I believe I am. What is society but a collection of individuals? Look at our community." Gretchen was thinking of her religious order, but Ray applied the word to his parish community.

"Yeah, it's true. I used to think that I could save my parish if I was just good enough." He looked at them self-consciously and added, "Messiah complex!"

"Hmm, you reminded me of something my old novice director told me." Gretchen turned her face to the sun. "She told me the bottom line is that we had to save only ourselves."

"Gretch! That's so selfish. I mean isn't our ministry all about saving others?"

"No, Beck," Ray said. "It's about serving others and trying to lighten their loads if we can until they get their sense of direction. God saves, remember?"

"Well, then we can't even save ourselves!" Becky looked challengingly at Gretchen.

Gretchen did an unusual thing then. She accepted the correction. "I think you're right. I suppose what I should have said was that we are responsible individually for working toward that wholeness so that we can receive God's salvation." They paused again as a gentle breeze blew across the lake and brushed their faces. Gretchen continued in a quiet voice, "I think Suzie must have been healing here, but some part of her wasn't ready."

"I'm angry about that. I can't help thinking she was a hypocrite," Becky confessed and looked away, dejected.

"If you think of her being hypocritical, I can understand that you're angry, Beck." Ray stretched out his legs, knocking over his plastic cup. Gretchen sat on herself not to reach out and set it right. "I think that it's hard to change ourselves. I look at Bob Murphy lying there, addicted to drugs. He's messed himself up. I think underneath is a boy who wants to have a normal life, but he took a wrong turn. It's going to take a whole lot of work on his part to reverse that wrong turn. If I understand it right, the only way is for him to get whole, like Gretchen says. He hasn't been dealing with pain up front. Instead, he tried to find a means to alleviate his pain when all it did was cover over it."

"Unless you carry your cross and come after me," Gretchen quoted.

"Yeah, in a way, that's right. But the gospel you quote isn't the only gospel that's being preached. Bob was an altar boy and he went to a Catholic school, so he heard that gospel. It didn't seem to matter. He found a better way, or so he thought. We don't do well with pain, do we?"

They sat quietly. They instinctively watched the wind as it rippled the water. Finally, Ray glanced at his watch and sighed. "It's just so peaceful here."

"I know. I hate to go back." Gretchen pushed herself to her knees, but Ray was already standing and holding out a hand to her. She hesitated and then decided to take it. He pulled her up and then reached toward Becky, who remained sitting, looking at the water.

"I've got it! Gretch, we own this place, don't we?"

"Yes, the community owns it." Gretchen wanted to be precise.

"Well, I think we should ask Agnes to let us have the use of this place. Look, we could come out here for our monthly weekend of prayer, at least."

"Becky, that's a very good idea." Gretchen felt her shoulders rise as though they had been sagging.

"Would you accept a visit Sunday afternoons? I'd come say Mass for you, if you would." Ray was still holding his hand toward Becky, who took it now and jerked him forward.

"Whoa!" Ray stumbled forward a few steps before he caught his balance. "Was that your yes or were you trying to drown me?"

Becky looked at Gretchen who nodded. "That's a firm yes, Ray. Won't that be neat!"

They began walking toward the woods then, but as they reached the end of the clearing, they all turned to take one last look. "It's so beautiful," Becky said while Gretchen and Ray nodded in agreement. As they walked through the woods, the sound of their steps breaking twigs frightened two rabbits, which whizzed in blurry fur through the woods away from them.

"That startled me. I think I'm nervous after what happened." Becky had jumped at the movement of the rabbits and fallen against Gretchen, who somehow managed to keep balance for both of them.

They finally made their way back to the cottage and packed up the car. It was time to head back to the city. They stood outside the car, looking around as they had on arriving. "It's hard to leave," Ray said and they all quietly got into the car.

As Ray pulled away, Gretchen said quietly, "We'll be back!" Then she let her head lie back on the curve of the back seat and closed her eyes. She felt at peace.

Ray let his eyes take in the scenery as much as he could with the winding drive through the woods. When they finally turned onto the pavement of the road, Becky looked for a distraction. She felt a terrible sadness at leaving. That's when she noticed the newspaper that had been untouched on the seat between Ray and her.

"My God!" Becky stared with her mouth open. The others looked at her, waiting for her to explain. She continued to read intently.

"Becky, what is it?" Gretchen sounded impatient.

"They've arrested the murderer—the suspect in Maria's murder."

Once again the other two looked at her, Gretchen leaning forward from the back seat, desirous of snatching the paper away from Becky. Becky began to read the article aloud. When she'd finished, she folded the paper so that a photograph showed. "Look, isn't that Mr. Hogan?"

Gretchen squinted to see, but the tiny dots were too fuzzy. At last, she had a reason to take the paper from Becky. "Yes, it is. My God, I can't believe it."

"But they aren't saying who it is?" Ray's mind was racing, and he had hardly been able to keep up with the words Becky had been reading.

"I guess I'm just relieved that this person is behind bars. I think the school won't feel so scary."

That's when Ray realized that he had to come clean with them about Duffy. He waited until they reached the interstate. Becky was bug-eyed with the news about Duffy. Gretchen was appalled and felt responsible. Her mind went immediately to what might have been, how vulnerable the schoolgirls had been under her care. Inwardly, she berated herself.

Ray sensed her anguish. He spent his energy trying to explain how he himself had no idea that Duffy was a threat to anyone. He took responsibility for Duffy's hiring and tried to lighten Gretchen's sense of responsibility.

Ray didn't feel he'd made any particular headway with Gretchen as he pulled up to the convent. They saw the car parked at the curb at the same time. "That looks like Hogan's car," Ray said as he pulled up behind it. Much as he needed to get to the church to set up for the Holy Saturday service, he saw a greater priority in hearing what Hogan had to say.

Hogan got out of the car as they were getting out of Ray's. "Good afternoon," he said. "I figured you'd be coming soon, being the services are scheduled for 9:00 tonight."

"You thought right," Ray shook Terry's extended hand.

"May I have a word with all of you?"

"Come in, Mr. Hogan." They walked to the door of the convent and waited for Gretchen to unlock it. Ray told Hogan that they'd been to a picnic in the woods, feeling obliged to explain why he was carrying a cooler.

Without hesitation, Gretchen led them into the parlor and sat down. "We read the paper, Mr. Hogan. Can you tell us about this suspect?"

"I can indeed, Sister. I want to apologize for not doing it sooner. I tried to call earlier, but there was no answer. I just decided to drop by later. I haven't been here but five minutes.

They looked at him pointedly, and he realized his social protocol was getting in the way. "I want to catch you up on the entire case first."

Ray intervened, "I told them about Duffy."

Terry nodded. "Well, I think you are aware of the fact that several bloody footprints were discovered." He had looked directly at Gretchen who affirmed his understanding. Becky, however, was hearing this for the first time.

"Of course, Sr. Susie's were one set. Duffy's were another. You did tell them that Duffy meant no harm nor did any harm to Sr. Maria?" He glanced at Ray who nodded affirmatively. "That left two other footprints. One set of these prints belonged to the person who knocked out Sr. Maria with that keg, that bank of hers. Robbery appears to have been the motive."

"You mean he killed her by accident?" Becky was listening in earnest.

"No, he didn't kill her, but he did assault her with a deadly weapon. We'll charge Robert Murphy with assault, but, being a first offense, he'll be sent for drug rehab and likely be paroled."

They were all shocked, uttering a mixture of monosyllables that were meaningless save to relay their shock. Ray stood, reeling with the news. "I, I, I just visited Bob and the Murphys at the hospital. He was strung out on drugs. My God!"

"We'll serve the warrant on Monday, Fr. Ray. You might want to prepare the Murphys."

"You said that Bob isn't the killer. Then who is?" Gretchen felt the tension in every muscle that had been so relaxed from the day's activities.

"Sr. Gretchen, we have charged one of your teachers. John Hotchkiss."

Gretchen sat there with her mouth open, staring at Terry. "Hotchkiss? Why?"

"Best I can tell from his confession is that he was on a bender. Sr. Maria had caught him with his alcohol in the school, and he felt certain she was going to tell you and he would lose his job. The man's brain is pickled. I think he came on the scene right after Bob Murphy left in a hurry, high as a kite and scared out of his wits. Hotchkiss probably thought she was already dead and given his polluted state and resentment, he just blew a gasket and kicked her hard several times."

"That beast!" Gretchen was red-faced. Becky was ashen, but she reached over and let her hand lightly rest on Gretchen's arm. Gretchen felt herself calm under the touch.

Terry noted but disregarded Gretchen's angry outburst. "He has confessed and will be charged with second degree murder. The evidence all points to him."

They sat for a few moments, trying to digest it all. Then Gretchen looked up at Terry Hogan. "Thank you for coming to tell us in person."

She said it so quietly that Terry knew she'd had a terrible emotional shock. "I wanted to be the one to break this to you. I know that this is very painful, but I know that you needed to know for other reasons." He looked around at them. "You've got a school to run too."

Terry felt that he'd said the obvious and felt a bit stupid for doing so, but they nodded.

"I'll be going now, but I just want you to know that, uh," Terry cleared his throat and continued, "I'll keep you in my prayers."

That night, the Easter fire seemed surrounded by terrible darkness. In the darkened nave, as each person lit a taper from the paschal candle, the light seemed to hurt Gretchen's eyes.

They were still red from the long cry she'd had after Terry Hogan had left them.

Chapter 44

When Terry Hogan reached home that night, he had developed a plan. First of all, he was taking several days off for comp time. He planned to spend a lot of that time with Millie and to take in some cross-country practices his son would be engaged in. He could hardly wait to break the news. He planned to give them his good news, and then he planned to do something else, which might not sit quite as well with his family. He hoped that Millie would support him.

On Easter morning, the sun was shining, removing the chill of winter with finality. Ray's heart was saddened because he knew he'd have to break the news to the Murphys and the sooner the better. As he shaved, a thought struck him. It might work, and it just might bring some hope to a family that sorely needed it. Ray patted his face with a towel and checked the time. Yes, he could get it in before the 10:00 AM Easter Sunday Mass. He patted Mack on the head, and the dog, cocking his head quizzically, watched him as he descended the stairs two and a time.

Gretchen sat at breakfast, watching Becky as she spread strawberry jam carefully on her toast. "I guess we were both too distracted to think of doing any shopping for Easter."

Becky looked up. "We've enough in the freezer to make do. I'm defrosting a roast."

"I guess you're a little more with it than I am."

"Don't be so hard on yourself, Gretch. You've a lot to think about. I was thinking that if it's all right with you, I could take the

English classes for a week. That'll give you time to find someone more permanently. I mean, for the rest of the semester."

"Becky." Gretchen looked at her with relief and with admiration. "You'd do that?"

"Sure, Gretch. I guess we're in this together. I figure I can handle the job next year if you want."

Gretchen smiled then. She suddenly felt that she wasn't carrying the burden alone any longer. "Becky." She paused then because tears were starting in her eyes. She tried to look directly at Becky in spite of her emotion. "Thank you."

Becky came around the table, leaned over and hugged her. "I know it's been tough."

Gretchen was looking down, but her hand reached out and found Becky's. "I feel so responsible. I kept putting up with that man. I feel in some way I killed her."

"Like how we're all responsible for Jesus's death? We are, and we aren't." Gretchen didn't respond, but she did hear what Becky was saying. Becky waited and then continued, "I loved Maria. She was the sunshine in our lives, so I want to hate them for taking that away from us, Gretchen. But it's no good. It just keeps me anchored to that one night. I have to live, and I want to live. Here. With you and with Tillie too."

Gretchen realized that she had always felt that anyone who came to this miserably poor and spiritually derelict neighborhood had never really said they wanted to be there. They just came to minister to the needy. She pulled away so that she could look into Becky's eyes, which she studied for a minute. "You want to be here?"

"Yes. I thought of wanting to be like Suzie, but I realize that I have to be more like Jesus. I have to do my 'public life' too." Becky went back to the chair she'd occupied opposite Gretchen. "Oh, I plan to take to the woods when I can. I think that Jesus went to the mountaintop to pray and rest because he needed to. These people can't get away, but I have to. That way I can maintain my "juices" so that I can give the people here something, the fruits of my prayer."

"Becky, I have to say that you sound a little like Mechtilde. Do you think I can handle two of you?" Gretchen smiled, looked down and then back up with a more serious look. "I have to forgive that despicable man, don't I?"

"Yes, and so do I." Becky returned to her seat opposite Gretchen, looked thoughtfully at her plate and then met Gretchen's eyes. "Only, Gretchen, I think you have to forgive yourself most of all."

They looked at one another a long time. Gretchen knew that Becky was referring to her harshness with Maria. Finally, she said, "Yes."

The clock chimed in the hall. Gretchen stirred. "My goodness, Becky, here we sit in our robes. We've just an hour to Mass! Quick. You take your shower, and I'll do the clean up." Becky jumped up and scooted in her slippers across the kitchen floor with her dishes to pile them in the sink. "And Becky, let's invite Ray for dinner."

Ray had stood in front of his congregation. The songs and readings dictated an alleluia mood, but Ray was always struck at the mood of the people in the readings. They were frightened and uncertain. He preached about this conflict between the liturgical mood and the historical mood. He believed that was the tension that he and everyone else felt that Sunday morning. Ray began by stating that Easter does not remove the pain of loneliness, uncertainty, and loss. Not, that is, until we encounter Jesus and believe in spite of the absurdity of believing.

Ray felt himself deeply moved as he spoke to his congregation. He spoke his words from an inner conviction; it didn't matter whether they understood, but he felt the intensity of their quiet, as if they were holding their collective breath. As he spoke, his eyes met the eyes of Jim Murphy, of Gretchen, of Mrs. Duffy, ashen-faced but sober.

As he stood outside the church doors after Mass, greeting his congregation, he was touched as several thanked him for his words. "That was a good one, Father," Murphy said as he roughly jerked Ray's hand in what passed for a handshake. Mrs. Murphy nodded with a brave smile as she herded her two boys along after their father. Mrs. Duffy, who kept her eyes down until she came to him, looked imploringly at him. He smiled at her and then opened his arms and hugged her. He saw her face change and the eyes tear up. "Thank you, Father, thank you," she said as she walked away uncertainly.

Terry Hogan introduced his wife and children and then asked if he could see Ray for a moment. The family went to their parked car and Terry walked along the side of the church where he waited until Ray was free and then Ray, fully clothed in the bright gold-colored vestments walked along the side of the church. They walked beside one another a few more steps and then stopped at the telephone pole, the site where drunks relieved themselves or steadied themselves as they stumbled homeward.

"Ray, I hope you don't mind my just showing up like this."

"For Mass? Terry!"

"Well, I know. I just wanted you to know that I plan to come with my family at least once a month. I want my children not to lose sight of the poor. I've been telling my wife that they need to see reality, but I'd confused that with the crime I see in my job. The reality is that some folks have nice things, like my family, out in the 'burbs. Well, lots of others don't have that. I want my kids to know that part of reality too."

"That's great, Terry."

"Afterward, we can go help out in a soup kitchen. I figure the one over at St. Hildegarde's is still in operation?"

"Oh, yes. And I believe they'll have another priest there this time next week."

"That's good for you. Overwork can make dull people of us, you know, Ray. Say, Ray, what else is happening? I mean did you get to the Murphys yet?"

"Why, yes, I saw them this morning. Betty Murphy took it very hard. I think she finally understood that her boy didn't set out to hurt Sr. Maria. I offered the job of janitor to Jim Murphy though."

"Really? Do you think that will work?"

"Well, I told him that he had to attend AA meetings at St. Hildegarde's as a component of the job and that he had to be sober for a week before he could come to work. He seems to have been really shook up by all this. He promised he would. Betty told me quietly as I was leaving that he'd been sober since Bob was put in the hospital. Maybe we have a chance with him."

Just then Gretchen and Becky came hurriedly down the street toward the two men. Becky was pushing Mechtilde in her wheelchair. "Look who's here!" Ray smiled and spread his arms in greeting. Mechtilde placed her hands on either side of Ray's face as he bent to kiss her. Her eyes were soft and gentle, and as Ray looked at her, he realized how much he had missed her. Terry bent down to shake the woman's hand. She smiled lovingly at him. Then she announced, "It's good to be home again. I think I see signs of resurrection here."

They smiled at her, thinking that perhaps she was speaking of the feastday. She seemed to understand their failure to grasp her meaning. "No, there!" Her finger pointed to the sidewalk just where the telephone pole entered the ground, next to her wheelchair. A single jonquil bloomed amid the dust and dirt of the city.

About the Author

C.S. Callahan has a great love of writing. The Irish in her loves telling a story (she wrote her first novel, alas, still unpublished, as a teen). She hones her skills as an English teacher at the high school and college levels. Her natural story-telling was disciplined by the pursuit of a Master's degree in English from St. Louis University.

If you haven't guessed already, C.S. Callahan is a nun. She is a member of Companions in the Infinite Love, which operates Windridge Solitude, a place of sanity in a hurried world. In fact, all royalties for Hellbent, her third novel, will go to Windridge Solitude to assure that its peace and quiet remain available for those who seek it.